A GENTLEMAN'S RELISH

to Kathleen love from john

A GENTLEMAN'S RELISH

Madingley

John Murray   *14. 7. 06*

Flambard**Press**

First published in Great Britain in 2006 by Flambard Press
Stable Cottage, East Fourstones, Hexham NE47 5DX
www.flambardpress.co.uk

Typeset by BookType
Cover Design by Gainford Design Associates
Front-cover photograph reproduced by permission of
Hulton Archive/Getty Images
Printed in Great Britain by Cromwell Press, Trowbridge, Wiltshire

A CIP catalogue record for this book
is available from the British Library.

ISBN-13: 978-1-873226-81-0
ISBN-10: 1-873226-81-0

Flambard Press wishes to thank Arts Council England
for its financial support.

Flambard Press is a member of Inpress,
and of Independent Northern Publishers.

For Rick Kemp of Steeleye Span, who first introduced me.

Also to the special memory of Monty who died on the 21st May 2005. Another gentleman who knew all about relish.

'The great thing about the world is that it is full of people.
Human nature is great stuff . . .'
  Peadar O'Donnell, Donegal novelist (1893–1987)

'Wot a game it is!' said the elder Mr Weller, with a chuckle.
'A reg'lar prodigy son.'
  Charles Dickens, *The Pickwick Papers*

One

I was leafing my way through the numerous appendices of my 1942 Etymological Dictionary, printed in Bungay in Suffolk in accordance with Wartime Economy Standards, when suddenly I came upon the following:

SPECIAL DEVICES AND HOW TO USE THEM

1. Figure of Speech
The use of fanciful ideas or unusual words instead of literal terms, for the sake of greater effect.

I stopped in my tracks, threw down the battered old book, and as if in response to an examination question, or a peremptory demand from my mad, pedantic father, Bill, I improvised a vivid example drawn from life: 'I, George Geraghty, would sooner be forced to empty the city drains in mid-August in downtown Calcutta – *without* standard issue workman's gloves – than to watch a gushing TV science programme devoted to gleaming futuristic gadgets.'

Last night I had sat and watched the first five minutes of *Tomorrow's World*, bored to stultification as the twin presenters drooled and dribbled over the wondrous structural and aerodynamic possibilities of the automobile in the imminent twenty-first century. The bleary hangover effect of all that millennial intoxication was still heavy in my addled old brain, and I made a mental memo to stop watching the TV altogether.

I returned to my dictionary and took in another dozen or so special devices including Miosis, Metalepsis, Circumlocution and . . . Sarcasm.

2. Personification
Figure in which inanimate objects are endowed with the human faculties such as speech, sight and hearing.

Oh yes? Well that was definitely child's play. All I had to do was to feel my age and my rheumatism and express myself with some modest vehemence: 'My Fascist of a Back is tormenting me. Also, while we're at it, my Oppressive Legs, my Cruel Ankles and these Merciless Bastards of Feet.'

3. Metonymy
Figure in which an object is described by something closely connected with it, in a figurative sense.

Not quite as easy, that one. I pondered the matter for a good five seconds. The result was far from inspiring, but then it was almost sixty years since I had last trotted out these rhetorical definitions.

'How about,' I asked the empty sitting room, '"The heedless North Cumbrian sky is bloody well pissing it down, this unkind May morning"?'

Clever dick that I am, it occurred to me that there you had metonymy and personification and anthropomorphism all in the same sentence. Though it struck me as well that the ponderous definitions were a great deal less impressive than the Greek and Latin terms themselves. Metonymy, for example, was a beautiful word, whereas its technical definition was more like an attack of verbal dysentery or rhetorical gout.

This rigmarole with the dictionary suddenly made me stop and think. Not least because, now that I am seventy-two years old and in dubious shape, I am at that age where one should be taking stock. If I take stock of the matter of human confidence, and how it manifests itself in words and speech, I find that the world as I know it is a very uncertain place. For instance, I know some very bright, original and successful individuals who feel painfully ashamed of the fact that they can't remember the difference between adjectives and adverbs, between nouns and pronouns, between definite and indefinite articles, between 'owing to' and 'due to'. Who make bloody idiots of themselves by saying, *It is I, George, standing out here in the rain,* rather than, *It's me stuck out here, you stupid bastard, Geraghty!* Even my wife Jane, who had far more brains, not to say native gumption, than nine tenths of our contemporaries, even Jane Geraghty always rued the fact that she did not possess the treasure of a university degree. But surely it didn't matter a damn, I always snapped at her impatiently, and even supposing it did, most people assumed that articulate, argumentative Jane must possess at least a dozen degrees awarded by six different universities. Likewise her first lover, a herringbone-suited Ministry of Agriculture botanist called Timothy Constant, suffered from the delusion that it is *what* one says, the paltry substance of one's hesitant, dithering speech, that holds the key to social popularity. Whereas I can't have been more than twenty years old when I realised that the truth of the matter was quite the opposite. For in the last event it doesn't really matter a damn about the actual content of one's conversation. Self-evidently some of the most impressive people in the world are rarely seen to open their mouths; instead their poker-faced silence speaks magnetic volumes. Meanwhile others gush torrents of facts, jokes, anecdotes, imaginative hypotheses, psychological theories, highbrow opinions etc., completely oblivious to the fact that everyone around them is dying for them to shut their dreary traps.

I poured myself an early evening whisky and returned to the printed page.

4. Synecdoche
A form of metonymy in which the name substituted conveys practically the same meaning as the word it stands for.

Ahum . . .

My dictionary quoted *the pen is mightier than the sword*, which apparently first made its appearance in Lord Lytton's *Richelieu*. I exhaled my indignant scepticism after taking a large sip of the Old Sheep Dip single malt. Ballocks, ballocks, and more ballocks, I muttered, signifying that Lord Lytton was babbling jabberwocky rather than synecdoche. Because, and you only needed to take a quick look at today's *Guardian*, wasn't it a blistering truism that the sword was *always* mightier than the ridiculous pen, historically and universally? I speak with a definite personal authority, after all. As someone who once endeavoured with his puny charcoal and slender drawing-pen to pierce the impregnable hides of some of the world's most disgusting rogues, I should know better than most. While I suppose my insolent cartoons of Stalin's show trials in the Forties and Fifties might have incensed many a purblind British commie, they obviously did less than nothing to halt the process at the source. For that to happen you needed power shifts, revolutions, cataclysmic changes, tanks and guns (or the threat of them), not to speak of the restoration of an independent judiciary as opposed to the arbitrary whims of a lunatic. Meanwhile the world-shaking artist toiling at home with his biting satirical pen and his biting satirical paper is both a romantic and pathetic fallacy.

I turned back to the dictionary and read the definition of zeugma. With a lump in my throat I reflected that my best friend, the erstwhile celebrity artist Joseph Ignatius Clifton, as well as being a Grade A alcoholic by his early twenties was also addicted to zeugma. He would say, *I like to take my time, my liberties, my poor little women for a ride, and my Old Jack Riley snuff.* And indeed he did take industrial quantities of OJR, as well as getting through a bottle of Paddy's every single day of his life. He was thirty-three when he died in a tiny terraced house in Limerick in the summer of 1953. It's more than likely he had cancer of the nasopharyngeal tract as well as cirrhosis of the liver. He took so much bloody snuff there were regular falls of charcoal from his whiskery nostrils. He was both vastly gifted and vastly wounded, though stoically silent about the origin of those wounds. I liked him more than anything because he was so remorselessly abusive towards his eminent patrons and their sumptuous galleries. Once to his face he called slippery Timothy de Vere, the youthful proprietor of The Waterford Galleries, a most promising young arselicker, a rapacious boy philanthropist, a gifted juvenile poltroon, and so on. That is, like his old pal Jazz Geraghty, he loved oxymoron in every shape and form. The two of us also liked to toy with punning, the wilder and madder the better. We also loved alliteration. We couldn't talk straight, you see, we could only talk bent. As for the matter of bathos, Clifton once told me in his run-down rooms in Dublin's Ranelagh after the War, 'I spent over a bloody hour on the single flicker of sunlight above that ugly tinker woman's eye. I toiled until the exhaustion overtook the exultation which had consumed the original moiety of moderate excitement. Then, finally satisfied, I rolled off down the stairs and *took meself a cathartic forty-minute shite.*'

So much for this cheerful business of nostalgia. In the meantime, my back continued its relentless torture. I'd swallowed my maximum ration of the little white painkillers and still the bastard was giving me hell. As a palliative of sorts, I decided to read a page or two of something pastoral and anodyne; Robert Louis Stevenson's *Travels on a Donkey*. To heighten the soothing effect I would have Radio 3 on as background accompaniment. Downing a generous slug of that other analgesic, Old Sheep Dip, I opened up the *Radio Times* and scanned the radio schedules.

I have been a Radio 3 and before that a Third Programme addict since the early 1950s. Radio 3, which defiantly plays fine classical music for seventeen hours every day of the year, seems to me one of those stupendous things, like limitless

13

free chocolate or sex on demand and without hazard, that normally only occur in dreams. Yet BBC Radio 3 *exists*, is philosophically real, and is in the phenomenal world, such as we know it. It is not the stuff of dreams, no matter how stiffly aloof it may seem from the rest of our vulgar world. And while we're on this particular subject, and so that you should learn something about me that very few people know, let me share with you an absolutely incredible but true story about myself and the Third Programme . . .

These days the classical programme might just serve as a senile distraction, but once upon a time it was a regular accompaniment to something quite the opposite. Let me explain as candidly as I can. As tit for tat for my wife's adultery, in 1951 I was having a fitful affair with my wife's best friend, Francesca (Frankie) Charne. Frankie Charne was petite to the point of tiny, jet-black-haired, and of a frighteningly independent spirit. She played the fool and she played the men. She played hard to get and easy to lose. My father, Bill Geraghty, who spoke some fifty-five languages, once told me that in one or two classical tongues, for example Sanskrit, there is a curious verb form that indicates 'to play the x'. Frankie Charne definitely 'played the x' for George Geraghty in 1951 in her perfumed silk-cushioned harem of a Maida Vale flat. When she went to bed with me she let me do more or less everything I asked for, quite a hefty checklist as far as I recall. And this was no anachronistic mid-century acquiescence to the superior sex. It was simply doing to me as she expected to be done by. One day for example she asked me to shower her gorgeous bare behind with fifty-three lingering kisses. Which I did with some dogged effort and with her doing the rhythmic counting. Afterwards I informed her with complete sincerity that she had the most beautiful buttocks of any woman in Maida Vale.

But why fifty-three, I asked her. Why not, said Frankie, what I really meant was fifteen thousand! And, she gloated, Jane Geraghty will surely hate me if ever she finds out I asked her proud young husband to kiss my little arse. She has Constant the government botanist to do her bidding, I said sourly, and I expect he kisses her arse on demand, if only metaphorically. Oh that weedy little chap who collects antique bottles, said Frankie. Exactly. Would you mind kissing my how-d'ye-do right here, no there, no exactly *there*, Frankie darling? Jane doesn't care for that business at all and I can't pretend I don't hanker after the rarely attainable. Why does he collect old bottles, asked Frankie, indicating that she would like me to kiss her own how-d'ye-do, and indeed we could do all this delectable osculatory stuff simultaneously and reciprocally. Because he is a squirrel who loves to hoard, I snorted. Actually some of his bottles are quite beautiful and are worth a bloody packet. He has an 1881 ginger beer bottle from Stow on the Wold worth at least twenty guineas, Jane reckons.

Lovely, she said, as I made myself familiar with every last lineament of her how-d'ye-do. Then lying on my back and gulping in some air, I added, he also has some of those white ones with glass marbles inside them in lieu of stoppers. Aha, purred Frankie, after asking me to resume the languorous kissing of her stupendous young bottom. They are called cods, spelt possibly with two ds. To get at your beer or lemonade you bang the bottom of the bottle and the cod flies out. Hence the derivation of the term codswallop. I read about that in my etymological dick, the one that Jane bought me for my twenty-first at the start of the War.

Say that again, cried Frankie loudly, obviously hugely stirred, as the saliva in her mouth began flowing like a gushing mountain stream. I groaned at her well-known lascivious obsession with naughty words, but complied. Dick, I shouted. *Dick, dick, dick*! No, she murmured, eyes closed, and most impatiently. Oh, okey doke, I said. *Etymological dick. Etymological* dick. *Etym* . . . No, Francesca snarled. Not *that*. What then, I asked her tersely. About *banging bottoms*, said Frankie. Okey doke, I said. Banging *bottoms*, banging *bottoms*, banging *bottoms*. Marvellous, cried Frankie deliriously, your words are driving me mad, darling Georgie boy! Even better, say *bots*, George. *Bots*, I said sheepishly. No, *banging* bots, Frankie snapped. OK, banging bots, banging bots, banging bots. Ayuuuugh, said Frankie, even better, she hissed at me in a very frightening wide-eyed manner, say banging *botties*. Must I, I groaned, oh, OK, banging *botties*, Frankie . . .

Crikey, gurgled little Frankie, I think I might be about to come. Okey doke, I said, and possibly me next. Leave out the banging, said Frankie, and just say *botties* over and over again, George. OK. *Botties, botties, botties, botties*. Say, Frankie's perfect ickle dahling sweetie botty, Georgie. Okey doke, okey doke, I said . . .

But it was too late. Frankie's own rehearsal of the request had brought her to her climax. She howled and yowled and shrieked and tore both her hair and mine.

The point of that preposterous anecdote is this. Throughout our frantic lovemaking Frankie had her enormous Bush wireless on and we were being serenaded by some chaste, celestial Baroque organ music on our favourite station, the Third. Quite incredibly, exactly as Frankie came to her climax, the lovely organ music came to its. There ensued a pregnant pause of total silence. Whereupon the announcer – was it the funereal Victor Hallam forty years ago, or someone else? – said in those ineffable sarcophagus tones only ever heard on the Third: 'Well, that was *shite*.'

Frankie and I lay there absolutely astonished. His extraordinary and uncalled-for statement floated in the air above our naked bodies.

'No, it wasn't,' snorted Frankie indignantly. 'It was terrific, that organ prelude. It was Bach or whasisname, Buxtehude, wasn't it, Georgie?'

'Samuel Scheidt who was born in 1587 and died in 1654 . . .' the announcer continued. 'Schütz, Schein and Scheidt are the trio of alliterative contemporaries who are frequently linked together. A pupil of Sweelinck's, the composer's last years were extremely tragic. No less than four of his children died of the plague, and he himself was buried in a pauper's grave.'

'Oh,' said childless Frankie Charne with a genuine sorrow. 'Poor old Scheidt. The poor old chap.'

No one believes that story of course. Neither when I tell it to one or two discreet acquaintances, nor when Frankie broadcasts it whenever she is drunk at a party and complete with all the appropriate actions. Yet as the richly compromised son of the womanising polyglot Bill Geraghty, I could tell you dozens of stories a great deal more extravagant. But there's time enough before I embark on the horrifying saga of Bill's lifelong philandering and his harrowing biography of continuously unfulfilled promise. Before which, and without delay, I need to tell you about my own related disappointment, which came about through foolishly poking my nose inside the *Radio Times* that sombre May evening in 1992 . . .

This is how it happened. Old malcontent Geraghty with squinting, surly grimace poring over outspread pages of *RT* for tonight's R3 schedule. Frescobaldi or 'Gaspard de la Nuit'? Ritter or Respighi? Cole Porter or Kodály? P. Grainger or S. Reich or J. Cage? Sir Hamilton Harty or M. Clemens non Papa (aka Jacques Clement, and not be confused with the poet Jacobus Papa)? . . .

Suddenly I froze with shock as if I was about to have a cardiac arrest. After which I found myself dancing up and down in my old leather armchair and expressing noisy amazement at what I was reading. My over-reaction was dramatic not to say histrionic, but bear in mind that I had been waiting for an event like this one for at least a quarter of a century . . .

On Radio Three, in precisely thirty minutes time, there was to be an hour-long documentary about the most famous satirical cartoonist of them all, that genius of a German, George Grosz . . .

Of course Grosz (I blush as I humbly point out that the great man and I share the same initials) was one of my crucial influences when I was a precociously successful and gleefully savage young cartoonist. Without bothering to disguise it, I parodied and plagiarised both his remarkable graphic technique and his scabrous and uncompromising political bile. As a result and under my pen name 'Jazz', I enjoyed an exalted if limited period of notoriety and national newspaper fame. It began when I was just a virgin lad at the RCA at the start of the War, peaked along with my failing marriage by the winter of 1955, finally plummeting to a deadly if predictable nadir by the middle of the 1960s. Long before the current notoriety of Steve Bell, Martin Rowson and Ralph Steadman, Jazz Geraghty was notorious for the anarchic cruelty and ferocious gusto of his cartoons. Day after day, in virtually every important newspaper and journal, I rudely defamed and excoriated the likes of Churchill, Stalin, Kennedy, Macmillan, as well as the lesser and drearier fry of Sandys, Gaitskell, Butler and Mikoyan. I also wrote the first-ever book about Grosz in English, which was published here in 1949 and very flatteringly reviewed on both sides of the Atlantic. Forty years on and with the frankness of hindsight, I can admit that my little effort was far from being rigorously systematic and not at all a work of sedulous scholarship. I suppose you could say it was in the now-vanished tradition of passionate *belles lettres*, full of the fearless subjectivity and unembarrassed spontaneity of a young enthusiastic war-generation artist in his late twenties.

Naturally my slim little opus with its rather overblown title (*Grosz, Courageous Scourge of the Monsters*) had been comprehensively superseded in the last forty-three years. It had been out of print since 1954 and I had seen it only a couple of times in the bargain bins of dusty second-hand bookshops. Notwithstanding, it was me and me alone, Jazz Geraghty, who'd first waved the flag for Grosz and inaugurated a home-grown satirical style that dared to show its vicious teeth. What caused me a quite unbearable physical excitement at the moment – the *Radio Times* was actually trembling in my hands – was the contents of the little publicity column at the top of today's schedule. There it explained that tonight's programme would include archive recordings, not only of Grosz's German and American contemporaries, but of *his pioneering British admirers also*. No specific names were mentioned, but as the publicity column was only a paragraph long, I was not concerned by that. As I'd given the first ever radio talk on George Grosz on the Third back in 1949 (to coincide with my book's publication) I was more than sure to be one of the principal highlights . . .

Highside, Mallsburn, Cumbria CA6 6VZ. 19.05 p.m., 24.05.1992

These time and place coordinates need to be stated with some clinical accuracy. At that hour and on that day at that address and with that postcode I sat alone and desolate in the gloaming of my little sitting room. I had no desire whatever to switch the electric light on and dispel the weight of leaden gloom . . .

Like a fool to beat all fools, I'd sat through the entire sixty minutes, hoping against hope that my youthful strident voice would be heard again across the 1990s airwaves. There is no fool like an old one, and especially one who has tasted fame but now can only taste his rather aqueous senile bile. There hadn't been a single reference, however oblique, to me or to my little work on Grosz. There hadn't been a ghost of a mention of 'the English Grosz' (*Sunday Times*, June 1948, *ibid*. July 1956, *ibid*. October 1958). Instead of the opinions of iconoclastic Geraghty, they had managed to unearth a single crackly recording of an appalling postwar broadcaster, a flamboyant old homosexual called Tenebris Forrester. T. P.

Forrester (ARCA) had taught during the War at the Slade where he would invariably deliver his lectures with his dog lying asleep on the desk in front of him. His dog, a Pekinese he'd christened Mencius, was not the only one driven to somnolence by these lectures. It was generally assumed that the peke would have made a far finer draughtsman than his doting master. 'Tenny' possessed a fluting lisp, a liquid yet sibilant delivery, a baroque and unembarrassed campness of manner that would have shocked anyone innocently tuning in tonight in 1992, never mind prehistoric 1942. His glib two-minute pronouncement on 'the uh fewociouss and invawiably febwile cawicaturess of the uncompwomisingwy antagonithtic Josh uh Gwoss', I recognised immediately as being recycled from his earlier wireless series 'European Art in the Thirties'. I had last heard tonight's extract somewhere around the summer of 1947 or possibly 1948. It had seemed very meagre entertainment then, and time had not been kind to it. Harder to swallow in my case, the bulk of the 'archive' recordings were from the Sixties and Seventies, and consisted of the rambling non-sequiturs of two languidly inexpressive art critics, both with double-barrelled names, who had written for the *New Statesman* and *Spectator* respectively. With the honourable exception of that combative old anarchist Herbert Read, there wasn't an ounce of visceral passion to be heard from any of the English commentators or critics.

The programme had been structured the way they all are these days, on the computerised patchwork pattern. With minimal linking commentary, it consisted of twenty experts all doggedly named at the start, their interviews cut up into bite-size portions, then given a random shuffle. Their voices were given no subsequent attribution so that apart from the falsetto squawks of Tenny Forrester it was largely impossible to determine who was opining what. I only knew it was Herbert Read at one point because I had attended one of his early RCA lectures. The wretched R3 producer had gone for a cross between an avant-garde sound collage and a too-close parody of *The Navy Larks*, and I hoped the bugger would be the first to be sacked in any future exercise in BBC downsizing.

Knocking off the wireless with my fist rather than my thumb, I tried to console myself as best I could. I wouldn't have been seen, by which I mean heard, *dead*, on that terrible bloody cut-and-paste impromptu! As radio documentaries go, and most of them nowadays are rather less enjoyable than listening to the bath emptying, it had been a travesty! Little more than a vapid showcase for snot-nosed thirty-year-old Oxbridge dons and cut-glass buffoons of mincing blue-rinse art critics (Careful, Jazz! I could hear Jane telling me with a chuckle, less bile and definitely less spleen, or you'll give yourself a bloody heart attack!). George Grosz for one would have laughed his head off if he'd tuned in through the 1992 airwaves. He would have thought it was a fifth-rate bourgeois soap opera instead of a meaningful tribute to an artist who invariably spilt blood when he drew.

But, I muttered almost tearfully as I poured myself more malt, even though it was a useless bloody radio documentary *I should still have been bloody well on it*!

Five minutes later I was halfway through the bottle of Old Sheep Dip, furiously composing an outraged letter to the presenter and the producer. Examining the *Radio Times* I saw that the former was called Quentin DeWitt and the producer was called Amanda Kazantzakis. Baffled by those two imposing foreign handles, I was tempted to sign myself as *Yours, Attila the Hun*, but I realised that this remote Cumbrian address and the gratuitous chauvinism might seriously weaken my case. Nevertheless, my letter poured out cathartically and angrily, and I was sure it would read like Jonathan Swift or Tobias Smollett at the very least.

I re-read it slowly next to the desk light . . .

And I found myself blushing with a painful sensation of dismal anticlimax. Far from being fantastically forceful, my catalogue of complaints read like the incoherent and peevish sour grapes of some obscure provincial has-been . . .

I screwed it up tight and flung it into the bin. Then I wrestled with something I wrestle with at least thirty or forty times every day of my life. The unglamorous and fatuous anguish, that is, of being so comprehensively *ignored*, having once been the darling of the English thinking public. This invisibility of mine seemed such an irreversible condition, it even made me resentful of all I had once had. It would have been better, all considered, if I had never made it to the top but had languished in the shadows as a graphic designer or one of those seafront caricaturists who at least have some genuine contact with the public. A reputation that had ended thirty years ago was not a reputation, it was a mirage, and no one can feed for ever on the thinness of the past. Worse still, my individual case was hardly a rarity, it was as common as muck. Weren't there after all hundreds of individuals famous in the papers and on radio back in the Fifties whom absolutely no one remembered now? Whether authors, artists, serious musicians or clownish variety acts, they survived only as dimly remembered historical phantoms. For example, who in 1992 cared about the writers Charles Morgan and Howard Spring, the testy broadcaster Gilbert Harding, the antipodean zither player Shirley Abicair, the lusty crooners Ronnie Hilton and Dennis Lotis, not to speak of the glamorous songstress Anne Shelton and the even more glamorous Jill Day? Likewise Jazz Geraghty might have been the willing scourge, the vicarious bad boy, the satirical mascot for the postwar intellectual left, but that was all he'd ever bloody been . . .

It was not as if my drawing skills had chosen to atrophy with age, nor had my caricatures become any less cruel, but for God knows what reason my style was suddenly perceived to be *dated*. It is instructive, by the way, how these perceptions seem to come from nowhere, then within a few months become the standard received opinion. One or two of the older editors kept me on out of stubborn loyalty and old-fashioned principle, but the others and especially the young ones decided to hurriedly dispose of this war-generation geriatric. Too much fussy graphic detail, they would inform me sniffily in a two-line memo, not enough forceful economy of line. The same, alas, goes for your top-heavy satirical content. Too much of a laboured manifesto in every single cartoon, George, not enough that is slickly focused, suggested, loaded, explosive . . .

To make things worse, it was all a recapitulation of my family history. My crude and inevitable fate, if that was what it was, was written into my genes. The principal obsession of my very gifted father, Bill Geraghty, was his more than justified gall at his unrecognised talent and his unfulfilled intellectual vocation. In fact I'm certain it was this private tragedy, this corrosive plasma of disappointment coursing every day through Bill's veins, which fuelled his amazing carnality. Put simply, if Bill Geraghty hadn't been an obsessive womaniser, I am sure he would have been inside a mental-hospital straitjacket by the age of thirty-five.

Suddenly, with uncanny vividness, I pictured him as he was that day in 1945, the very last time I saw him. Startled by the strange intensity of this twilight vision, I examined the wartime cut of his crumpled old tweed suit, as if it might tell me something significant about his unfathomable inner nature. I also noted his full shock of jet black hair, without a single wisp of grey. He was smiling his friendly if always circumspect smile. I looked at his discoloured teeth and the crumb-laden-bird-table nature of his extravagant moustache. Spontaneously I imagined him in characteristic mode, humorously opening his mouth to come out with a racy pun in Mandarin Chinese or a suggestive double-entendre in Sanskrit or an obscene oath in Catalan. After which he would grin and offer a loud and unbowdlerised translation to his blushing listeners, and if there were a vicar in the room he would repeat each line for twice the effect.

Bill Geraghty had exceptional gifts as a linguist and if luck had been on his side ought to have won himself a pampered academic sinecure. With no struggle at all he had gained a Congratulatory First in Greats at Magdalen back in 1911. Acknowledging which, the gowned and majestic Fellows of the SCR had clapped him furiously until their palms had blistered. They had also toasted him in Latin, Greek and Norman French, and soaked him in 1891 Madeira by way of hearty approbation. Nevertheless, an obvious All Souls candidate, he'd been refused his Fellowship, and had never got over the insult, not even to his dying day. Only two years later, by 1913, my father had effectively vanished into a nameless obscurity, adopting his lifelong position as a freakishly overqualified proofreader employed by an Abingdon printer. At Losty's Printers he had earned his bread by employing about one thousandth of his mental faculties. He survived this precipitous fall by exercising his redundant erudition in whatever way he could (he read at least twenty books a week) and also by exercising his phenomenal libido . . .

Appalling as it was, the reason for the exclusion was obvious. It had not gone well from the start, even during the rapturous clapping in the Magdalen SCR. Badly coordinated and comically clumsy, in bowing low to the Fellows young Bill had tripped over an astrakhan rug and spilt every drop of his priceless Madeira. After that, it was a miracle he'd got as far as the All Souls viva. There prattling an unquenchable torrent, he'd sprayed claret-coloured spittle over four of his interrogators. Of course it sounds ridiculous that those two vaudeville incidents together should have barred him from his academic vocation, but so it was and his is not the only case I've heard of. Afterwards he heard that the blinded All Souls men had awarded him a beta minus minus for the spittle, and that one of the Magdalen dons had tried to drop him to a gamma plus query minus minus for the devastated Madeira.

From that day forward my father detested all exclusive Masonic organisations inhabited by men. From 1911 onwards Bill Geraghty devoted himself to the pursuit of the woman in the street.

Two

My father's father was called Stanforth Geraghty, and he was an overweight Berkshire lawyer and a man of many parts. By many parts, I mean he had more hobbies than are good for one, and had taught himself a baffling medley of random skills via the circulating and subscription libraries. Stanforth died in 1924, so my memories of him are few and possibly imagined. I seem to remember being driven home very late one night in my Uncle Winston's brand-new motor car, after a visit to a very large house. Before that a comically fat old man, whose nose was very bloated and whose bulbous hairy ears stuck out at unequal angles, waved his hand and blew me generous kisses as the car left Reading for Oxford. This peculiar wheezing chap had given a pack of beautifully illustrated playing cards to my mother and told her they were exclusively for the use of the boy. I gazed at them sleepily in the back of Uncle Winston's car. They had sepia pictures of tender country lanes, gentle country houses, dreamy woodland scenes. Not having the faintest idea what one did with them, I spent many an afternoon simply staring at the pictures and arranging them into a tentative fairy story involving young boys and girls, forests, lanes and . . . mansions.

Stanforth Geraghty encouraged my father to have a go at anything, or rather to pitch his ball at everything. As well as persevering at school, Bill should read up on everything of intellectual interest or possible profit in his leisure hours. If he were to follow in Stanforth's footsteps he must have plenty of pursuits. An unexhaustive list included: collecting lepidoptera and arachnida; mycology; marbling; croquet; the study of cacti; Arabic; sword fencing; agricultural fencing; numismatics; genealogy; country dancing; country-wine making; philately; topiary; sculpture; philology; Chinese calligraphy; Japanese cooking; volumetric chemical analysis; world religions; psychology; collecting rare seaweeds; and the study of canal navigation systems across the world.

My father must have loved his father more than he cared to demonstrate in public. They were never at odds in any serious way, apart from the time Bill tried to wear a canary-yellow bow tie at my cousin Edgar's christening in 1915. Stanforth said he would personally garrotte Bill if he thought he was getting away with what he called an ochre halter at a family ceremony. So Bill refused to attend the christening and relations cooled for a month or so. Nevertheless as twin rapacious autodidacts they were natural allies and were unlikely to drift apart over a lurid dicky. After Stanforth's death Bill quarrelled with young Winston and his two stout and unattractive sisters, Bingy and Madge. Stanforth, a life-long atheist, had insisted on being cremated but had left no precise instructions as to what should be done with his ashes. As the eldest child, Bill, with characteristic unilateral conviction, insisted on keeping hold of the ashes *himself.* With the liberal enough proviso that any of his mourning siblings could come and pay their respects to this funeral urn – reasonable notice being given – at our pleasant old terrace on the Banbury Road.

Bingy was a born-again evangelist and said that Bill was not only mad but sacrilegious. She said that it was as good as putting Stanforth in some spiritual limbo if he did not have their father's ashes properly interred. Madge, who had a poorly concealed sherry addiction, said that she didn't mind Bill keeping hold of Pop's ashes as long as she could visit the urn at any time of day or night. No, like hell, her brother remonstrated peremptorily. He wanted at least seventy-two hours notice *and* in writing and as per postmark. Madge gargled a large draught of Harvey's and accused my father of

27

being obsessive, controlling, and a stinking paterfamilias. My father stalked out of the Reading mansion where Stanforth had spent the last thirty years of his life and said he would talk no more to inebriated and unwomanly women. He was just able to catch Winston, the baby of the family, accusing him of being a lordly arrogant fathead. Bald young Winston ran after him to seize the urn, but my father simply turned on his axis, and said that if Winston or either of the girls tried to go against his wishes he would fling the urn down now, regardless, on the hard grey paving. And then the considerable wind blowing outside would disperse Pop's ashes everywhere and nowhere. Stanforth Geraghty would revert to the four quarters and/or the Void. Would that be a happier solution, Winsy?

'No it wouldn't,' panted Winston. 'But you've still no right to keep my father on the mantelpiece like a private trophy or some blasted ornamental sweet jar!'

In fact Stanforth's ashes were deposited in Bill and Hetty's bedroom wardrobe. They sat there for fifteen years, from the winter of 1924 until the eve of the War in 1939. They were stored well to the back of the capacious Victorian antique and were soon swathed and obliterated by my mother's long evening dresses and my father's numerous expensive tweed-suits. Over that fifteen-year entombment, in that wardrobe sarcophagus, they were rapidly forgotten about. Bill had almost nothing to do with his immediate family, and whenever they were obliged to cross paths, should he notice any untoward huffiness, he would put it down to the laughable personal failings of his bald little brother and fat little sisters. Bingy the evangelist had married a Protestant missionary and gone off to the Camargue to try to gain some Romany converts. Madge, still a boozer, over the years had gradually availed herself of a string of love-hungry gentlemen in her Finchley flat. She ran a little florist's business in West Hampstead and employed a dogged but dozy young woman to supervise the shop. Madge generally stayed in the back in her cosy little parlour, Pomeranian lapdog and Bristol Cream to hand, and many an attractive or unattractive male, purchasing fresh blooms for a frivolous or solemn occasion, was invited in the back for a private celebration or a private condolence. They were encouraged to fondle the Pomeranian and in doing so found themselves against their oddly hypnotised wills fondling Madge's heaving, gigantic bosom. Before they knew it the hypnosis would conduct them to the flat and to the swaying florist's bedroom. Bill, whose favourite playwright was Ben Jonson, growlingly referred to her as an abominable odalisque, an immitigable jade, an irredeemable punk and a damn embarrassing bally tapstress.

One day half a dozen members of the Oxford Home Guard knocked at our door, presented my father with a rubber gas mask, and invited him to join the ARP.

'You what?' my father answered blankly, not to say shiftily, as if they might be duns or even bailiffs dressed in camouflage.

He stared at their helmets and rifles, eventually laughed in their faces, and said not only was he forty-nine years old, he had a serious weakness of the lungs caused by infant tuberculosis. This was swiftly confirmed by a medical board examination a fortnight later, but it cut no ice as far as any patriotic duties were concerned. Bill said very well, he would join their blasted ARP but was damned if he was going to wear that bloody cannibal death mask they had offered him. He would sooner choke on Jerry bombs and/or canisters than waltz around like some blighted gargoyle out of *Twenty Thousand Leagues Under the Sea*. True to his word he trotted upstairs to stow the gas mask somewhere where it would cease to exist. Quite unwittingly perhaps, he decided his big bedroom wardrobe was the ideal candidate. Rummaging around its creaking base he quickly came across an irritating obstruction. Characteristically impatient at meeting the brainless resistance of the physical world, Bill battered and chastised the offending object with the odious gas mask. In doing which, he sent flying the dusty old urn, which immediately rolled forward and cascaded a heap of its contents across the bedroom floor.

It took Bill quite some time to make any sense of the odd-looking rubbish that was his father. Mice? Dry rot? Wet rot? Illicit picnics by visiting nephews on Hetty's side, Compton and Bentinck? Then the singular shape of the urn seemed to strike a significant chord, and at once Bill understood the infuriating puzzle.

'Dad!' he gasped with rancour. 'Look at the bloody pig's mess you've made of our bedroom carpet! Have you the faintest idea of how much bloody proofreading it took to buy that Isfahan rug from the Walton Street Antiques?'

He shouted down excitedly to Hetty. I was training at the RCA at the time and it was she who told me the history of Stanforth's long-lost ashes. Dad decided not to keep the paternal urn, which on inspection turned out to be something rather collectable. He took it down to Walton Street Antiques and, with the twenty pounds gained, hurried across to Blackwell's and purchased *A Grammar of Colloquial Lettish* and *An Introduction to Modern Albanian (both Gheg and Tosk Considered)*.

Before that he ordered Hetty to sweep up his father's ashes and to put them in a suitable receptacle. Having nothing of a specialist nature to hand, Hetty put them inside a brown paper bag, the one that had held the weekend joint from the butcher in Oxford market. My mother was highly intelligent but also prone to vagueness and distraction. As her memory was not her strong point she had sufficient sense to write on the bag *Stanforth, Not Knitting Remnants*. Bill gave his cursory approval but somehow the absence of any dignified ceramics to hold his father's last remains struck him as inappropriate, possibly worthy of criticism. Sooner than fuss about finding a second-hand urn, he decided the time was ripe to bury his dad immediately. The next day, a Sunday, he took his wife and the ashes along to Port

Meadow in search of a quiet spot by the river. Before which, he decided to stop off at a pub on Plantation Road for a quick drink, not so much to settle his nerves as to operate a kind of funeral tea in reverse. Hetty sat opposite him looking very uncomfortable and nursing a brandy. Bill clutched a double whisky in one hand and his father, in the carrier bag, in the other. He had bought himself a cigar along St Giles and now puffed at it in a speculative way.

'Do you think it's right?' he suddenly asked Hetty, though without really addressing her. Her ready vagueness and his natural self-centredness matched each other symmetrically. She irritated him if ever she talked at length and he always let her know it. But despite his attempts at husbandly tyranny, she never took him seriously or moderated her natural volubility.

'I think it's preferable to the last arrangement,' she said. 'Now that I think about it, I feel a belated chill. Bingy might be an odd little thing with her feverish Pentecostal ranting, but it isn't all that acceptable to keep human ashes in a mouldy old wardrobe for fifteen years. Not unless they had been brought back from the Colonies as some sort of macabre memento. Like a tiger skin or a shrunken head or something just as sinister . . .'

Bill held up his hand impatiently. 'I didn't mean this bag of ashes. That's all as right as rain as far as I'm concerned. We'll trot down shortly and tip Pop in the river at Port Meadow, the stretch by the lock where he and I used to stroll together many a time. Surely a place where anyone with a touch of poetry would be delighted to be dispersed. What could be better than a gently flowing river to carry one's father into . . . into . . . ?'

'The sea?' suggested my mother. 'Though isn't Oxford further from it than everywhere else in the country?'

'Into a peaceful oblivion,' snorted Bill. 'But I wasn't meaning any of that in the first place. No, I meant that caption in the *Daily Mail* that chap's holding there. *War imminent*. Think that's right, Hetty?'

My mother looked uncertain then downed her brandy in one fortifying swallow. 'But isn't that why they gave you the gas mask and told you to join the ARP?'

'Oh was it?' asked Bill. 'D'you really think so?'

'I believe that was their logic. I gather they are handing out gas masks to almost everyone.'

'Mm, I suppose they see it as some sort of foolproof precaution. Covering themselves, just in case, so that no one can accuse them of negligence. Personally I don't feel worried in the slightest. I have no feelings whatsoever of impending crisis.'

My mother suddenly hissed, 'Bill Geraghty! Stop what you're doing! For God's sake!'

My father stared at her in amazement. He felt himself colouring over he knew not what.

'You what?' he snapped. 'Look, old girl, we're agreed already about what we're going to do with old Pop.'

'Your poor father! I mean . . . a second cremation, Bill!'

Bill lifted his head aggressively. 'What the blasted hell are you on about, Hetty?'

'Just look at what you're *doing*!'

Bill Geraghty looked and saw that he was flicking the ash from his Cuban cigar. Not even noticing the nearby ashtray, he was cheerfully tapping it into the carrier bag holding Stanforth's ashes.

They left the pub in furtive haste, all eyes following them suspiciously. Hetty was flushed and Bill was stuttering his sarcastic indignation. Perfectly natural to mix one lot of blasted ash with another lot of blasted ash. Stanforth was a bloody atheist after all. He would have been just as satisfied if his son had slung his ashes out for the corporation refuse chaps. Nonsense, Hetty shot back, as she strode a yard ahead of my puffing father. No one would want to be put out in the dustbins like so much dirty rubbish. Why, it upset people having their dead dogs taken away in an ash cart, never mind one of England's most distinguished lawyers. The argument continued as they made their way across Port Meadow. Hetty for one was relieved to see it was all but deserted. Far ahead in the distance there was a young man in a flat cap flinging a stick for a lively Alsatian. Bill halted and panted and opined that death, that old chestnut, was a lot of ballyhoohaa. The formal burial service, the whole business of church interment and cremation, was a heck of a lot of needless palaver not to mention expense. Personally, Hetty, he would prefer to be buried according to the Zoroastrian manner, just as the Indian Parsees did it in Bombay. After death Bill Geraghty would like to be laid on an elevated slab in the open air and let the carrion make their lunch of him.

'No!' said Hetty, appalled.

'It'd be more than appropriate in my dad's case. Pop always loved to feed the songbirds down in Reading.'

My mother said queasily, 'Throwing sponge cake for a robin isn't the same as letting vultures tear at your corpse.'

'Oh buck up, Hetty,' Bill admonished. 'Please don't turn so ridiculously green, when I'm talking to you. I for one would love to be laid on a Tower of Silence. Before you say it, I know I'm not a Parsee, nor am I of any religious faith. But let's say if I were to have a belief, I would be more likely to be a Zoroastrian than anything else, if only because of their sensible attitude to corpses. My mind's made up, Hetty, I've thought about this particular question for several years. Only your predictable squeamishness has kept me quiet up to this point. I'm telling you now, when I die I want to be put on a slab and have the birds devour me.'

'Don't talk so utterly absurd! There are no Towers of Silence in Oxford. Nor are there any vultures!'

My father riposted darkly, 'There is All Souls College, Hetty! There are plenty of vultures living at large in dear old Oxford. Know what I mean?'

'But if we put your corpse upon a slab,' she objected, 'a blackbird or a robin would simply ignore it. They would much sooner have a go at a peanut.'

'Well a crow wouldn't,' Bill insisted. 'Especially a carrion crow. It would almost certainly go for my eyes first . . .'

'Bill!' cried Hetty. 'I'm going home! At once!'

Bill thrust out his cigar and waved it in her face. 'Will you please stop changing colour like a lollipop, woman, when I'm telling you about something important? I promise you I intend to have it put as a special codicil in my will.'

They had reached a secluded part of the river. Like a sentry on parade my father halted and thrust out his chin to command a respectful silence. He was now obliged, he informed her, to commence an appropriate final ceremony. He had racked his brains, he candidly admitted, for three whole days, trying to think of a fitting speech to mark the dispersal of Pop's ashes into the river. A bit of choice poetry seemed appropriate on a theoretical level. Unfortunately Stanforth, though extremely well read, despised all poetry as womanish, if not effeminate. He'd likely have welcomed a chapter or so of his idol Wilkie Collins before his remains were scattered, but somehow that seemed too gloomy, too funereal by far. Stanforth Geraghty had been a cheerful man, as well as being a man with a phenomenal memory. As well as being a brilliant legal mind and hence being justifiably very pleased with himself all round. But if one thing were to characterise Stanforth, it was that he hated wasting time and always enjoyed learning something new in any of his chosen fields. Bearing all of which in mind, Bill had found him just the thing on the shelves of an Abingdon bookshop.

It was true that Stanforth had always delighted to feed the garden birds. It was also true, though known only to his son as a shared secret, that if Stanforth had had more leisure he'd have kept some colourful cage birds as an enjoyable hobby. They would have served not only as attractive, exotic pets, but for intriguing zoological and ethological study. Stanforth had once, incipiently feverish with Spanish flu, almost bought half a dozen cockatoos from a dealer in Reading.

Bill's ma had put her foot down of course and the flu in any case had kept him in bed for a month. Hetty hadn't the faintest idea why he was telling her any of this, nor why the prayer book he was fishing out was blindingly orange and yellow rather than the usual black.

He held aloft the brightly coloured volume, and began to read aloud to Stanforth and Hetty.

'Parrots, Dad,' he began with an unsure cough. 'You OK, Hetty?'

'No,' said Hetty, irritably, as she tried to make sense of his nonsense. 'No, I'm not. What on earth is that book in your hands?'

'A parrot book of course. What else?'

'You what?'

'A book on parrots. See the title on the front? *Caring for Your Parrot.*' Turning considerately to Stanforth in his carrier bag he added: 'I'm going to abridge this, Pop, or it'll take all blasted day.'

'You are mad!' said Hetty.

'*Parrots,*' he explained to the fresh air and Port Meadow, '*need clean water for both drinking and bathing. The latter must not be considered any less essential than the first. In the event of your parrot refusing to take a bath in the summer, he should have a quantity of tepid water sprinkled over him. However, avoid your parrot getting damp at all costs. Excessive dampness will invariably give your parrot gout.*'

'You don't say?' snarled my mother. 'They really can get gout can they?'

'*As for food,*' my father continued, without looking up, '*too much hemp is considered by some authorities to be a cause of overheating.*'

'Hemp?' echoed his wife with sudden confusion. She was worried that Stanforth would be as confused as herself by such recondite facts, not to speak of his funeral turning into a WEA lecture. 'You mean what those red-eyed holy fellows smoke out in India?'

Bill Geraghty glanced at her inscrutably, *'Once a day the parrot will look for his sop.'*

He paused as he decided that Hetty was warming to his inspired little funeral oration. He knew as much because she was tugging at his sleeve with sheer excitement.

'Bill –'

'Yes, yes. Glad you're starting to relax a bit, Hetty.'

'I don't want to alarm you, but that huge Alsatian is galloping this way!'

'Nonsense. Damn, I've lost my blasted place in *Caring for Your Parrot*. I'm sorry but it'll have to be a bit of a lightning précis from now on, Pop . . .'

He continued in a hoarse and solemn voice. *'Should your parrot catch a cold, he should be kept very warm indeed.* Quite right, until he's better of course, poor chap. *If he starts picking out his feathers, then you should provide him with a green capsicum.* And listen, this is quite remarkable, Pop. Did you know that if a parrot shows signs of a weak digestion, then a rusty nail in his drinking water is a perfect remedy? Personally, I'd have thought it'd have given old Polly lockjaw.'

'I really don't like the look of that Alsatian! It's so . . .'

'I've got this other book in my rucksack, Pop. *Caring for Your Pigeons.* You know, I really do think you should have indulged yourself more in the way of keeping birds. I feel that you always stinted yourself unreasonably there. I know you always said that keeping pigeons smacked of smelly working men and foul-mouthed grimy colliers . . .'

'Bill! That horrible dog is running straight at us! Its jaws are bared wide open and it's dripping saliva.'

'Poppycock,' scoffed Bill. 'It's heading for its blasted stick, nothing else.'

'It's –'

'The Carrier has an abnormal development of beak and eye wattles. The Barb is rather a heavy wattled bird. The wattle may be said to be his chief point.'

'Bill!' cried Hetty. 'He's coming straight for us!'

'*Pouters are also regarded as high-class pigeons, and are so named because of the development of the crop which is of a globular form. As much as a hundred pounds has been paid for a specially well-bred pouter.*'

'Bill!' she shrieked.

'*Grrr!*'

The Alsatian, a vigorous and massive bitch in its prime, took a flying leap at the carrier bag.

My father went sprawling on the grass. My mother screamed her hysteria and implored the deserted meadow for aid. Refusing to part with his carrier bag, Bill attempted to fend off the dog with angry blows from his bird book. As he lunged and parried, he bawled: '*Get off my father*, you *cur*! Be off, sir! Why, you bugger . . . you hideous bugger! *Down*, sir! *Down, sir*! Down! I said *down*!'

'Agh! He's got hold of your father, Bill!'

'Over my dead body, Hetty!'

'Agh! He's worrying Pop!'

Worrying was the appropriate verb. The Alsatian had finally torn the butcher's bag from Bill's fist. Possibly because it still smelt of its original contents, the dog proceeded to masticate the bag, and all of Stanforth, in four voracious gulps.

'Ooh!' sobbed my mother. 'My God! The dog's eaten your father!'

'I'll have it shot!' roared Bill. 'I'll have the blasted beast destroyed, I promise.'

Hetty turned in horror to the approaching owner. 'I say, you, the gentleman, the man who owns this dog! Your dog's just swallowed my husband's father.'

The dog owner was a thirty-year-old factory hand from Cowley. He looked remarkably unflustered by the scene before him and there wasn't a trace of guilt upon his stolid features. Like everyone else in this town he was well used to university eccentricity and took it in his stride; viz. with utter contempt. If it wasn't the loud-mouthed stuck-up bloody students, it was these pathetic toffee la-di-das parading about doing barmy bloody things like reading aloud *to the river*. Just like this spreadeagled posh fool here with his air-ace moustache. Spouting bloody poetry out of a knapsack and puffing away like Lord Snooty at an outsize cigar. Holding up a grubby old carrier bag and waving it around like an orchestra baton. Ordinary Oxford townsfolk wouldn't dare to carry on like that in public, or they'd be arrested and stuck in the madhouse.

Which is precisely what he told my affronted parents, and added that it served them bloody right for aggravating his bitch Cora in the first place.

'If Cora has gone and eaten his dad,' he sneered, 'then I'm . . . I'm the Master of All Souls.'

'Eh?' cried my father, shuddering at those too inflammatory words. 'I'll have you put in charge, man!'

'Hah! You and whose army? And what are you going to tell them? You're not even scratched as far as I can see.'

'You and your bloody dog! I'll have you both put in charge. And let me tell you something of the utmost importance, should I? It's the *Warden*, not the Master of All Souls.'

'You what? I don't give a –'

'Don't you know that much? You, the Warden of All Souls? How dare you suggest anything of the kind? A common working man like yourself.'

At that the proud working man advanced with an incredulous expression. 'Common! I'm supposed to be common, am I? Well I'll show you, you toffee-nosed bastard!'

He bent down to my father, still flailing on the ground. Without flinching he seized the ends of Bill's moustache and as if they were the strings of a yo-yo, began to pull them along opposing axes with all the strength he could muster.

'Aaagh! Aaaagghgh! AAAGHGHGHGH!'

No one would have imagined that a stringy old proofreader could have emitted such a lionlike roar. The torture was not a quick matter either. The Cowley man kept on his pitiless twirling for what seemed an age. My mother howled with panic as she wondered if this horrible young brute would ever stop. Despite all his efforts neither moustache seemed to be coming out by its roots, and she worried that Bill Geraghty, like the would-be regicide Damiens, would eventually be torn in two . . .

At last he released his hold. The moustache bristles were arrayed like two miniature bird nests upon his outspread palms. He put his red face a quarter of an inch away from Bill's.

'Don't you know there'll be a war on soon?' he sneered. 'And here's you busy fooling about chanting *poetry* to a bloody *river*. Prancing about like an imbecile and telling the world that your dad lives in a carrier bag.'

We were left a reasonable inheritance by Stanforth, though not enough to keep us in the style Bill Geraghty would have preferred. Education being the indisputable household deity, my father sent me to a costly prep school and later to a fee-paying day school. It took up the bulk of his savings, of course, and the income from his proofreading had to be eked out very sensibly. Unfortunately neither of my parents had much in the way of sense, so we struggled along by a kind of fitful serendipity. Bill, for example, would blow five guineas on a new Ottoman Turkish dictionary, afterwards instituting a family diet of mock goose and fried turnips for an entire week. Likewise he would peremptorily decree that the electric lights should be switched off if even a speck of daylight was visible in the morning room. It didn't seem to bother him if this was the room where I was trying to draw a botanical specimen for my prep-school head, Miss Pettifer. In the end, hardly able to see my hand, I found it easier to go outside into the garden in the icy wind and draw my spring snowdrop *al fresco*. It might be grey and my mittened fingers might be trembling with the cold, but at least I could see the flower that I was sketching.

Not that Miss Pettifer was any stringent art critic. She ran a small mixed school just outside Witney, and the curriculum was an extravagant mix of the rote, the senseless, and the anarchic. By the age of seven we were doing at least a hundred sums and two lengthy English comprehension exercises every single morning. Come early afternoon, reeling, dazed and defenceless, we would be allowed the last hour and a half to do some kind of aimless, unsupervised activity. Living close to Witney, I was generally allowed to return home for the weekends though invariably burdened by a lorryload of homework. Bill admired the Herculean quantity of sums and comprehension, and he also admired Miss Amanda Pettifer. Miss Pettifer was certainly redoubtable. She was big and sturdy and had a fierce hacksawed haircut which must in retrospect have been her chosen lesbian adornment. Apropos which her doting partner, Miss Bellowes the Deputy Head, wore daringly tight black trousers and the thickest daubs of lipstick I have ever seen. Incredible as it sounds, in front of us forty pupils, Miss Pettifer would refer to blushing Miss Bellowes as 'my little wife'. She also spoke of her as 'my right-arm man', 'my third limb', and 'my price-less, precious one'. Inevitably I babbled some of this to my parents who, preoccupied as always, were remarkably unperturbed. Bill snortingly referred to them as two fine strapping bouncy girls, and also remarked that Bellowes was an appealingly jokey sort of surname. In fact, he added, she rather put him in mind of 'a splendid pair of bellows' and surely the merest glimpse of her by any red-blooded prep-school master ought to be enough 'to raise any dying fire'. I found this incendiary metaphor much too baffling and Hetty, I noticed, had turned very pale.

All weekend and for most of the holidays, I was usually kept busy with homework. But even during our lunch, it was Bill's obsessive habit to pose me questions related to his own fussy interests. He despaired of the fact that I showed no interest in foreign languages, but was pleased that English grammar and comprehension were twin staples at Witney. Last week Miss Bellowes in a very resonant and sultry voice had introduced us to Parts of Speech and Punctuation. Bill Geraghty, the polyglot proofreader, now went a step further. Anticipating the demanding entrance requirements of Bedlington School three years on, he attempted to lead me through the byzantine mazes of Clause Analysis.

'Clauses, Georgie,' he barked at me over Sunday roast. 'Now who can tell me what a clause is, eh?'

'Birds have them,' scowled Hetty. 'And they also have those things called beaks. Do ask him something harder, if you're going to ruin our lunch with your interrogations.'

'D'you mind,' snapped Bill. 'It happens to be one of the most crucial elements in the English language. I'm talking about the sentence itself, no less. Sentences, Georgie, break down into lesser units called clauses, as any fool knows, even those who are hopeless linguists like yourself. Just let me think of a suitable example. *The dog ran quickly, in order to get at his juicy bone.* Right. Which is the main clause in that sentence? Simplicity itself, I promise you.'

I took a stab at the peas and carrots and also took a stab at the main clause. '"Bone" is.'

'You *what?*'

'No, it's not,' I said, blushing, '"Quickly" is, Dad.'

'You fool!' he snorted. 'How on earth can a single word be a clause?'

'Ar . . .'

'A clause, you duffer, is a *discrete unit of sense* in a sentence. Or at any rate that is always true of the main clause. Now then, Georgie. Which bit of my dog sentence makes discrete sense?'

Hetty, always game when it came to puzzles and quizzes suggested, '"In order to"?'

'Gah,' he barked at her through a mouthful of beef. 'You

41

are nearly forty, Hetty, and you don't even know what "discrete sense" means?'

My mother was quick off the mark with her response. 'I know all about discretion,' she snapped. 'I have always had to show it with a devious husband like you.'

I saw Bill Geraghty blush purple, and I understood nothing.

'Don't embarrass the child, will you, woman, with your blasted *doubles entendres*. Now listen, George, old man. "The dog ran quickly" makes adequate grammatical sense on its own and is therefore the main clause. Bearing that in mind, what do you call the other bit of the sentence, the bit that isn't the main clause?'

'An apostrophe?' I said.

'Doh!' he bawled. 'Don't you see, you idiot, that the other bit *depends* on the first bit. The "in order to get at his bone" bit, depends on the dog running quickly . . .'

'No, it doesn't,' interrupted my mother. 'The dog could have run slowly and it would still have got its bone. *Festina lente*, surely.'

'You are both insane,' he shouted at the pair of us. 'Listen here, George, the other bit, the "in order to" bit depends on the main clause and is thus called a "dependent" clause. However, it has an alternative name which you may not have heard of. I'll give you a helpful clue, and, please, Hetty, will you keep silence, as I feel you have nothing at all sensible to contribute to this discussion.' He turned back to me with a struggling alacrity. 'George, old boy, if you are in the army and you're a lieutenant, what do you call the ranks below you?'

I looked at my lamb chop and furrowed my brow. 'Privates?'

He almost threw his fork at me. 'You what! Private Clause? Are you serious, you young imbecile?'

'Corporals?'

'Corporal Clause?' he bellowed. 'Don't just babble anything, use your intelligence if you have any. I'm talking about the word that describes the lower ranks generally, and specifically with regard to you, the lieutenant.'

I put down my cutlery and stared at him transfixed. 'Lazy?'

He got up from his chair and walked across to give me a thorough shaking. 'Eh? Why not try "dirty"? Or "common"? Or "ragged", while you're at it?'

'Dirty . . . comm . . .' I stammered.

'Gah! SUBORDINATE, you young fool! The MAIN clause and the SUBORDINATE clause. Dammit, I was versed in clause analysis when I was a scrap of four or five, as I recall. Not a great overgrown lump of seven like you! "In order to etc. etc." is the *subordinate* clause.'

Soon after that I began to make great effort with clause analysis, if only so that I could eat my meals in peace. However, the more I mugged it up, the more Bill felt obliged to ask harder and harder questions, some of which I doubt Ridout himself could have answered. One lunchtime my father asked me to supply him with a subject noun clause and an object noun clause, always regarded as the most elusive examples. Judge of my amazement when Hetty – who had obviously been doing some homework re the doings of her husband as well as English grammar – slyly pipped me to the post.

My father's example of a subject noun clause was, *That the wasted state of the city was all the fault of the emperor, seemed clear enough to his wife.*

Hetty, who had been drinking a good deal more wine than her usual ration, leant across the table and muttered: '*That you are the author of an extra-marital affair, is surely a proven fact.*'

I had no idea what that meant, though of course my brainy father did. His bushy hair seemed to stand on end, and he was as blazing as a turkey comb.

'Eh?' he gasped. 'For Pete's sake, Hetty, I'm trying to coach Georgie here through his entrance papers! Is this the appropriate time to beard me in my lair with this hearsay damn inflammatory stuff?' Hotly refocusing on his selfless parental task he said, 'Georgie boy, I want you to supply me with an object noun clause.'

Hetty refilled her wine glass and blurted: 'Here's a prime example. *I know, George, that your father is regularly fornicating with Angie Foy!* And I can analyse that clause by clause, my poor little son. Main clause, *I know*. Subordinate clause, *that your father is grubbily and clandestinely fornicating with Angie Foy*. The second clause is the object of the first clause. And what is it that I know? I know *it*. I know the bloody truth, Georgie!'

'Will you shut up!' roared my father, turning from puce to green. 'Georgie, go to your room.'

I pointed out that I had had no lunch as yet. Bill hesitated, then said I could stay where I was as long as I promised not to listen to my mother's frantic babblings. He sat there looking direly put out, though not remotely guilt-stricken. Rather, he looked like an unfairly-done-by family man. Dazed by all this spontaneous candour from his drunken wife, he scratched forlornly at his chin. There was only one thing that was going to help matters at the moment, and that was for him to grill me about verb adjuncts and adjectival adjuncts.

Hetty broke in swiftly. 'I can supply you with some verb adjuncts, Bill Geraghty! I've been reading Ridout's *English Grammar* on the sly, and I can give it to you verbatim. Do you want it paraphrased or précised, my dear lying husband?'

Bill flushed as he was obliged perforce to opt for a précis. 'Dammit, Hetty! Please draw it mild, will you, in front of the little chap?'

My mother hammered on relentlessly. '"Behind closed doors at the Abingdon publisher's" is the verbal adjunct to the fornicating. Also, "several times a week" judging by your extended workload and your volunteering for all the evening overtime. I can also supply some adjectival adjuncts. How to describe delectable Angie Foy? Twenty-eight and florid. Large of hip and small of heart. Massive rotund titties and . . .'

'Hetty Geraghty!' thundered my father. 'How dare you talk filthy smut like that in front of our boy?'

My mother shouted contemptuously, 'Don't try to hinder me, Bill, when I'm finally getting to understand the rules of grammar. Though, I admit it's not always plain sailing and there are still things I'm getting stuck on. For example, I have no problems with understanding the predicate, but what about the copula? What about the *bloody old copula*, Bill?'

'Ar –'

'It sounds like an appropriate nickname for one of your blousy women. It sounds like what they ought to call Angie Foy behind her back. Copula Foy.'

I broke my silence and asked in a thrilled voice, 'What on earth are you both talking about?'

'Only grammar,' said Hetty, suddenly weeping into her wine. 'Only the grammar of life, poor little Georgie.'

'Clause analysis,' grunted Bill with a weary, almost done-for look. 'All we are doing is talking about clauses, old man. Though I really think it's time we talked about something else for once.'

Three

There was no more about object noun clauses after that. My father's lunchtime pedagogy became far more restrained, sporadic, and a good deal less intrusive. Hetty Geraghty continued to cope with her husband's sexual secrets by cultivating an aggressive wine consumption, though thankfully she paused at the brink and never became a serious alcoholic. Meanwhile I was permitted to play with the neighbours' children during the holidays, even though neither of my parents had any inclination for doorstep fraternising. Rather, Bill Geraghty continued to do six days a week proofreading in Abingdon, and his passion for voluntary overtime continued unabated. My mother had an assortment of women friends in various parts of Oxford, but I was the only effective point of contact with our neighbours on the Banbury Road. In 1932, when I was twelve, my best friend three doors along was called Thomas Tarkenter, a Roman Catholic and an impenitent daredevil. His father was an Oxford estate agent and his mother was a doctor in the Radcliffe Hospital. Tarkenter, like me, attended a fee-paying day school, in his case run by some soutaned Blessed Fathers in Summertown. St Bridget's was a magnificent Victorian edifice but a legendarily fearsome place of learning, with an unequalled reputation for driving the boys on to Oxbridge entrance. Tarkenter was thus an exceptionally bright twelve year old, as well as an exceptionally bad one.

One sunny April afternoon, the two of us were busy inside my father's aviary, his unselfconscious pride and joy. Bill Geraghty did not stint himself like my grandfather when it came to indulging a natural love of birds. For years now he had kept a touching little collection of gently chirruping budgerigars and finches in a shed next to the wall that separated us from the Bricketts. The Bricketts were also Roman Catholics, and Timothy Brickett, a thin and neurotic boy with a dual lisp and a pair of incredibly thin legs, was in the same form as Tarkenter. Thomas hated Brickett. It was bad enough that he was punily-built, borderline agoraphobic, and had a ludicrous speech defect, but he also had the cheek to cultivate an ostentatious piety. According to Tarkenter he went along to the school chapel every break and lunchtime, and prayed there at interminable length on his knees. His face looked starved of daylight, and in fact we rarely saw him along our stretch of the Banbury Road. Thomas Tarkenter would have loved to have given Timothy Brickett a good hiding, as he suspected him of being some kind of tenured school spy. It would obviously be hazardous to ambush him at St Bridget's, but Tarkenter regularly toyed with improbable schemes to attack him violently outside his house.

We cleaned out the half dozen cages and topped up the water bottles. Of the twenty little birds, Bill's favourite was a blue female budgerigar which he'd tenderly christened Mrs White. This was not as nonsensical as it sounds, for although five of Bill's budgies were blue, only one of them had distinctive white flecks along the rump. We stood there reverently at Mrs White's cage and stroked her mottled neck through the wires, and when she cocked her tiny intelligent head, we cooed at her almost as lovingly as her master Bill Geraghty would have.

Suddenly, incredibly, we heard the voice of Timothy Brickett fluting over the garden wall. This was so rare an event that we stopped our musical cooing and listened with taut attention. He was laboriously explaining something at monumental length to his businesslike harsh-voiced mother. With those lisping and puerile inflections he sounded like an emasculated version of *Just William*'s Violet Elizabeth Bott. As for his mother, she sounded like a glacial harridan out of

Bleak House or *Little Dorrit*. I was just about to guffaw with loud scorn when Tarkenter sternly hushed me.

'Shush,' he whispered. 'I think I've finally got the bastard at long last.'

I cupped my ear like Tarkenter, and listened to Brickett's sibilant lispings. He was proudly unfolding details of an excursion he was making next week with Father Joseph and four other favoured boys from St Bridget's choir. They had been invited to attend a lunchtime performance of Verdi's *Quattro Pezzi Sacri* at a church a couple of miles outside Banbury. As his mother grilled him for precise details of trains and return times, Tarkenter, with a look of exultation, was busy scribbling down the answers in the dirt below the wall.

'Verdi, Timothy?' asked Mrs Brickett. She ran a select accommodation agency in St Giles, and like another Richmal Crompton caricature always wore grim lorgnettes. 'I thought that Verdi only wrote extremely noisy operas?'

'But the Pedthee Thackeray,' replied her son, 'ith outth-tanding for itth peewiod. And for itth party, ath Father Jotheph theth.'

Once they had gone indoors, I let out my pent-up hysterics. But Tarkenter remained very serious as if struggling with complex computations. At last he said that he had worked out a plan of great subtlety for getting his own back on that lisping laughing stock. Last week someone, almost certainly Timothy Brickett, had snitched on him for smoking a Players Weights behind the cycle shed. Father Joseph had taken him into his study and given him six expert strokes across the hand with the ferrule. Tarkenter then paused to direct a mime act where I was Father Joseph and he was himself being caned. He also coached me on imitating the priest's voluptuous snorting and puffing as he lashed away with the ferrule, and added a lewd game of priestly pocket billiards occasioned by the ecstatic pleasure of administering a flogging.

Signalling an abrupt end to the horseplay, he explained his ingenious strategy.

He had decided to sneak off school next Wednesday, the day of the trip to the Verdi concert. Tarkenter would have no problems taking some short-notice leave as he had an eighteen-year-old cousin called Telford, who was both a gifted painter and an accomplished amateur forger. Thanks to Telford, Tarkenter possessed three years' supply of sick notes all supposedly signed by his father, none of which had ever been questioned by the Christian Brothers. And wasn't it a coincidence, he reminded me, that next Wednesday I happened to have a special day's holiday from Bedlington. It was the statutory annual reward requested by old boy Major Shott-Eckersley at our recent speech day. Wasn't it very opportune that I, George Geraghty, could be his assistant in the necessary retribution visited on Brickett.

'Eh?' I asked uneasily. 'What retribution? You aren't going to do anything criminal are you?'

He grunted cryptically. 'I haven't made my mind up yet about the finer details. I need to spend the weekend giving it careful thought.'

In the meantime he could not resist sketching out one or two broad strategies. Inclining his head obliquely, he said he supposed the sensible thing to do would be to exact vengeance at the railway station. According to Brickett, Father Joe and the choristers would be boarding the Banbury train at 10.25. Therefore Tarkenter and I would need to be lurking around invisible in their immediate vicinity. If we could manage to do that, there were all sorts of attractive possibilities. A bucket of dirty water to be tipped from the platform bridge? Or a brimming bucket of vomit? Or better still, excrement? The bucket of shit to be democratically strewn over Father Joseph as well, if he was fool enough to be lingering next to Brickett? Tarkenter looked thoughtful, then asked me if I was up to saving a few days' excrement for him. I frowned and said there would be no easy way of getting such a tell-tale extravagance past Bill and Hetty. Where the hell would I store each day's evacuation in any case? Shit being shit, wouldn't it make its pungent presence known wherever I tried to hide it?

Very well, he grunted. In that case he would get hold of some sort of garishly coloured dye, the kind that would take years to get out, if ever. I grinned my smirking approval but underneath I was seriously anxious about the limits he would go to. I was really terrified of any kind of lawbreaking, but had no desire to appear a feeble coward. We wandered back to the aviary and spent the rest of the afternoon looking at a book of Grosz's cartoons which Hetty had bought for my birthday. The text was in academic German which meant we understood very little, but the savagery of the satire and the succulent lustfulness of certain drawings certainly impressed us both. Hetty hadn't bothered to look inside its daunting pages, but Tarkenter and I gave it a good and sweaty going over that Saturday afternoon amongst the budgerigars.

Wednesday morning came with frightening rapidity. I didn't exactly lie to my mother. I told her I was going for a long and solitary walk on my day off, and might even take a few train numbers down at the station. Tarkenter and I had agreed to reconnoitre there, as it seemed safest not to be seen brazenly plotting together the full length of the Banbury Road. There he was looking inordinately relaxed as he waited outside the cheap little café near the station. As soon as I saw him I gave an incredulous shudder, because Tarkenter had chosen to disguise himself with a bright purple balaclava.

'What do you think of my camouflage?' he asked.

I scrutinised him warily. He looked like a grotesque, pint-size version of King Arthur's Gawain.

'Not much,' I said. 'You're probably the only person in the south of England wearing a purple balaclava today. It makes you stand out.'

Tarkenter screwed up his densely freckled face. 'Perhaps

you're right. Do you want to wear it instead?'

I demurred. The balaclava got irretrievably stuck around his temples as he tried to pull it off. Swearing violently as he fought with his unyielding ears, he tore it loose and stuffed it into his knapsack. Tarkenter was also playing the avid trainspotter and had filled his bag with all the blameless paraphernalia. He had packed himself a few fishpaste sandwiches, a small black exercise book and a turquoise propelling pencil.

He opened his bag wide, and invited me to look further. Inside was something very few trainspotters would have found any specialist use for. I gasped at the sight of a giant catapult, a really wicked-looking thing with a pouch the size of Tarkenter's fist. It was the kind of implement I was sure professional hunters, dead-eye dicks, would use for slaying wolves and coyotes, even bears, out on the Wild Frontier.

'Where the hell did you get that?' I asked. 'You could kill an elephant with it.'

'Quite,' he said coolly. 'It's a professional poacher's catapult. My cousin Telford goes out poaching with a builder called Tovis from Carterton. They drink together in The Stoat and this Tovis chap has invited him out lamping with his lurcher dogs. They train the headlights on Tovis's car onto the deer in the Carterton plantation, and immobilise them with the glare. Then they set their bloody great dogs on them.'

'Do they?' I said sadly.

'They also use bloody great catapults like this one. Telford gave me it for my twelfth birthday and said, "You keep this fucking object a fucking secret whatever you do."'

I assumed we must be scheduled to hunt crows or rats by the river later on, and looked forward to handling such a grown-up weapon. Meanwhile, roaming round the station with our platform tickets and our virtuous little notebooks, I became so distracted by the setting I quite forgot our punitive task. I even started to hum to myself as I stared at one or two stationary engines and jotted down their numbers and names. After ten minutes of this dogged annotation, I grew very hungry and suggested we go in the station café. Tarkenter looked pityingly at my neat little notebook, and reminded me of our original purpose.

'It's ten to ten,' he said sharply. 'They'll be here in ten minutes or less. We need to bloody secrete ourselves.'

Tarkenter had been down here on his own two days ago, and had made some discreet (balaclavaless, he swore) enquiries. The 10.25 to Banbury, he had confirmed, was virtually simultaneous with the 10.23 to London. Hence the bridge between the two platforms would be thronging with travellers any time after 10.15. The first part of his plan was for us to dally by a distant railway building facing the Osney road. Then once it got to quarter past, we would mill with the passengers halfway along the bridge, pretending to examine the locos below. Piously transcribing train numbers, we would hide ourselves up there until Father Joseph and his flock were gathered below on the north-heading platform. After that it was pure, or rather impure, child's play.

'Hang on,' I objected. 'How on earth do we know they'll bunch themselves right below us? For tipping your coloured dye onto them?'

Tarkenter's smirk was oddly overemphatic. 'I have an abnormally strong right arm, George. Feel that muscle there if you don't believe me. I can throw the full length of a rugger pitch if I need to, and my aim these days is absolutely unerring. I'm Captain of the Junior Shooting Club at St Brid's as a result. By a choice irony, it was Father Joe himself showed me how to hold a pistol and make myself a dead-eye dick.'

'Ah,' I said wonderingly. 'Ah I see.'

We strode rather too businesslike around that grimy station building which contained a number of poky, partitioned offices. Inside we could see a few diminutive men with ragged moustaches scribbling away and smoking Players with a baleful sort of resignation. They looked up and, seeing our rucksacks, swiftly ignored us. We retraced our steps clutching our alibi notebooks, and at every opening onto the platform took a wary squint for the arrival of Father Joe.

Sharp at ten the legendary priest appeared. He was at the very front of his group and in hale good mood, bantering in a playful, hectoring way with his five excitable young choristers. He had a wholesome, unsparing look about him, which would have convinced any of the public he was all a good priest should be. Perennially good-humoured, conspicuously candid, forever ready with a lively joke or a lightning sally. There was the dog end of a Capstan between his bearded lips, though of course his gossipy weedy charges weren't smoking. He looked an endearing man, did this Father Joseph, and I expressed the incongruous perception to Tarkenter. Tarkenter sneered and said I should see him slurping with pleasure when he got a boy to cry at his canings. Why, he added quickly, by way of analogy, your own father, Bill Geraghty, looks a sane, quite pleasant sort of gent from a distance, doesn't he? Closer inspection soon revealing he's rather a dizzy sort of eccentric crackpot, eh? Not trying to be insulting, George, but your old man is rather bloody peculiar, isn't he?

'Oh yes,' I agreed. 'There's no doubt at all about that.'

Brickett was good and prominent amongst Father Joseph's beaming sycophants, those two or three who hung on his every word. Tarkenter stared hard at his worst enemy and made an obscene conjecture related to Brickett's facial pallor and Father Joseph's difficult vow of chastity. Then he turned to me, looking every inch the ruthless juvenile mercenary, and whispered: 'Come on, guv. We've got highly important work to do.'

I felt hysterical as I pictured splattering that smug bunch below with a shower of indelible dye. I also felt a finite amount of panic in my chest and bowels and an ineffable sense of hovering retribution. I was not of their queer Roman

Catholic school, and therefore not under their aegis. They had regular lessons in things like Sacred Music and Martyrology which meant they were almost as peculiar as my father. Nonetheless, it was inevitable that Father Joseph would be able to exact retribution via my headmaster, Dr Lawless. And of course if Tarkenter's parents were to learn of our crime, so would mine. All they had to do was walk three doors down the Banbury Road to get their hands on two repulsive reprobates for the price of one.

We stood with thumping hearts on the crowded bridge above the platform. Slowly we squeezed our way to the steps descending to the Banbury side. Tarkenter asked me to stand and shield him, while he rummaged in his bag with impatient hands.

'Where did you end up getting the dye?' I asked. Then I noticed a remarkably fat woman with a floral scarf was staring at us quizzically. Peering up from the platform, she evidently had some intelligent doubts about two little schoolboys spreading themselves pivotally along a central thoroughfare.

'Oh I didn't bother to get any dye.'

'No?' I said, waiting for that woman to avert her piggish gaze. 'So what did you get? You haven't got a bag full of shit have you?'

Tarkenter sighed. 'Don't be such an idiot, George.'

I watched in a slowed-down dream as he took the poacher's catapult out of his bag. The bag I noticed pointlessly was dangling in the area of his privates.

'Oh God!' I gasped.

Tarkenter scrutinised me with an incredibly adult assurance. He was only twelve years old, but looked at least a hundred and twelve.

'Why on earth not?' he snorted. 'It won't sting him much more than Father Joe's ferrule. Probably a good bit less. I'm not intending to kill anyone, George. That is, I don't think I am . . .'

I watched nervelessly as he pulled out a small paper bag. I had noticed it earlier and assumed it held a tomato or a bit of cheese for his lunch. He opened it and took out something very odd. It was a four-inch piece of alloy metal bent into a perfect U shape. The ends were frighteningly, murderously sharp.

'What the hell is *that?*'

Give him his due Tarkenter hesitated, as if to tell the whole truth would be a philosophical error.

'It's only a staple, George.'

'A staple?' I echoed terrified. 'Don't talk such stinking ballocks. It's more like a bloody six-inch nail.'

Tarkenter sighed at my ignorance of all things practical and mechanical.

'No, I promise you it's an industrial staple. In fact its proper name is masonry staple. It's used for fixing pipes on gable ends and so on.'

I shuddered tetanically. 'Is that a fact? And what the hell are you going to do with it? You're not –?'

Tarkenter offered no further explanations. He took hold of the glittering staple and put it inside the swinging pouch. Peering like a studious architect through the bridge's iron-work, he pointed his weapon expertly over the twittering choristers below. In every respect he was more like a Swiss archer with a six-foot crossbow than a freckled little school-boy with a six-inch catty.

'You'll kill one of them,' I whimpered. 'You will, Tarkenter!'

'Good,' he murmured softly. 'The less of that lot, the better.'

'Tarkenter,' I gibbered. 'We'll both be put in reformatory for the next twenty years.'

He turned and examined my terror with a little sanguine pity. 'Well it won't be any worse than St Brid's. And at least they won't pretend they're doing it for the good of my eternal soul.'

I began to babble a torrent of threats and pleadings, hoping to make him halt and reflect at this terrible existential abyss. I thought that if I distracted him with my rapid eloquence, he would absently unstring his poacher's crossbow and forget his mad revenge. Surely if I kept on debating, for example the moral coordinates of firing industrial rivets at one's peers, the Banbury train would chug away before he had a chance to maim. And surely, not even Thomas Tarkenter was mad enough to risk twenty years in borstal all because of a stunted milksop with a pair of pipe-cleaner legs?

A second later I heard the loudest scream anyone has ever heard from human lips. It sounded like someone contesting a prize audition for a box-office-record-breaking horror movie. It sounded so horrible, so hellish, so reverberant, I thought the station roof was going to crash upon our heads. Instantly the pair of us took to our heels. As per the master strategist's prior instructions, we raced off in opposite directions. Later, by a byzantine ox-bow route, I was scheduled to join him beside the Osney towpath. At the reconnoissance point we were to leisurely swap intelligence about the 'dye' escapade, guzzle our well-earned elevenses, and spend the rest of the day roaming the length of the river.

I had been ordered by the same expert to make a calm, unhurried progress in the direction of Oxpens. Indignant at his fatuous command, I tore up the middle of the road as if pursued by the entire Oxford police force. That horrible scream reverberated inside me as I ran. It was at least ten minutes before I judged myself to be at an adequate distance and stopped to pant behind a deserted warehouse. As well as panting, I jabbered aloud my terror and indignation.

If that staple, I babbled, was embedded in Brickett's skull, he was definitely a corpse by now. Or supposing, just supposing, it had sunk into one of Father Joe's ballocks? That agonised cry had sounded soprano and schoolboyish, but perhaps the missile had pierced the chaste man's gonads and made him an instant castrato? Or what if it had horrifically entered the poor priest's eye, as with King Harold (or was it Harald Hardrada?). Murdering a Catholic priest, I moaned, what would be the secular and/or eternal punishment for that? And, if we'd killed him, did that make Father Joseph a Catholic martyr? Had it in retrospect been his ordained fate to die, in order to protect the faith against a balaclavaed idolater, an unrepentant masturbator, an illegal weapons dealer, a shameless friend and consort of Protestants?

I took the zigzagging loop to Osney that Tarkenter had decreed. En route, I dodged in and out of deserted doorways convinced any second I'd be grabbed by a six-foot policeman. I was expecting Thomas Tarkenter to be in the same sort of terror, instead of which I found him boredly twanging the catapult elastic and whistling with an unfeigned calm. He looked up from his tranquil thoughts and gave a bland Churchillian wave of two fingers. Indeed he gazed at me rather absently, as if I wasn't really a significant part of his larger meditations.

'How come,' I bawled at him, 'you aren't petrified out of your wits? The police might be on to us at any bloody minute.'

He said, 'God, you look white, Geraghty. You look like your own ghost.'

I answered tearfully, 'I feel like one. I never wanted to be a fucking assassin, Tarkenter. We've probably killed little Brickett with that horrible bloody staple.'

He looked without cynicism at my upset. 'Unfortunately we haven't. We've only wounded Boston D'Arcy instead.'

I flinched and scowled at that ridiculous name. 'Who the hell is Boston bloody D'Arcy?'

Boston D'Arcy was yet another chorister fairy, or so Tarkenter bluffly categorised him. Like Brickett he was fake pious and like Brickett always white in the chops. Because of, opined Tarkenter, that same pathetic prepubertal onanism. He was another of Father Joe's willing catamites, was his next insinuation. Tarkenter actually used the term 'catamite', as he had a precocious literary appetite, and already knew an enormous amount about the dark underbelly of human affairs. At any rate he had dallied long enough behind the station to identify the scream as that of D'Arcy. The fairy chorister had copped the masonry staple in his upper thigh. The little catamite was young enough and stupid enough to wear short trousers, and the staple had had no option but to bed itself inside his bare leg.

'Did you see any blood?' I asked.

'Torrential streams of it. Oh stop trembling, George, I'm just joking. No, it just seemed to go incredibly purple and disgustingly swollen.'

'Oh God . . .'

'Then of course Father Joe took charge of things. First of all he knelt down on the platform and said a hurried prayer. Then I heard him send someone off to get the station master. To get Boston D'Arcy some immediate First Aid, I suppose.'

And also the railway police, I shouted bitterly. After which no doubt the ordinary police, the Oxfordshire CID, the whole bloody lot. Not forgetting a phone call to the Radcliffe Hospital, I added, where Tarkenter's own mother worked. And what was likely to happen when they traced the two idiotic culprits? Two ridiculous, absurdly conspicuous twelve-year-old truanting trainspotters. One a truant proper, the other his evil Protestant accomplice. Assuming she was still there when the police began investigations, that ugly fat woman who had stared at us would also prove an invaluable witness.

Tarkenter looked shrewdly sceptical. 'It won't get as far as that. A nurse'll soon sort D'Arcy out. A huge needle up the arse for tetanus is the worst the little bum boy will face. Pity I can't watch it all from behind the hospital screen.'

'Maybe your mother will give him it,' I said thoughtfully.

'She's a gynaecologist, Geraghty. She only deals with women's arses.'

Tarkenter spent the rest of the day by the river with his catapult. I was too terrified to do anything, and I told him I was going home to read my George Grosz. It was the only thing I could think of that would distract me for the next crucial twenty-four hours. He shook his head dismissively, then said that if by a fluke he was traced and apprehended he would swear on oath the pair of us were innocent. But supposing they subjected him to any sort of mental pressure or physical torture and he cracked, he would take all the blame on himself.

'Thank you very much,' I grunted, and I set off home with drooping shoulders.

Bill Geraghty was toiling late as ever at Abingdon that evening. During supper I kept clearing my throat and sighing plaintively, desperate to tell my mother what I'd done. But maddeningly she kept on clearing her own throat, as if desperate to confide something else to me. In the end I groaned so deafeningly she asked me if I was ill, and I embraced the suggestion immediately. I was in any case falling prey to the physical manifestations of guilt and terror. I really thought I was coming down with something serious, I sighed to her, in a flat and tragic tone. She ordered me to bed at once, and I tottered gratefully upstairs. I staggered into bed with Grosz, then listened dismayed as my mother wept softly in the bathroom.

I stayed off school the next day, as pale and fretful as a wintry sky. Lying in bed I made plans to run away from home and wander the countryside as an unhappy guilt-ridden tramp. I was convinced that D'Arcy would get gangrene in his leg and it would have to be amputated. I was certain that Tarkenter would receive the flogging of his life from Father Joseph. Perhaps they would have to thrash him more than just the once? Perhaps they would beat him senseless once a week for the next twelve months, with a double quantity at

Easter and on Saints' Days.

That evening at around six o'clock there was a loud hammering at the door. At once I dived beneath the bedclothes. Bill Geraghty had never subscribed to corporal punishment, but I knew he would feel obliged to give me a royal hiding for yesterday's wickedness. I heard Hetty talking very solemnly at the door and then in a disappointed voice ushering someone inside. Their twin steps moved in the direction of the stairs and two inaudible murmurs chimed together. A menacing creaking followed as they ascended upstairs. The footsteps ceased and an eerie quiet ensued. I lay there quaking like a stricken rabbit. Then came a hideous rat-a-tat-tat and the sound of someone clearing his throat.

I tried to say 'come in', but it came out as: 'Gguuh.'

The door began to open inch by inch as if being propelled by a sinister hand. I expected a pitiless trilbied detective, or possibly half a dozen. The door was fully open yet no one had entered the room. I stared terrified at this phantom entrance. Then a dwarfish figure rushed into the room and, hurtling towards me, shouted: '*Putain*! Ere come M'sieur Maigret!'

I foamed at the mouth, 'Bastard! You bastard bastard bastard, bloody *bastard*!'

'*Comment?*'

'I nearly died of bloody terror.'

Tarkenter arched his eyebrows and surveyed me like a shrewd clinician. Ill with his puny nerves was his instant mental diagnosis. Yet I detected a fleeting sympathy, as if he assumed that to be a worm like me must be a very debilitating condition.

'What's happened?' I said surlily. 'Do they know it was us?'

He puckered his lips and sat down on my bed. Then he picked up the Grosz cartoons and leafed through them salaciously. I glared at his teasing silence.

'Well?'

'Yes.'

'Oh my God. Oh my God.'

Tarkenter took some of my invalid's grapes and began to swing them idly.

'They soon found out it was me who used the catapult. Given how brainless they are in every other respect, I was amazed by such lightning efficiency. I was called in by Father Joseph first thing this morning. He told me that the witnesses the police had questioned all spoke of a second boy being present. Half the railway station saw us there unfortunately.'

'But they can't have done,' I said in a childish squeak. 'We hid ourselves so carefully.'

'Of course I denied it all immediately. I said that I was on my own all day long. I categorically rebutted any involvement, but Father Joe didn't bother with any legal process after that. It had been proved, he said, that I had truanted because, believe it or not, the school cook's brother lives at Osney Mead and he'd seen me down there. He'd been out walking his blasted dog and seen me firing my catty at the starlings. In fact he had the cheek to tell me to stop it, so I told him to fuck off.'

'You –'

'How was I to know it was the cook's brother? Or that he could easily identify me to Father Joe? Father Joe turned that on me, but I said, no sir, the truth was it was the cook's brother who had told *me* to fuck off. That enraged Father Joe out of all proportion. He knew I was lying and he knew that I knew that, and it made him apoplectic. I said yes, agreed I had a catapult, but no I hadn't been down there at the station. And I said even if I had been there I wouldn't have used that dirty great nail they took out of Boston D'Arcy's leg. It could easily have killed someone, ammunition like that, I told the Father. I said I didn't want to spend my life in a punitive reformatory and that only a complete fool would have shot something like that with a catapult as powerful as mine.'

'What did he say to that?' I asked numbly.

'He said he was going to flog me for the truancy, irrespective. Also, having consulted with two other Brothers and the Senior Brother, he would give me an additional flogging for injuring Boston D'Arcy with that terrible staple. Even though I denied it, he was completely satisfied of my guilt. I wasn't going to let him have his way as easily as that, of course. But just as I was furiously protesting my innocence, in ran a Fifth Former with a message from the secretary. Father Joe looked at it and almost wept with joy. He turned to me smirking and told me to stay put and quake for a few minutes, and off he ran, the soutaned bastard. After about two minutes he came racing back with an enormous grin. A telephone message had just come through from the Oxford station master. And guess what?'

'I can't imagine,' I said. 'I don't even want to imagine.'

'Where we fired the catapult, one of the railwaymen had found a purple balaclava.'

I made a little howling sound on his behalf. I didn't dare ask what had followed. It was strange he showed no signs of it, but surely he must have been beaten to a pulp.

'It even had my name stitched on it! Father Joseph was so jubilant. He licked his lips and said he was half tempted to make me wear the balaclava as a penitential hood when he flogged me. He told me he was going to flog me publicly in front of the assembled school. After consulting with the other Brothers he was going to give me the unheard of total of ten strokes on the left hand and twenty strokes on the right hand, the one that had held the catapult sling.'

'Oh Tarkenter,' I groaned. 'Show me your hands.'

He opened his small and delicate palms. There was no trace whatever of any weals. They were perfectly unscathed.

I said angrily, 'What's going on? I don't understand.'

He smiled. 'There's a simple explanation. Even though I was proven guilty and therefore deserved a severe flogging, I wasn't flogged. Somebody *else* was flogged instead of me, George!'

I glared at him. 'Ballocks, Tarkenter.'

'No it's not, Geraghty. They flogged that stupid bugger *Brickett* instead.'

I shot out of bed and seized his unscathed hands. 'Don't keep on *lying* to me, Tarkenter.'

'Tch tch, George! I promise!'

'Promise all you bloody like! Stop talking bloody nonsense.'

He said drily, 'It's not nonsense at all if you're a good Roman Catholic. It makes sense if you swallow it all hook, line and sinker. That fool Brickett went up to Father Joe at lunch time and pleaded for the honour of being punished *in my place.*'

'I –'

'Brickett had soon learnt about my imminent public flogging. Luckily he didn't know that my staple had been intended specifically for him. Maybe it'd have been different if he had. But he informed his hero Father Joseph, who announced it proudly to all of us, that *he wished to take Tarkenter's flogging upon himself*. Brickett wished to take my awful crime, my terrible sin, upon himself. As a spiritual penance, as a humble act of atonement.'

I stared at him in absolute consternation. I told Tarkenter I thought that his religion was . . . what was the word? Demented. Bloody crazy. I said that I couldn't believe that any priest would be so mad as to let a boy be flogged for another boy's crime. Surely if Tarkenter had almost killed or seriously injured Boston D'Arcy, that fool Brickett wouldn't have been allowed to step into his shoes?

'Who knows?' said Tarkenter yawning. 'Though I was seriously tempted to tell Father Joe that Brickett deserved to be burnt at the stake – in the middle of St Brid's quadrangle at any rate – for heresy. He was taking my sins upon his shoulders in an imitation of the sacred saints themselves. Sheer presumption and blatant heresy, isn't it? But I didn't. I thought it was better to see Brickett getting flogged after all.

It saved me from wasting any more staples, apart from anything else.'

I asked him fearfully, 'What did they do to Brickett?'

'Father Joe gave him thirty vicious strokes with the ferrule. He lammed him as hard as he could, his very favourite pupil. Brickett's hands were the most unbelievable mess by the end of it. He screamed his little head off and muttered umpteen prayers while it was happening. I noticed that he didn't even lisp when he screamed. It must have taken a good quarter of an hour, all that flogging, but it seemed to last about a year. Everyone watching was rooted to the spot. Nobody laughed, as they might well have done. No one loves Brickett but they were all stupefied by his sacrifice. They realised what it was to be an apprentice Catholic martyr. At the end of it Father Joseph hugged him and said he was a great spirit. Brickett was in a hell of a state, crying his eyes out, but we heard him say thank you to Father Joe for allowing him to take a poor sinner's place.'

Four

A major crisis befell my father in the summer of 1936. I was a shy and diffident sixteen year old by then, and Hetty as far as I could guess had almost worked herself up to seeking a divorce. It was Bill's terrible tragedy which seemed to change my mother's decision at the last minute. Even an unworldly teenager had noticed her becoming unsubtly infatuated with a new acquaintance of her younger sister, my Aunty Greer. Aunty Greer was a stringy six-foot-tall cello teacher who lived near Henley and had a number of startlingly progressive metropolitan friends. Amongst them were a forty-five-year-old poet called Geoffrey Hass who incredibly wore twin monocles rather than a single pair of specs, and a sixty-five-year-old composer of avant-garde atonal music called William Pimblett. Bill had met them two or three times at parties given by Greer, and had been spectacularly rude to both. Once William Pimblett, whose bloated old ears were as hairy as a retriever's, played a stark and lethal forty-minute piano sonata, a crude plagiaristic pilfering from Schoenberg. Throughout his smileless hammer-and-nails performance, Bill bared his mouth wide open and kept picking at his deliberately protruded front teeth like a prognathous beaver. It was aggressive sabotage of course rather than philistine ignorance. To my ear alone he referred to Pimblett as 'William Omelette, Ponce of Darkness', and applauded his own double pun.

Hetty was shyly deferential towards the awful musician, but blushingly demonstrative when talking to Hass. Most males wearing monocles look like blimpish snobs or Woosterish toffs, but Geoffrey Hass was oddly enhanced by his pair. He was the only monocle wearer I have ever seen who didn't need to grimace to keep them in place. They looked as if they had jumped of their own volition into his eye sockets, overjoyed at finding a distinguished home. Also Hass minus his monocles was a strikingly handsome man and he knew it. Also he could plainly see the tension between the Geraghty couple and doubtless had heard about Bill's oddities from Greer. Also both Hass and my father were competitive failures, for where Bill had enormous brains but no commensurate academic glory, Hass was reckoned an original poet whose gifts remained stubbornly unrecognised. He had published only two very slim and limited editions in the last fifteen years. I had actually gone out and purchased one of them, entitled *Cicisbeo*, and at sixteen had been enormously impressed. In one poem alone he had managed to use the following obscure words: 'ursine', 'bassinets', 'Cicerone', 'palanquin' and 'nugatory'. Later I showed the poem to Bill who snorted and denounced him as a 'meretricious invert' or 'if not a sodomite in practice, certainly one in bloody disguise'.

'Modern poets,' he leered as he slapped the slim tome shut, 'are in the main flagrant intellectual charlatans too damn shiftless to harness their meagre musings into an enduring form. Surely by 1936, George, any author who is a serious artist rolls up his shirt sleeves and gets stuck into honest and diamond-hard *prose*. Into forceful and workman-like chapters, that is, instead of all these putrid bloody stanzas.'

'You really don't think much of Geoffrey's poetry?' I said disappointed.

'Pah! A proper writer would distil said pithy reflections into red-blooded prose, instead of skulking behind his own shadow with these ugly little broken-backed verses. The damn gall the man has to stand up in a pleasant middle-class living room like Greer's and spew it all out, this witless Masonic gobbledeygook, as brazen as any prancing troubadour. Fat lot I care about his palanquins and his bloody bassinets, eh? Why the hell should I care about 'em? He's babbling on about some sylvan woodland fol-de-rol so really he's only talking about fairy hammocks and fairy perambulators. With the stress on the fairy which is aptly enough in the possessive case, ha ha. A bloody giveaway his "poetic" vocabulary. That beggar Hass prefers lolling on his London sofa and penning scrappy bagatelles of posturing trash to sweating industriously at his desk writing something worth reading. Why didn't he put a vivid, punchy sort of alternative like "shake-me-down" or "truckle bed" instead of "palanquin", eh? Doesn't have the same slithery womanish sleight-of-hand, not sufficiently fairyfied, eh? As for any scintilla of supposed meaning apropos these verses, George, it is all the most opaque and lacklustre bosh. In my view if an author chap is convinced he has something first rate to tell us, let him damn well put it all down in black and white, let him slap it down for all to see like a man.

'I maintain that any chap with the nerve to declare himself a serious poet in 1936 ought to be creating an incendiary conflagration like Byron or Wordsworth or Shelley. A fearless revolutionary or a womanising madman, not a bleary bimonocled nancy with a broken soprano whinge like Hass's. Just supposing we forced that pathetic fool Hass to write *exactly* what he meant in honest lucid prose instead of his impenetrable verse. Then, supposing you and me, boy, supposing we two Geraghtys examined the finished offering under an imaginary lexical/artistic/aesthetic microscope. What do you think we would see?'

'I –'

'My prediction would be . . . nothing. Not a bloody thing. Not a tittle. An empty screaming page, George.'

Pleased with his stanchless phillipic he rose from his armchair and said he was going outside for a breath of air. Picturing the object of his ridicule, for a few seconds I pondered my father's own cuckolding. Bill's philandering was so blatant the restraint shown by Hetty with Hass must have duped him completely. Clearly he had no idea what she got up to down in Henley-on-Thames. He took his whisky and his cigar and shambled out with that crouched and lurching gait, a bit like a dog sneaking off to do some mischief. I also thought he looked very much like a well-to-do bookie's runner or a smartly-attired small-time crook. Even at sixteen I realised that people can't easily hide their true and frightening natures, not even by the way they amble into the garden.

When my father returned it was without any flourish or sprightliness. He came back walking very slowly indeed. I watched in alarm as I saw he was doing something I had never seen him do. Bill Geraghty was crying. Profuse and frantic tears were running down his heavy, wilful face. For a second or two I had terrible thoughts that he'd had a telegram about something dreadful and had received it out there by the garden gate. Perhaps, oh God, my mother had been killed on the train to Henley. His shoulders were shaking convulsively, his face twisted with a pitiful grief, the tears plopping down onto his outstretched palm.

'What is it?' I stammered. 'What's happened?'

'It's . . . her . . .' he sobbed. 'Oh it's her . . . it's my darling.'

My heart began to pound with incredible violence. It was my mother. Something terrible must have happened to the only other sane person in the house. I felt as if my head were going to split in two at the unbearable thought.

'Is it my mother?' I gasped.

He stared incensed through his tears. 'Of course not. It's nothing to do with her. It's far more . . . it's too . . . it's too . . .' His voice broke as he sputtered and hiccupped. 'It's . . . it's . . . poor poor Mrs White . . .'

I trembled with the massive exultation of knowing I still had a mother. I was also enraged with my absurd bloody father for letting me think otherwise, even for two seconds. But as Bill approached, I saw the little budgerigar lying dead in his hand. It was his legendary love, his little favourite, his angelic Mrs White.

'Oh,' I said doubtfully. 'Oh that's . . . that's quite sad.'

He stared open-mouthed, quite frightened by my idiotic adjective. I looked guiltily at the object of his love and saw it to be tiny, inert, indescribably graceful. The longer I gazed, the more I saw of an inexplicable and unyielding pathos. I stared at that tiny gracefulness and wondered if that was the same thing my father saw. I could scarcely believe that with his randomly scattered sensitivities he could possibly perceive anything like me. If he was capable of observing a pitiless pathos in the corpse of Mrs White, then he should be capable of discerning it elsewhere. For example, in the endless marital suffering of his wife.

'Oh, George,' he wept. 'What shall I do? What shall I do now that she's gone?'

I had the strongest premonition. I felt as if I was hearing the voice he would use if Hetty were to run off to gay Paris or gorgeous Rome with Geoffrey Hass. Or if, without giving him reasonable notice, she were to die of an accident or an illness. But keenly as I felt it, I knew it was not an accurate parallel. Because I knew in the last event he had always loved a bird, Mrs White, more than he had ever loved my mother, Mrs Geraghty. He had forever been leading bemused visitors and wary relatives into his garden aviary to demonstrate his matchless little treasure with the baffling name. He had openly doted on his angelic blue budgerigar, but never on his wife or his only son George.

'Oh the poor old gal,' he stammered through his tears. 'Oh the poor old poor old little gal.'

I murmured nervously, 'Is she . . . what do you think she died of, Dad?'

He glared at my ignorance. 'Old bloody age, what d'you think? Nothing more pernicious for a little cage bird than to be piling on the years. Mrs White was as old as the Mendips in budgie terms.'

For the next twenty-four hours he was inconsolable. He took Mrs White upstairs with him and spent the afternoon and evening locked away in his study. At first an unearthly silence emanated from his room. Hetty arrived home about six, supposedly from an afternoon of helping Greer with the design of her Henley garden. She smelt of an unusually pungent perfume which I thought might have been Greer's or possibly Hass's. I looked at her uneasily as I explained Bill's recent bereavement. With a guilty flush she dashed upstairs and hammered on the study door. After an eternity Bill mumbled that he had a wish to be quite alone with Mrs White, that he was in fact holding her wake, and we probably wouldn't see him till the morning. Also, he muttered in the weirdest though sincerest tones we had ever heard, he wasn't sure that life itself had much to hold now that Mrs White was gone. Oh not to panic, he added listlessly, he wasn't the wretched *felo de se* type, but he didn't expect to surface from deep mourning for at least a week.

But what about your work, Hetty demanded, what was she supposed to say to Mr Losty, his print manager at Abingdon?

'Tell him Bill Geraghty is in deep mourning,' shouted my father, 'for the finest little act of creation in the whole of bloody Oxford.'

I stood outside the door with Hetty, and we had the bizarre experience of hearing him talking to his dead bird. Renouncing all theatricality, he addressed a tender, resonant elegy to Mrs White. He told her everything he remembered of her history, described in precise meteorological detail the weather on the day he bought her, then the necessarily sensitive manner in which he had introduced her to all his other birds. He talked about her little blue mirror on which in blue ink he had inscribed her name, and which he would bury beside her as if she were an avine Pharaoh. He spoke of her absolute specialness, the very private place she occupied in his affections. He pointed out that he was not a man for throwing his love around any old where, that he was a very private person, someone of whom hardly anyone knew the subtle depths. Least of all, he snorted emphatically, his immediate family. Mrs White, he informed her, was certainly one of the very few who had been granted a view of his complex emotional recesses. I watched my mother's face at that, and she looked both remorseful and embittered.

'Do you think . . ?' I began downstairs, as the two of us ate supper without him.

'What?' she said abstractedly.

'Do you think my father is mad?'

Hetty flickered from her mournful reverie. She rested her face on her fingers and pondered.

'I think he is most definitely an unusual man. Yet your father is remarkably true to himself in his own way. Mad or not, he manages to earn a living and to keep his family.'

'But he's talking to a dead budgie . . .'

'Yes but he knows it's dead, George. That's what really matters. He doesn't think it's listening from the beyond.'

The next morning Bill emerged from his study and ordered us to accompany him on a solemn pilgrimage. He was going to bury Mrs White, and he felt it only right the whole family should attend as a measure of the gravest respect. We assumed he meant stepping out into the garden, but he advised us no, we would need our topcoats and possibly our gumboots. When he said bury he hadn't meant literal interment. No, what he meant was a ceremony of dispersal. He was going to take Mrs White down to Port Meadow and cast her into the same bit of river where poor old Stanforth had been cast.

Hetty looked at him pityingly. 'Your father was eaten by an Alsatian, Bill. He never actually got as far as the river.'

'Eh?' he mumbled. 'Oh, I'd forgotten that. Still the original intention was there at any rate.'

I asked with interest, 'How are you going to do the

71

incineration? I mean you'll have to turn her into ashes first, won't you?'

'Don't be so obscene!' he barked at me. 'I'm not going to touch a feather on her precious head. I'll tip her in there just as she is in her lovely perfection. Inside a heavy funeral casket of course, just to make sure she sinks. See, I've already got her here inside this box.'

My mother gasped at the luxurious sarcophagus he showed us. 'That little box is the finest Wedgewood china. It was one of my nicest wedding presents! It cost my mother eight guineas . . .'

The casket co-recipient was furious. He clenched his fists and looked ready to take a punch at her. 'The greatest love of my life is worth more than any amount of filthy lucre, Hetty! You know very well I would pay several king's ransoms to have her cheeping and lovebirding to me on her swing again. Just the way it used to be until yesterday after-noon . . .'

And he broke down again at the terrible prospect of a life without Mrs White. Hetty scowled and reached resentfully for her best raincoat. We followed him slowly, foolishly down to Port Meadow. I looked on with the cold fascination of an amateur anthropologist, but Hetty nursed a mounting anger with every step. At Bill Geraghty's funeral eight years later, she took me to one side and said that it was that day more than any, the day of Mrs White's funeral, when she had been agonising over a move to London with Geoffrey Hass. She was confident enough that I could look after myself adequately at sixteen, but fearful that Bill would end up so disordered after his cagebird bereavement they would have to put him under lock and key.

Bill made a resolute military progress towards the river. I flinched as he stepped in two cowpats and didn't even notice. He had reached the bank five minutes before us, and he surveyed our tardiness as serious mourners with distaste. Once we were assembled he reached into his pocket and came out with the Book of Common Prayer. I held back a sneeze and realised I would have to stifle a fit of hysterics. Hetty glared at him and said if he thought she was about to endure an entire burial service for the benefit of a budgerigar she was going immediately. Even Stanforth Geraghty hadn't been granted that luxury, irrespective of rapacious Alsatians. Bill silenced her with a lordly shush and calmly explained that because it was the Ninth Sunday after Easter he was not only going to do the full Morning Prayer but also the complete Litany: all that as well as the ordinary burial service.

'The standard burial service only takes twenty minutes, Hetty. You'll agree that's not enough for Mrs White, a cruel insult to her treasured memory. I did ring that clownish clergyman Beatty on Woodstock Road to see if he would do it for me but he told me to go and see a doctor pronto. So, if the established church says it won't see to the love of my life, I will have to give her the full pageantry she deserves. The whole thing should last about an hour and a half, according to the dress rehearsal I did in my study. Then as an appropriate funeral tea, I thought a spot of lunch in the Randolph, this being such an exceptional occasion.'

Hetty gaped at his fatuous earnestness. 'An hour-and-a-half service? But you aren't even a clergyman! You aren't even a lay reader. You don't even go to church! And you seriously intend to chant every single bit of that endless thing called the Litany for a bloody *cage bird*. It sounds like absolute sacrilege to me.'

Bill growled impatiently, 'I tell you our nearest parson, that spindly leftwing imbecile Beatty, refused to bury Mrs White. If he won't do his sacred duty, I shall have to be the blasted invocator in his stead.'

Hetty turned tail and walked off without a word. I shrugged my shoulders and smiled at him reassuringly. I stayed there with my dishevelled father and became his exclusive congregation.

For the first twenty minutes at any rate. Until Bill, clutching

Mrs White in her Wedgwood casket, turned to address the river with the unabbreviated Litany. It was then I took to my heels before he had the chance to see me flee . . .

He languished in a profound misery for about a month. The simple business of feeding all his budgerigars and finches was enough to remind him of the darling who was missing and to redouble his grief. Once he asked me in a tearful voice to do the mournful job instead, and even talked wildly of getting rid of his aviary.

One morning looking very shocked and unkempt, he told me that he had dreamt of Mrs White coming back to life again. In this vivid, prophetic and unsettling dream, Mrs White had talked to him at considerable length.

I asked him spellbound, 'Really? What did she say?'

He answered with an entranced expression, 'The sweetest words anyone has ever spoken, George! Mrs White looked at her grieving old master and came out with the purest and gentlest of sounds. What she said to me was oh so . . . so magical . . . so infinitely profound . . .'

I persisted, 'But what exactly did she say?'

'That's the unfathomable mystery, lad. Her speech was perfection itself, so it didn't seem to matter when I couldn't make out any cogent sense as such. She was having her say oh so eloquently, and it was so extraordinarily beautiful everything she was communicating from the ah . . . from the other side of the, ah, the divide. But I'm damned if I can recall any actual, significant content. It's driving me half crazy, because it all seemed of the utmost prophetic importance at the time.'

Soon it got to the stage where he was talking of going to the nearest Spiritualist Church in order to get a more lucid, possibly publishable account from Mrs White. His all-consuming grief rattled Hetty sufficiently for her to cease her trips to Henley, and with that she grew irritable with her son as well as her husband. The following weekend they had one almighty tearful row over his stubborn obsession with the dead bird. Bill stalked out of the house ranting and swearing and promising never to return, not even if she bloody well begged him. He returned, still ranting, at two in the morning, yet a few days later a mysterious sanguine calm suddenly became evident in my father's behaviour. The storm had broken at long last, and that leaden cloud of grief had dissipated. Bill ceased to blanch and sob every time anyone mentioned the words 'Mrs', 'bird' or 'death' in any innocent context. He had been back at Losty's for some time, but now he was up in the mornings without struggle and even whistling as he left the house. Hetty also began to smile again but was lingeringly resentful of certain missed opportunities. No doubt Geoffrey Hass had found someone else to enchant with his mesmerising monocles and his difficult poetry. However, she resumed her visits to London and Henley, and a new and devious wilfulness, fragile as it was, began to show in her voice and her expression. I sometimes wondered if she had found herself drawn by default to the atonal severity of William Pimblett, the old man with the gun-dog ears and the horrible music. She started to smoke heavily and to drink with abandon. Bill as ever was crassly oblivious of that smouldering rebellion in his wife, much too intent on celebrating release from the misery of his bereavement.

Anyone might wonder how a boy of sixteen managed to endure the instability of such a marriage. In reality, sulky as I often was, I was mostly indifferent to their ridiculous melodramas. I felt sorry for my mother when she wept in secret but stonily concluded that the problem, the tragedy, was hers, not mine. How could I possibly solve the absurdity of their married life and the absurdity of my father's personality? In any case I didn't really believe that my father was real. He seemed more of an implausible theatrical caricature than anyone I had ever met. Because Bill wasn't entirely real, he wasn't really credible as an agent in my destiny. I sternly brushed him off and decided that my trajectory through life would be determined by my own deeds, efforts and desires, not through anything he had inculcated. Besides, Bill Geraghty was no longer an inculcator. He had tried hard enough with his fatuous lunchtime drill ten years ago, but that was all dead history. I had made a private pact with myself that, as soon as it was feasible, I would have as little to do with Bill and Hetty as possible. I would make myself financially independent by the age of twenty-one, and would visit them only out of inclination, not out of economic necessity.

One August evening I was mooning in the garden with a copy of Rilke's poetry when there was a loud knocking at the front door. It was so loud I jumped with apprehension, not to say a diffuse, irrational sense of guilt. Bill Geraghty was nowhere to be seen of course. As evidence of his rapid emotional recovery, my mercurial father was back to his twelve-hour shifts at Abingdon. On an evening like this he would probably have called in at The Lamb and Flag for a slow gin and tonic. Hetty was outside on her knees weeding her bedding plants, though I was quite confident her thoughts were down in NW3 with the decadent prewar avant-garde.

'Will you go?' she shouted to me wearily. 'I'm covered with all this bloody soil. Whoever it is, ask them to hammer less aggressively next time. Such ridiculous bloody rudeness to batter on a door like that.'

I walked through into the hallway. Through the dimpled glass of the door I could make out a trilby hat and a vast bobbing head. I assumed at once it could only be the plain-clothes police and I opened with foreboding.

A squat fat man of about fifty was stood outside. He wasn't my picture of a plain-clothes policeman, but he certainly looked alarming. It was a sticky summer night and he was sporting a vivid crimson shirt of a cheap and crude design. It was the kind of garment you would buy on a market stall or from a shifty salesman touting at the door. His sleeves were rolled up and on one beefy arm there was an outsize tattoo enclosing a heart with a name on it. The name was 'Maisie'. He had a cork-tipped Craven A in his restless lips and was squinting aggressively at the smoke percolating up his nose. He stared at me with insolent suspicion and I could hardly return his gaze. Far from being a man of the law, he looked more like an unabashed and unstable Oxford criminal.

'Is this the Geraghty place?' he croaked in a harsh and tarry register. His fingers were black with nicotine as if he got through a hundred Cravens a day.

'Yes,' I managed.

'And who are you then? Are you the lad?'

'I'm not my father,' I said hastily.

The large man guffawed and he touched his tattoo with a meditative caress.

'Nor would you want to be. No one would want to be in his boots right now for a crock of gold. But it's him what I want to see.'

I tried to gather some composure and to repel this uncouth phantom.

'You can't,' I sighed with a fluttering heart.

'Why the hell not?'

'Because he's still at work.'

The phantom glanced at its tattoo and smirked. 'And at his work they said he should be home by now. They told me with such honest serious faces that he caught the five o'clock into Oxford. So one of the two parties has to be messing with the facts, and in this case it might well be you. I'll bet you your old man has a whole string of ready-made fairytales to flummox the husbands. Come on, son, why would any white-collar blighter be toiling away at eight o'clock of a boiling summer night?'

'He's a proofreader,' I stammered. 'The workload varies

terrifically.'

'Terrifically! Haw! Haw! I bet it bloody does.'

'But it does,' I said.

'Pah! I've been asking about. I've been talking to one or two observant folk, barflies and nosy old women and lay-abouts in the Abingdon pubs. You'd be surprised to see how he goes and spreads it about all over the place. Abingdon's not a very big town but he's turned it into a bleedin Sod em and a Gomorrer. Your Dad . . . let's just check this for accuracy before we take any action . . . your father Bill Geraghty works where?'

'Abingdon,' I squeaked terrified. 'Losty's Printers and Publishers.'

'So does my missus,' he said glowering. 'Jack Losty's her boss as well.'

I looked agog and felt aghast. 'Does she really?'

He mimicked my accent cruelly. 'Yaas. Rea-ll-eeh she do, young squire. She really do work at Jack Losty's, young sir. Or at least she did till today, but I've gone and given her notice in. Then I took her home as fast as I could drag her, and followed her round the kitchen and the sitting room and left her with a few lasting reminders. Then I informed our lads Derry and Mike about her secret life and they got very mad and gave their old mum a bit of a dance lesson as well. It's partly my own fault I admit. I should have listened to my own suspicions. Everyone should always listen to their suspi-cions, young Lord Fondleroyce. Always. I let her go out to work in an office among a lot of men when I didn't really feel happy about it. I was right to feel uneasy, wasn't I? Your father, Lord bless him, has gone and proved me right. Women weren't meant to go out and bloody mix among men, not when there are cave men Cast an Oafers like your Dad about.'

I gawped at this homo pithecanthropus who was referring to Bill as a cave man. I tried to say something pertinent, but nothing would come out.

'He dips his dirty wick, your wicked dirty dad! Dirty, dirty, dirty, dirty little Bill! He sticks it bloody everywhere, does Bill. Half of the women at Losty's, half of the barmaids in bloody Abingdon. There's only one practical solution for persistent Donjunes like him. He needs to be gelded. Especially and more than anything because he's a toff, and he's arrogant enough to go messing with the local working class. Look, you tell him. If he wants to go spreading it like pox or measles, let him do it with your mum's posh sister or your mum's posh sister's posh sister-in-law etc. etc., and especially if she's a bleedin snooty dowcha or a bleedin right on.'

I was about to tell him that Greer had no sister-in-law when Hetty came up behind me. I decided to shoot inside and leave them to it, but they both put arresting hands upon my shoulders.

'What does this person want?' barked Hetty, haughtier than Marie Antoinette by a factor of ten.

From the Abingdon man: 'You stay there, boy! Just in case I lose my temper with your poor dear mamaaa.'

'In case you what?' choked Hetty.

'He,' I translated rapidly, 'he wants Dad. He ah . . . he thinks Dad . . . he thinks that seemingly Dad and . . . apparently his . . . his wife . . .'

Hetty's flush was barely visible. Breathing hard to regain her tempo she scrutinised this overheated roustabout.

'Mr . . ?'

'Thorne. Barrie Thorne. Look, I don't want any patronising glares from the likes of you, lady. You won't care to hear it, but I've been put forward to train as a Cowley union rep and I'm not afraid of any bugger these days. I'm forced to write all these little essays about sosighty and give little talks to the class and use plenty of big words and it's changed me already in ways you can't imagine. Don't you see, it's types like you that should be squirming and doing the apologies, not me? Your wonderful husband, milady, is working all his overtime only so's he can molest half the women in

Abingdon. He's just finished doing his ugly, nasty business with my wife. I've decorated her in two-tone blue for it, and I'm sorry but I intend to do likewise with your sneaky husband. Your boy says he's still slaving at Losty's and at Losty's, guess what, they swear he's gone back to his smart residence in North Oxford. I'm going to stand here at your front door till he shows his sly little weasel face. Either he's hiding inside, or he's prancing his way up St Giles, but either way I'm waiting here to give him his reward.'

Hetty stopped his searing monologue with an enigmatic gesture. She raised her palm majestically and to my amazement assumed a mask of glassy charm.

'Mr Thorne. Wait just one second, will you? You've had a stuffy train journey and an appallingly long hike up the Banbury Road. You look worn out and it's such a roasting evening. I'll just go inside and get my husband. He's up there working in his study, but I'm quite sure he'll sort things out to your satisfaction. I'll be back with him in a trice.'

She swept away and Thorne looked on with grudging admiration.

'Loyal to your old man, eh son? Telling lots of helpful lies for the crafty old bleeder. It's not going to save him from crude natural justice though.'

I was flabbergasted. How on earth did she propose to produce Bill out of nowhere? Was she just going to ring for the police? I waited for the sound of furtive dialling but none came. We heard her calling cheerfully upstairs to an incorporeal husband. After a brief pause she relayed that he would be down with Mr Thorne in just a jiffy. Then from the dim hallway she gave us a strangely resolute smile and disappeared towards the kitchen. I was boggled but Barrie Thorne was enthusiastically smashing his fist into his palm. He orated fatalistically about the perpetual war of the inevitably opposed classes, the workers versus the public schools, the unions versus the bosses, the shop floor versus the bone-idle tycoons.

I nodded politely at his dialectic and waited to see what would happen. I had decided she must have gone round the back of the garden to get help from Tarkenter's father. A rather hopeless strategy in my view, as Walter Tarkenter, the lanky, testy estate agent, would surely run a mile from Barrie Thorne. And even supposing Walter had the courage to accompany her, the Abingdon Marxist would assume this gangly toff was Geraghty and promptly floor him on the spot.

Just as Thorne began to get restive, Hetty returned in an extraordinarily shuffling manner from the kitchen. It was quite uncanny. She was jerkily mincing towards us like a clumsy geisha girl while gazing very attentively at her bound and fettered feet. I frowned at the ridiculous sight, and Thorne scratched his ugly chin, bemused. Equally bizarrely, she had her hands behind her back in a demure, imploring gesture. She looked as if she were about to bow and seek the union rep's forgiveness as well as the sparing of her husband's neck.

'George,' she whispered in a faltering voice. 'Can you . . . can you please go and shout of your father again?'

Thorne scowled his exasperation. 'What the soddin hell's going on? Are you two jokers having me on? Look, I'm going to make my own investigation . . .'

Still in that crazy Mikado posture, Hetty squared up to him and thundered: 'What in *hell* do you mean?'

Thorne blinked at her moderately warily. 'I mean you bloody well get him down here in the next two seconds! Or I'm going up those stairs to get him myself.'

Hetty was stricken but resolute. She looked him full in the eye and said: 'In that case, Mr Thorne, you'd better step inside. Just step inside and wait down in the hall.'

After which it was all like a Mack Sennett film. Thorne wiped his streaming forehead as he entered. My mother lunged forward as if to deliver a kiss upon his perspiration, but proffered something that was not a kiss. In a single hallucinatory movement she produced a vast object from behind her back and smashed it with full force across the Abingdon agitator's terrified countenance.

'Arrrggggh!' screamed Barrie Thorne at the hideousness of that blow.

As in a slowed-down film, quantities of liquid started to spurt like engine oil from his snorting nostrils . . .

It was incredible. My polite middle-class mother had smashed a working man in the chops with a colossal cast-iron *frying pan* . . .

Before he had a chance to stanch the torrent, Hetty bundled him roughly outside. Floored by an outsize skillet, the union representative could scarcely urge the justice of his case. He tottered sideways like a crumpled marionette, then collapsed with a thud on the pavement. Hetty leant over him businesslike and raised the pan to deal him a second smash.

'Bloody hell!' I screamed. 'Don't do it!'

Our reeling visitor supported me in this: 'No! No, no! Don't bloody do it!'

My mother shrieked at him, '*Bugger off at once*. Go on. Before I *kill* you! You common, obscene, overweight, utterly horrible and unpleasant man! How dare you! How *dare* you come creating such an embarrassing, revolting scene at my front door? How *dare* you in front of my young son with your disgusting bloody insolence! I swear on oath I'll hit you twice as hard if you don't *fuck off* immediately.'

It was the first time I had ever heard that verb on my mother's lips. She was so enraged she was foaming at the mouth like a mare. She swayed high above him but with the pan dangling an inch from his nose. Thorne squirmed beneath her, panting.

'Goohhh,' he groaned. 'You're mad as hell the pair of you.'

Hetty blazed afresh. She brandished her skillet and swore in a manner I'd have thought quite impossible. Where with her sedate Godalming upbringing had she ever heard the words 'prick' and 'shagger', for crying out loud? She spat and wiped her hands like an Aberdeen fishwife, then slammed the door in his mess of a face. Panting and wild-eyed, she turned and waggled her frying pan at me.

'Say nothing,' she hissed. 'Say *nothing* of this to your ridiculous bloody father.'

Five

I stayed silent about the pan-floored husband but my mother did not. There was an incendiary confrontation that evening when Bill rolled in breezily from The Lamb and Flag. They ordered me upstairs of course, but I listened enchanted on the staircase and caught every last curious detail. With the steely intuition of an adolescent I saw what an absolute fabricator my father was. Without a second's hesitation he denied all knowledge of Maisie Thorne, not to mention the umpteen overheated Abingdon barmaids that her husband had thrown in poor George's face.

'But,' my father protested, 'I don't even enter half the pubs of Abingdon. So how could I seduce half the blessed barmaids?'

'*Blessed?*' my mother stormed. 'Blessed?' she repeated, half insane. 'Say "bloody" like a real man will you? Stop acting like some goofish music-hall performer, or I'll flatten you as well! Say bloody, bloody, bloody . . .'

Bill reproved her with a liquid piety. 'Please don't swear, Hetty. I can't say I care for the sound of a respectable woman cursing.'

As my mother made serious attempts to strangle him, my father protested that she wanted it both ways. She wanted him to talk like a man, whatever that meant, yet condemned his spurious identity as a notional Lothario. As he improvised thus I realised that whatever she threw at him he would find some way of denying it, however preposterous. Bill would swear that black was white because that was his philosophical mode, his epistemological scale. To that extent my father was exactly like a child, like a very small boy for whom the fantasy is as true as the fact. If Bill Geraghty were to decide that it snowed all year round in Arizona, then indubitably it did. Likewise, if store-room copulation with Maisie Thorne was just a garish dream, not a garish deed, that was all there was to it. Because Bill Geraghty chose to see it thus, it was true. Because like a magician he conjured it so, it was his truth.

Hetty snarled at him, 'So what was that obscene man so excited about? What possessed him to come all that way to confront an innocent man on his own doorstep?'

'Criminal deception,' said my father sternly. 'Putrid detective-novel blackmail of the most flagrant kind. I'm clearly in a different social league from the rest of Losty's staff, so perhaps he thought I'd prove a milkable pot of gold. Do you really think, Hetty, that I would soil our marriage by canoodling with the wife of some revolting ship's stoker sporting a puce shirt and a heart-shaped tattoo?'

'Yes I do,' said my mother coolly. 'Yes I do think so. You have no sensible discretion whatever and when it comes to other women your taste can be extremely vulgar. I've seen you smirking and primping at the tartier type of barmaid many a time in an Oxford pub. Also your inclinations in the marriage bed are no longer restrained and decent ones. Over the years you have learnt some things you never knew when we first got married. Certain types of kiss, for example.'

He gasped in dismay. 'Shush, Hetty! Draw it mild!'

My mother shouted, 'You never used to shove your cigarry tongue down my throat in the ferocious, quite disgusting way you do these days . . .'

Bill Geraghty grew very huffy and attributed his amatory excesses to his extensive reading in an extensive number of languages. With Sanskrit and Arabic firmly under his belt he could whistle through the *Kamasutra* and *The Perfumed Garden* as fast as you like. Hetty snapped back that they didn't smoke cigars in ancient bloody India and he could keep his lies for some other bloody fool. What's more, and from now on, he must be back at home six o'clock sharp every evening. What, gasped my father in real horror. How can I poss–. Hetty said that if he didn't get himself home at a regular hour she would make an appointment to see Mr Losty and demand that for the sake of her marriage her husband be spared doing any overtime. And that was assuming he'd ever done any bona fide overtime, she snorted. There was a fair chance poor old Losty wouldn't know what the hell Bill Geraghty's wife was talking about.

Thus Bill was ignominiously grounded for that last period of my living at home. He trailed his way back obediently on the five o'clock, gulped a half of bitter in town, then pounded his way resentfully up the Banbury Road. Hetty meanwhile exacted a measured revenge and spent most of her days away from the house. As well as Greer and her outré chums in Henley, she visited her sister's pacifist and theosophical acquaintances in Banbury, Warwick and Stratford. Usually but not always she would be back in time for dinner when she would chasten her husband with her bravado and her scorn. Should he complain about her galli-vanting, she'd mutter cryptically about back wages and retrospective dues. Later of course the War put a stop to her husband's straitened schedule, as the propaganda cause genuinely obliged him to work all sorts of hours. In any case Bill soon found a way round these oppressive constraints, no doubt by meticulously planned lunchtime assignations. Nonetheless he was tense and half-demented for about a month, before the air around us cleared and I realised he had found a means of sexual ventilation.

During that month of rigorous grounding, his domestic behaviour grew impressively unhinged. First of all he decided to expand his aviary by adding a shed dedicated to the legendary memory of Mrs White. He christened it 'The White House' without any sense of irony, and decided, instead of obtaining more budgies, to acquire some cocka-toos, cockatiels and parrots. In all he acquired six of each, but instead of naming them Buster, Captain and so on, decided to pay homage to the second great love of his life. His new friends were subjected to the interesting nomenclature of things linguistic . . .

The largest male cockatiel was not called Gerald, but Gerund, and his female cockatoo was called Absolute. A very noisy male parrot he dubbed Deponent. Other innocent pollys he christened Indicative, Active, Future Perfect, Passive and . . . Supine. He addressed some darting cockatiels as Nominative, Accusative, Genitive, Dative and Ablative. Five of his smiling, blinking prize cockatoos were christened Particle, Article, Definite, Indefinite and Correlative.

'Definite and Indefinite have been mating,' he informed me cryptically one windy autumn evening. His hair was stood wildly on end after he had crawled under a row of nest boxes to get at Deponent's lost toy. He looked outstandingly deranged and made no effort to straighten his mad-professor appearance. 'If they have any offspring,' he went on, 'what shall I call them, Geegee?'

'Call 'em Variable Suffix, Invariable Suffix, Infinitive and ah . . . Gerundive . . .' I rattled off smoothly.

Bill snorted at this gratuitous competitive tone. He grunted: 'Absurd bloody names for infant parrots, Variable Suffix and Invariable Suffix. And how do you think little Gerund is going to feel if he thinks I've shouted his name to a baby cockatoo you would wish to greet as "Gerundive". Worse still, when the same cockatoo grows tall he will scarcely care to clash in mid-air with a strapping great cockatiel who mistakes his name for an abbreviated form of an adolescent cockatoo's. Will he, feller me lad?'

'Ah . . .'

The next day he brought home a full-grown tortoise. He had already christened it Participle, having acquired it in a pet shop in Abingdon for a bargain half a crown. Participle dawdled out in the garden during the day and as far as anyone could see had found himself the perfect berth with doting Bill. However Bill loved to bring him into the sitting room in the evenings, and was wont to make extravagant inferences from negligible attempts on Participle's part to contribute to the family dialogue.

'Good old boy,' Bill cooed one evening as I was busy preparing a portfolio for the entrance examination to the RCA. I was feeling a little sick in the stomach because tomorrow I had to take the train up to London to be interviewed by a distinguished panel. I sighed as I examined a still life of a bowl of fruit, worrying that the orange was so much more vivid than the apple. I should have drawn two oranges and to buggery with the bloody apple. Also the peach looked too lush and too suggestive, too much like a pair of glistening, furry pink buttocks. Bill had already earnestly pointed this out to me and for once he was right.

'Good old chap,' Bill repeated. 'You know, George, Participle is such a cunning chap.'

'Mm,' I murmured as I looked balefully at a charcoal sketch entitled *Blackwell's on Bonfire Night*. The jumping jacks that the skinny children had ignited on the Broad Street pavement were a damn sight more convincing than the bookshop's hurrying customers. The trouble was that I tried to have a go at everything instead of sticking to my single forte. My obsessive fascination with the outrageous Grosz had led me along a highly specific artistic route, and I had already drawn my own conclusions. What I did best was caricature, grotesque and insulting caricature. However, that was a completely unexaminable skill as far as English art colleges were concerned, even the most distinguished and far-sighted.

'Definitely,' Bill opined sagely. 'Old Participle's the kind of chap whose mind we assume we can read very easily. But really old Participle is profoundly inscrutable.'

I looked at Participle and thought that by his doleful and weary mien he was probably battling with a stomach ache.

'Some fools,' Bill continued, 'think that Participle has

absolutely nothing going on upstairs. But in my opinion Participle has a very shrewd eye for the rest of us. I think, for example, he looks at me, his master, and senses that there's a chap whose distinctive talents are grossly undervalued. There's a chap, thinks Participle, who could have been Warden of All Souls had the cards been properly played.'

I looked at my father worriedly. 'But how would a tortoise ever know that All Souls existed?'

Bill glowered at me. 'I took him past the bloody place when I brought him back from Abingdon. I had to call in at the gents outfitters on High Street to settle a bill. Afterwards I carried him by the side of All Souls and I couldn't resist lambasting the heartless place as I strolled past. After I'd finished my say, Participle craned his neck and gave me the most knowing glance of penetrating sympathy. It's as if he knows on some profound mysterious level the state of things better than any blasted human.'

I shrugged off my father and continued examining my drawings. Some of them were bloody appalling, oh God, some of them I would have to fling in the Isis or the Cherwell, even if it meant ditching half my portfolio. I put the least embarrassing specimens to one side and wondered if I ought to train as a bank clerk or a commis chef instead. Or perhaps, courtesy of the good offices of Bill, as a printer's proofreader? Angrily berating myself, I was suddenly startled by a curious sensation of primitive disgust. I looked down in utter perplexity as I continued to feel the clammiest, most unpleasant stimulation around my left ankle.

At first I could make little sense of what I saw. Until, no matter how hard I tried to discount it, the unpalatable truth was undeniable . . .

Participle, Bill's tortoise, was trying to *mount* my ankle . . .

'Oh my God!' I shouted angrily. 'Dad! Look at . . . look at what he's bloody well doing.'

Bill stared at the pair of us, leg-shaking son and shambling, clamorous reptile. He slapped his trouser leg and guffawed: 'Wild old fellow. He does that to me as well. He's such a relentless old beggar for his how's-your-father. In fact I should say Participle's the most virile tortoise in Oxford.'

I snarled, 'But surely he's not meant to do that.' With a struggle I prised my leg free of Participle's passionate claws. Then I lifted him to chest level, searching for some organ I could reasonably chastise. Participle looked at me very dolefully and I hadn't the heart to whack at his person. With a grunt I handed him back to his chuckling master.

'Of course he's meant to do it! All we men are meant to do "that", as you call it. The blasted species needs to perpetuate, doesn't it? And there's only one tool or measuring instrument can manage that feat of creative magic, lad. And it's not a stick of artist's charcoal, you know, not even the ones they wield at your Royal bloody College.'

I flushed at his sneering and advised him to get Participle a girlfriend, if that was the case. Bill became silent while gazing at me piercingly. Then, apropos his tortoise's singular shrewdness at understanding the humans within his purview, he offered a provocative hypothesis:

'Participle was just trying to *tell* you something, old boy.'

I reddened once more and snapped, 'What on earth are you talking about?'

'Anyone,' my father opined, 'can see that as a bursting lad of eighteen it is time you were plunging your stick of charcoal into the sinuous folds of a fecund young poppet.'

'You what!' I said, turning purple.

My father examined my embarrassment bemused. 'Bah. Old Participle can see what the age-old problem is. He takes one swift dekko at you, and says to himself, aha, there's a young chap who needs to be sinking his how's-your-father into someone's how's-your-ma. Then, not having any speech faculties, Participle conveys his fatherly advice to you by a brilliant feat of mime.'

'Oh shut up!' I spat at him. 'A tortoise knows nothing about me, for God's sake.'

'Don't you believe it! Old Participle can diagnose a frustrated youth at ten paces. Willing you into remedial action, he dashes across . . .'

I snorted mirthlessly, 'He doesn't dash.'

'In his own terms, Participle does. He wants to communicate some sound advice to a vulnerable young man like yourself. By the way I've noticed, George, that lately you've been burying your youthful head in Schopenhauer and Spengler and all those anguished German coves. Doubtless in your innocence you imagine that all your adolescent tension and turmoil are somehow connected to the impenetrable business of philosophy. Hence you determinedly fret yourself to no avail about the meaning of life, the daunting questions of ethics and absolutes and all that keg of blasted worms. By contrast this sanguine little chap on my knee called Participle is altogether shrewder, and knows damn fine that if you had a twice-weekly leg over with some billowing young girlie you wouldn't be blushing every time an innocent little tortoise happens to mount you. Participle, take my word for it, George, is only trying to *help* . . .'

In that summer of 1938, I went up to the RCA and gave a blinder of an interview. As Participle had noted, I was bursting with pent-up nervousness, and my eloquence was correspondingly massive. Everything I knew about the history of Fine Art, which was far from encyclopaedic, came bubbling out with unstoppable fluency. I could see that the old men in the droopy bow ties and the one young woman with the heavy spectacles and the wipsy hair were surprised and most impressed. My slim little portfolio was examined with indulgent tolerance, and they murmured politely about 'definite promise', and added courteous adjectives like 'workmanlike' and 'dexterous'.

I had refused to attempt Oxford entrance despite Bill's urging me to read Greats and let the painting bug evaporate as all nonsense must eventually do. My father would not accept that anyone, even a sexually frustrated teenager, could seriously believe that art was either a manly academic subject or a means to profitable employment. However, unlike Tarkenter's father, he made no attempt to outlaw my vocation. Tarkenter had already expressed the impressive ambition of becoming an acclaimed professional photographer. He was intent on fashion journalism at the age of sixteen, and when his father demanded why such a preposterous leaning, he artlessly replied that he adored attractive young women and would like a job that allowed him to be near as many as possible at any one time. Walter Tarkenter was deeply orthodox RC and he struck his son across the ear for his impiety. He tried to force him into studying Law at Cambridge, but Tarkenter foiled that by leaving home and going to live with his deviant cousin, that forger and poacher called Telford.

The scholarship at the RCA was in the bag, and Hetty was flushed and excited on my behalf. She gave me a five-pound note and told me to go out with Tarkenter and enjoy myself in the Oxford pubs. Bill was still enduring his period of grounding and failed to offer any audible congratulations. Consoling himself with his chattering cagebirds, his behaviour was becoming more florid by the day. Throughout that month of enforced fidelity, he was busy teaching every one of his birds to speak. His willing students not only had their unusual grammatical names, they were also being coached by my father to speak in different languages, most of them dead. He had paid a joiner to construct some tiny study cubicles in each of his sheds, and by dint of partitioned rehearsals was managing to give all his birds a solo tutorial. Before such things as Oxford Language Schools existed, Bill Geraghty had one flourishing halfway up the Banbury Road.

He taught alert little Gerund a few sentences of lewd dockside Basque. His cockatiel Ablative became proficient in uttering Mediaeval Monastic Armenian. To listen as I did late at night in a paraffin-illumined aviary to a tiny cockatiel declaiming a solemn Psalm in Old Armenian was not so much touching as . . . incredibly eerie. Deponent, the crimson parrot, was coached in Classical Chinese and was soon repeating some of the weightier sayings of Mencius. The cockatiel Nominative became precociously fluent in the numerals, ordinals and days of the week in Romany, and Accusative rattled away gamely at the incomparable tenth-century Persian of Firdausi's *Shah-Nama*. Bill stopped him after the first dozen stanzas of the kingly saga but boasted that Accusative would have mastered the whole damn lot if he'd had all the time in the world to tutor him. As for Particle and Article, the two prize cockatoos mimicked respectively *Colloquial Bengali for Instructing Your Cook* as edited by Retired Lt-Colonel Kelso Pickering of Muttra and published in the same place in 1921, and a short fifty-stanza Sanskrit treatise on elephant veterinary science printed in Poona in 1888 and entitled the *Gajayurveda*.

In effect Bill had manufactured his own private Babel in his aviaries, for if one bird started off, the others usually followed suit. The agglutinative Basque of Bilbao dockers fought it out with classically inflected Church Armenian. Sino-Tibetan Chinese battled for syntactical supremacy with Indo-European Farsi. The twittering racket at times was so dissonant and hellish that even the birds seemed dazed by the collision of idioms, phonetics and semantics. I could just about guess which language was which, but only my polyglot father understood what was being cheeped and parrotted. His innocent birds, of course, could only mimic, they had no idea whether their words were sacred or profane, living or dead. Bill, presiding over his Babel with the zest of a composer, was obviously pleased as punch with his unparalleled creation. Snatches of avine Sanskrit elaborated a *yogacurna* or magic powder for alleviating sore feet in elephants, and clashed with its linguistic relative Romany in which Nominative announced that six two-year-old ponies were being sold at Appleby Horsefair for twenty guineas each on the 15th of May. Gerund meanwhile chipped in that some spawn of an incestuous whore from the worst Bilbao slum had stacked a pallet like a drunken pansy and would cripple the next guy who shifted it. At which point, listening to Bill's translation, I said puzzled: 'I can understand you knowing Firdausi and Mencius and Romany from reading the relevant books. But given it's unprintable, how on earth did you ever learn swear-word Basque? Did you and mother honeymoon in Spain?'

Not bloody likely, scoffed Bill. For a man of fifty-five languages my father was remarkably poorly-travelled, even narrowly provincial. His favourite holidays were in tranquil boarding houses in Cromer rather than rented villas in Sicily. But twenty years ago Bill's scout at Magdalen, a high-spirited Scouser called Edgar, had been an ex-Merchant Navy man. Not only was Edgar an expert on dockland obscenity in Bilbao, but in Bombay, Surinam, Panama, Marseilles and countless other pungent ports of call.

'And the queer thing about foul language,' he added rather sternly, 'is that it is all much of a muchness in virtually every language, old or new. The identical idioms monotonously reflecting the repetitive and universal nature of the same obscenity. For example, howdyedoing a prostitute and the unspeakable howdyedoing your mother, being more or less interchangeable, and found in damn near every language known to man. Thank God my little Gerund has no understanding of Basque, much less any notion of assaulting his own mother.'

'Gerund's mother?' I said dimly.

'I never knew her,' sighed Bill. 'But the market dealer was certainly a reputable man. His cockatiels were never less than show material.'

As she observed the extraordinary success of Bill's language school, Hetty saw its feverish orchestration as a worrying omen. Her husband's actions were always at their oddest when his freedom was curtailed, and this clamorous polyglot jabbering from all these cockatoos and parrots seemed to be so many coded messages directed specifically at her. Their deafening babble was like the tidal babble of dammed-up passion inside Bill Geraghty. Sooner or later, if he didn't find release, Bill would either run out of birds or run out of languages. He was acquiring new students every weekend and adding on three new languages every week. Tomorrow he was threatening to buy a mynah and planning to teach it Hottentot throat clicks and Mongolian laryngeal yodelling.

'Dear God,' my mother sighed, as we left him to his birds and walked back to the house. 'You know, George –'

'Yes?'

'I've decided perhaps it's better for his state of mind if he's doing all those extra evenings at the printer's.'

'You've what?'

'Don't you think so too?'

There was a queer and endless silence. I looked at her accusingly yet she returned my gaze quite unperturbed. She knew that I knew what overtime stood for, in all its shabby and inglorious double entendre . . .

Hetty patted my cheek in a brisk and admonishing manner. 'Don't look quite so outraged. You're not exactly a child, George. Whether you like it or not, you are now a man. Thank God you show no signs of being like him though. I'm so pleased you've decided to become like someone else.'

Six

It was Wilhelmina van der Waal who saved me from being conscripted. One morning in her weekly drawing class she began rooting impudently through my portfolio as if she had every right to make an unannounced check on the progress of her indolent students. A moody widow in her mid-forties, she had trained at Utrecht and Leiden in the Twenties, and despite her proud Dutchness, had all the pedagogic rigour of a German Frau Professor. Luckily for her she spoke flawless unaccented English or she might have been taken for a clumsy German spy. In total silence she pulled out a recent drawing, one of several I'd done satirising the consequences of appeasement and the Munich agreement. This one happened to show an extremely vulgar depiction of the clerical leader of the Slovaks, Tiso, who in March of 1939, thanks to Hitler, had acquired himself a Fascist protectorate. It showed Tiso with crudely slavering lips, torn between kissing the emblems of holy office and kissing Hitler's protuberant backside. In the background was an inane marionette version of Chamberlain, his straggling unkempt moustache and vacant wooden eyes suggestive of extreme if senile debauchery. I blushed as she examined it, dubiously sniffing. She turned from my drawing to stare at me, then back to it, then back to me. I expected immediate reproof, as satirical drawing, the stuff of crude journalism, was not a permissible subject at the hallowed RCA. However Willy, as everyone called Mrs v der W, suddenly decided to give it her version of an extravagant plaudit. She grunted: 'This is not so bad at all, Mr Geraghty. Though the crude highlighting might possibly be improved if you were prepared to take the necessary pains.'

It might not have been the best of my drawings, but the highlighting happened to be its one flawless aspect. I answered politely, 'Thank you very much.'

She demanded with a frown, 'But how did you do it?'

'The highlighting?' I answered. 'I used bread pellets, Mrs van der Waal.'

'No,' she said sharply. 'Don't be so dim, young man. I mean how did you do the drawing itself?'

I blushed as the other students hearkened to the sight of Willy apparently seeking technical advice from one of their peers. As if I were disclosing a culpable formula, I whispered almost inaudibly: 'I started with rough pencil sketches, copying from photographs I'd snipped out of some old *News Chronicles*. One by one I made them as accurate as I could, and then started doing caricature versions by superimposing and erasing. Afterwards I took this fine drawing pen to them, Mrs van der Waal. It cost me all of three guineas. Then I did lots and lots of erasing as I went over every pencil line. Then –'

'I see,' she interrupted. 'Mm. Perhaps you should publish it. Why don't you send it to an important newspaper once you have improved the crude highlighting?'

Not all that humbly I pointed out I'd been doing just that as of the last six months. I had sold a total of six to places like the *New Statesman* and *Punch*. In fact it was a lurid *Statesman* cartoon, a bloody portrayal of the murder of the anti-Fascist Rosselli by *Action Française* thugs, that had paid for my drawing pen.

Later, as all the others were dispersing and I was lingering over the plaster cast of Nero she had told us to copy, Mrs van der Waal said: 'I would like you to come and drink coffee with me in three days time, Mr Geraghty.'

I blinked at her warily. 'Thank you but –'

'I live in Shepherd's Bush, 44B Tindale Avenue, in the upstairs flat. I have an obese cat called Tubal Cain who sits outside my door with a large bell on his neck. He miaows a lot, very plaintively, he's quite unmistakable. Come at precisely three o'clock Saturday afternoon, and please bring me any other work of yours which you think outstanding. I will probably give you Parisian Florentines saved from last Christmas with the coffee which will be Douwe Egbert sent from Utrecht by my maternal grandmother. She is 98 and once danced with Henrik Ibsen at a dinner party and she has an overweight cat which is also called Tubal Cain. I wish to see you on Saturday because I have an idea for your future.'

'You –?'

'No more! Till Saturday. Try in vain to imagine what it is that I am going to suggest. Meanwhile, George Geraghty, do take a bit more trouble with your highlights.'

It was the first time she had used my Christian name and I reddened like a pimpled adolescent. She smiled with a sisterly if awkward grimace which made her look a bit like a Dutch carthorse puckering its lips. I murmured vague thanks and wandered off in a daze. Tubal Cain was some minor character in the Old Testament and Willy wouldn't have been out of place in the Queen of Sheba's entourage. She was over twice my age but had an eccentric youthfulness, a Netherlandish briskness and vigour that made me think of imperial seafaring Holland. I imagined her taking cold baths in Shepherd's Bush whilst reading a novel by Louis Couperus and drawing a picture of Tubal Cain with her much-beringed left hand. She was middle-aged but her looks were oddly immature, austere yet florid and faintly vulgar. She was also very muscular and had the longest back I had ever seen on a woman.

Instead of going straight home I did what I always did. I took a bus to Bloomsbury and went into the Bijou Café. Since the mid-Thirties the faded ill-lit Bijou had been frequented mostly by East European refugees, including a great many Jews who had fled places like Ruthenia, the Bukovina and Tiso's Slovakia. I heard Rumanian and

Hungarian spoken alongside Yiddish and Ladino, and although I had none of Bill's linguistic brilliance, I enjoyed hearing this cosmopolitan Babel. Indeed I felt like a nominal and honorary foreigner, almost as if I were a refugee myself. Occasionally I wished my father were here to translate some of their impassioned conversations, though no doubt he would have been as critical about my Bijou draughtsmanship as Willy van der Waal.

I came to the Bijou Café partly to draw from life. I also came to record the harrowing remnants of cultures that were vanishing as the brutes of the world embarked upon their annihilation. I drew dozens upon dozens of refugee intellectuals, displaced doctors, morose dismissed professors, traumatised former nurses. Many of these sad people spoke fluent English and one or two told me their horrific tales. I sat in the corner with a black coffee and a pack of Strand and sketched non-stop with my pencil. To allay any justifiable paranoia that I might be some punitive government spy, I wore an ostentatious bright-red bow tie. As I was only nineteen, it was a tacit declaration of my complete harmlessness. After a while the regulars took no notice of me or sometimes they gave me a hesitant smile and came over to take a look at my efforts. Still the proud owner of my schoolboy purchases, George Grosz's *Über alles die Liebe* and *Die Gezeichneten*, I did what Grosz himself did as an apprentice. I drew more or less everything that moved, as well as everything that preferred to stand still. This Sunday I was planning to sketch some interesting wasteland I had glimpsed from the bus as it passed through Kilburn. In the space of ten seconds I had observed the gaping shell of an old factory, a couple of discarded rusty AJS's and two meths-swigging old derelicts engaged in a murderous argument.

Three days later I made my way to Shepherd's Bush, and with some effort found Tindale Avenue. The numbering was very puzzling and I walked up and down looking for 36 to 46, which apparently had been demolished. Trust old Willy to give me a bogus address, I thought, as an interesting practical joke. Or out of sheer eccentricity to forget her own number. Eventually I asked a stout policeman and he pointed out the missing houses lurking down what looked like an obscure side road.

The door was wide open and I walked up the staircase to the second-floor flat. Outside a large cat with a bell on its neck was miaowing dolorously. I stooped to pat it and when it rolled on its back I tickled its belly. At once it shot out sharp claws and took a deep scratch of my finger.

'Why, you little bast–!'

The door opened before I could clout the little savage. Willy poked her head out, her heavy lipstick covered in Florentine crumbs. She spotted my bleeding finger and tutted: 'Tubal Cain is usually quite gentle but can also be gratuitously aggressive. They say that pets are often like their owners, of course. Personally I think it is owners who tend to mimic their pets. At least it is definitely the case for the imitative and invariably too passive English.' She stared at me challengingly as if wishing me to rebut the stereotype. 'From what I've heard, all you English students think I am much too aggressive and severe?'

'Oh no,' I demurred, sucking my wounded finger.

'Don't lie, Mr Geraghty. Of course you all do! I am very severe, of course I am. You young people are at the finest art college in your country and you must expect great demands from your teachers. We are obliged to be your superegos, as most of you are nothing but raw ego, and some of you don't even possess that notional requirement of the driven artist. None of you can possibly make any headway unless you are working at least a dozen hours a day. Only a tenth of you do so as far as I can estimate. However your own drawing is so strikingly promising, you obviously do work very hard?'

'Yes,' I winced, as Tubal Cain began to purr and tear at my trouser leg. His claws went deep into my skin and he began to flex them luxuriously.

'You are the only student I have ever invited to my flat here. I hope you acknowledge the supreme and baffling honour. No other RCA student in history has ever been attacked by tubby little Tubal Cain.'

Hesitantly she touched my shoulder, then led me into her flat which was lushly furnished. The colours were deep and ponderously heavy: magenta, mauve, soporific crimsons. There were Persian rugs and Turkish carpets, and a few fine copies of Hindu bronzes sat on a tall mahogany chest. Between the Indian gods which served as oversize book ends she had a row of philosophy books written in French, German and Dutch. I stared at them wonderingly until Willy said she was attending some philosophy lectures instituted by the RCA in the vain hope of giving its students a rounded education. I smiled rather smugly and told her I attended the new literature lectures instead. Only last week I had gone along and listened to Somerset Maugham talking about the short story.

'Somerset Maugham?' she scoffed, spitting out a stray shard of Florentine. 'Short stories? But surely that must be some sort of pallid therapeutic hobby, hardly a taxing intellectual discipline? Novels and stories and so on are what one reads for idle relaxation, not for exercising and fortifying the immature mind. No, as a serious artist, George, you must definitely come along to these philosophy lectures. Next week there is one on syllogistic logic, given by my fellow countryman Julius van der Loon. Tell me, doesn't that whet your appetite, just the sound of those words?'

'Van der Loon?' I said stunned.

She snorted. 'Don't be so idiotic. I mean the syllogism and the logic. Does not the suggestive, by which I mean the allusive, poetry of the word "logic" give you a horripilating frisson, Mr Geraghty?'

'Ar . . .'

Adamant that she would personally frogmarch me to van der Loon's lectures, she jumped to more urgent concerns.

Where were the drawings she had asked to see, my best work of the last few years? I smiled awkwardly and brought out my portfolio with a shy little flourish. At nineteen I was certainly optimistic about my potential, but not at all complacent. In fact I had plenty to boast about if I had been smug. I genuinely enjoyed working an average of fourteen hours a day without a proper break. At not even twenty, I had proven or at any rate marketable talent. I could even boast a tentative confidence in my personal attractiveness, as I had already tired of two art-student girlfriends before they had got round to tiring of me.

Wilhelmina scrutinised the six cartoons I had published and another half dozen not yet sent out. She studied them with a very practised eye, peering at the smallest lines and even sniffing the paper like a tracker dog. At my age Willy had been training as a lithographer, and she still had the reddened watery eyes that come of staring for too long down a lens. She looked up and saw me noting that redness, and demonstrated the first signs of a fleeting bashfulness. She smiled uncertainly, and again, I told myself, she had the look of a moderately attractive carthorse.

'Mm,' she said at last. 'I don't like saying this kind of thing. It can ruin a young artist, pampering him with unqualified and hence facile praise. But these biting little drawings of yours are . . . how can I phrase it? . . . rather good.'

She had dithered over inserting the modifier 'very'? Though of course, right enough, she wouldn't have risked that, not even if I had been young Harmensz van Rijn Rembrandt and we had bumped into each other in the university parks in Leiden about three hundred years ago.

Without further ado Mrs van der Waal started to reveal her remarkable scheme for my future. I hadn't the vaguest notion of why she'd asked me here, but was hoping she would refer me to someone who could teach me more about caricature. All we had had so far was coffee and Florentines, but as I listened to her breathtaking cloak-and-dagger scenario I thought I must be drunk or dreaming.

Mevrouw explained it in a loud impassioned whisper. Barring a miracle, she said sternly, war with Nazi Germany was only weeks away. Bearing that in mind, certain officials from what would soon be known as the War Office had confidentially approached the Royal College senior staff. They had been instructed to single out the most brilliant of their students, those whose outstanding graphic skills might help contribute crucially to the war effort. So far fastidious Willy had earmarked only one of hers. Only young George Geraghty, in her opinion, merited the hyperbolic designation known as 'talented'. Yesterday she had telephoned a top-secret number and mentioned my name to a government official called Dorryfield.

'You mean,' I said suspiciously, 'someone like me doing British government propaganda?'

'What else?' she said tersely. 'If you'll pardon my vulgarity, your vicious little drawings of Messrs Tiso and Hitler will make those pitiless monsters piss themselves with rage. You are just the thing for your War Office, George.'

'But I insulted Neville Chamberlain in the *New Statesman* last month.'

She pouted her heavy lips at my naivety. 'Who cares about the likes of him? No one does, not even his friends, assuming he has any left. Certainly Winston Churchill must have been delighted if he saw your nasty cartoon. You haven't mocked Winnie himself yet I hope?'

'Not yet.'

'Good. In the case of Winnie you will have to wait until after the war.'

Not bothering with any glib dissimulation, I told Willy that her suggestion was quite impossible. For a start I would never be able to mock Fascists alone, I would want free rein to attack both sides of any totalitarian equation. After all, I was a satirical artist, and though satire might be discriminate, it was never particularly discriminating. Like my hero George

Grosz I felt myself morally obliged to take a swipe at cupidity and cruelty across the board and wherever I came across it. Willy stared at me with severe impatience. 'But Grosz himself was a propaganda man at one time. If he really is your hero, then you may easily follow suit?'

I answered just as impatiently, 'He was propaganda chief for the Dada movement, not the Weimar bloody Republic.'

'Exactly! Bourgeois imbecilic frolicking. Advanced clowning and buffoonery with Schwitters, Jung, Brecht, Weill and all the rest. While Germany burned, going through civil war, inflation and famine, Grosz and his like did merely play the fiddle. Patronised by rich self-abasing businessmen, they guzzled champagne and experimented with the occult, pah!, and turned on their grovelling patrons and called them stinking pigshit. Those pathetic Dada patrons lapped it all up and shouted for ever more brutal insults and vituperations. You, Mr Geraghty, have a much more important and more grown-up mission. You will produce exquisite propaganda leaflets that will help destroy Fascism before it succeeds in destroying us. In your new and vital work at the War Office, you will help to give hope to some of those sad refugee people that you like to draw in your Bijou Café . . .'

Ten minutes later we were locked in a ferocious carnal embrace. I'm not certain of the precise choreographic sequence, but I believe it had something to do with the purple nineteen-year-old fury with which I countered her defamation of Grosz. I told her how he had nearly been shot for desertion after the First World War and had faced jail for his early exhibitions. His drawings had been burnt by the Nazis as supreme examples of vile unAryan degeneracy. Also the *Propagandada*, who was currently living in the States, had already renounced his early Dada infatuation. Even when he was in the thick of it, Grosz was laughing at all the barmy occultists and plutocratic crackpots who had swarmed like flies around the tantalising new anarchy. More to the point, unlike me and Mrs van der Waal, Grosz had been through the trenches and had seen it all. After his discharge in 1916 he had devoted his energies to satirising the idiocy of war with countless shocking paradigms of the destruction and the total waste.

As Willy remained temporarily dumbstruck, I gave her one or two ready examples.

'Numerous harrowing drawings of emaciated German soldiers without their noses. A harassed hospital orderly emptying his bucket full of assorted bits of human flesh. A one-armed infantryman saluting with his good hand a complacent fat lady who's offering him a biscuit. Busy saluting, he's quite unable to take the biscuit, Mrs van der Waal . . .'

I halted my itemisation, embittered and defiant. But Willy was far from being put out. Instead of becoming angry and chucking me out of her flat, she began to clap her chubby palms and beamingly applauded me for being so *en colère*.

'What incendiary passion, Mr Geraghty! What impassioned humanity in a mere stripling like yourself. With that incandescent operatic countenance, you look the mirror image of Signor Rudolf Valentino. Even though of course you English as a nation are quite incapable of such a thing as emotion. Are you sure that British is your nationality? Is your name not really Garibaldi?'

I scowled, thinking she was making some baffling jest that compared me to a perforated biscuit. Willy proffered her consolation by hurriedly patting my peevish face. Then, before I could protest, she started feverishly embracing me . . .

'Gugh,' I gasped, as she forced her outsize tongue deep inside me. It was as if she were trying to drown or choke me as she lunged at my quaking uvula.

Seconds later she was forcing me to make incursions into her tulip-coloured cardigan and hand-embroidered Irish blouse. Simultaneously she lifted me some six inches from the ground and bore me like a trussed infant into her bedroom.

I had never made love to a Dutch carthorse before, and I found it very enlightening. Old enough to be my guardian aunt, Mevrouw van der Waal took no nonsense and showed me precisely how things must be done. Just as she'd censured my sloppy highlighting, so she tutted if I made a too brusque caress or attempted a too jerky shifting of my limbs. Impatient at one point with my ferrety zeal, she grabbed hold of my wrists and turned me sharply on my back. Then she clambered astride my stomach in order that she could move things at her chosen pace. This was all very well but she was a large woman and as she began bouncing ever more furiously on my guts and ribcage, I felt my teeth rattle and as if my belly might void superfluous wind. If I were fool enough to fart under her amorous batterings, I was sure she would finish me with a single rabbit-chop. But once she'd achieved her own climax, she set to satisfying me, and in ways one would hardly conceive. Wilhelmina wrapped her huge breasts about my face and percussed my frightened ears and guffawed wildly. Then she performed a slow and maddening ladder of kisses, from my toes up to the thighs, then jumping to the head, then back down to the hips. Only one outstanding part of me did Willy refuse to incorporate into her ladder. I pointed it out, this anomalous deficit, but Mevrouw refused to jump to my bidding. I was impressed and put out in equal measure . . .

Afterwards she stood by the window, smoking and staring through the parting of the curtains. I assumed she was surveying Shepherds Bush by night and wondered where its allure lay. Instead of dreary West London I was looking at the fine mountain of her tapering back and the full curves of her robust haunches. She had the sumptuous buttocks of a Renoir bather and I admired them with a painterly as well as layman's eye.

Willy glanced elliptically into her dressing-table mirror and saw my obvious enchantment.

'So you like my backside, Mr Geraghty? As a keen young artist you find it not unstimulating?'

'Yes indeed.'

As if from an RCA podium she demanded, 'Who, George, in the history of art, east or west, alive or dead, celebrated or forgotten, has painted the most succulent and delectable female bottom?'

Willy was not employing theatrical rhetoric, it was more like a PhD viva. It was just five minutes since we had been making love, and already she was talking like an automaton lecturer. I scratched my jaw and yawned and said I found it difficult to choose an absolute favourite. I mentioned Ingres, Schiele, Velazquez, George Grosz, and of course the ineffable Renoir.

'Auguste Renoir?' she echoed sarcastically. 'Him and his steatopygic odalisques.'

I made a quick translation. Whores with fat bums, was that what she was saying?

'But they weren't whores,' I protested. 'They were just young girls bathing.'

'Pah! Do you seriously imagine they were gambolling there in the river in the buff, just as smirking Auguste happened to be sauntering past? Renoir boasted to everyone that he painted with his penis, so undoubtedly they were his odalisques. Or if not, his unfortunate concubines.'

I snorted, 'I like his backsides anyway.'

'Tell me,' counter-snorted Willy. 'Do you paint with *your* penis, George?'

I swallowed and looked at her defensively. 'Up to a point.'

'Literally?' she guffawed harshly. 'You paint with your penis *up to a point?*'

I made a sour face and asked if I could have one of her cigarettes. She threw me the packet and turned back to her naked window-gazing. After an uncomfortable silence in which I almost nodded off, she addressed me in a distant and dreamlike tone.

'For me at the moment, my backside is a very serious matter.'

I stirred myself and noticed with horror that I had dropped fag ash all over her sheets. I rubbed it in to erase it but made it ten times worse. Mortified, I folded my skinny arms and tried to hide the outrageous mess with my elbows.

'Really?' I panted. 'Something wrong with it, Mrs . . . Wilhelmina? Haemorrhoids?'

She shook her head with ponderous exasperation. 'Such a naive little boy you are, for all your precocious talent. Of course there's nothing wrong with it physically. I'm not talking about my physical bottom, George. I am talking about its abstract nature.'

I was tempted to say I was about as interested in an abstract backside as I was in an abstract bar of chocolate or an abstract fiver. Thank God, I congratulated myself, that I was a penniless young artist and not a cloistered bloody pedant like Willy van der Waal.

'For the last two weeks I have spent much profitable time looking at my behind in the mirror. Not out of immature vanity, George, because I am contented enough with my extremely passable body. Clearly it's not a case of needing to frantically strip off to reassure myself as to my looks. I could see how goggly-eyed you were yourself by it just a few minutes ago. No, the reason for my obsessive buttock-gazing might strike you as odd, but then you haven't been to any of the RCA philosophy lectures. I have been to every one of them so far. Two weeks ago we had a brilliant though very ugly man called Cornelius Boor talking about epistemology, the philosophy of knowledge.'

In a fog of drowsiness, I nodded vacantly.

'Boor was talking particularly about duality and unity. About whether a physical object that is apparently single and unified can also be perceived as having a plural and differentiated nature. You will appreciate, George, that this is a regular consideration in certain sophisticated eastern philosophies, where the debatable divisions between Nature and Spirit, the Physical and the Immaterial, and so on and so forth, are of quite crucial distinction.'

She was waiting impatiently for my response. I said very dopily, 'Hmm?'

'The misperception of a snake as a rope is a famous epistemological example. A snake at a distance may be mistaken as a rope, or a rope may be likewise mistaken as a snake, and yet in each case there can only be one verifiable reality. Then there is the muddy, murky solipsism of the Mind and Body dichotomy. For how, George, can the mind be considered separate from the body, when we all know that if the head be removed from the body the mind goes with it too?'

'Oh,' I murmured. 'Oh I see.'

'Precisely! This is where the sight of my bare bum two weeks ago suddenly presented me with a glimpse of the numinous plenitude of supra-immanent aesthetic illumination.'

'Aha?'

'The image of my naked bottom in my grandmother's old Delft mirror presented me with the perfect paradigm. I suddenly saw, George, what I had never seen before. I, like you, all my life have gaily gone around referring to a single object, the bottom, the backside, the behind etc., as a *lone*, pristine and undifferentiated entity. But how can that possibly be the finish of the philosophical story? Surely it is just as true to say that it is not an "it" but is a "they", meaning the plurality that is evident as my *two* well-differentiated buttocks?'

Together we stared at those two well-differentiated buttocks and gaped at the enormity of the theoretical problem.

'On the rope and snake analogy, it is surely as much the one as the other. The "two-buttockness" is therefore as valid as the "one-bottomness"! For if a bum, as it always is, is dually bifurcated, then surely it can no longer boast of some fanciful epistemological unity.'

I sighed judiciously. 'Up to a point, Wilhelmina.'

'Surely a lone, autonomous buttock – that whose oneness is clearly irreducible – has as much existential right to assert that it is my *fons et origo*.'

'Of what?' I said flummoxed.

'Of the heuristic matrix that I inevitably perceive to be "that-upon-which-I-sit".'

I thought I might be getting the hang of this at last. I put in helpfully: 'But surely it's "those-upon-which-you-sit"?'

'What?'

'Surely your *two* autonomous buttocks are just as much your phenomenological matrix, Wilhelmina.'

Willy blinked her moist lithographer's eyes and clapped her hands exuberantly. She shouted: '*Genau*, as Emmanuel Kant might have said! And isn't it blindingly obvious? Only fatuous *a priori* reasoning would cede a spurious hegemony to a quasi-unified and pseudo-single backside.'

Feeling almost as crazy as she was, I interjected, 'Whereas, *a posteriori* . . .'

She paused as she evidently needed some strong audio-visual emphasis by this stage. Facing the mirror and with her vast horselike back to me, Willy seized both cheeks of her buttocks and pulled them apart dramatically. Then gasped: '*A posteriori* reasoning would argue for the two posteriors rather than the one posterior!'

'Yes,' I concurred warmly. 'Yes I bloody well think so too.'

Hoarse with excitement, she allowed both cheeks to twang back to their orthodox setting.

'But that is not the end of our story. We cannot talk of black and white but only shades of grey when it comes to the subtlest philosophy of the fundament. The most subtle, overarching, not to say reasonable model would in fact argue that "that-upon-which-I-sit" is neither singular nor dual . . .'

'No?' I said rather disappointed. 'Are you sure of that?'

'No, George. As with light and the quantum theory, the bum is neither the one nor the other but is obliged philosophically to be *both*.'

Apropos the crucial question of national security in wartime, all of this seems to me infinitely significant. After all it was this unlikely woman and no one else, this loquacious and indiscreet foreigner, who spent much of her time staring at the baffling disunity of her backside, it was she and she alone who was responsible for putting me in touch with the top-secret Ministry of Wartime Propaganda.

Seven

Before beginning work for Dorryfield, I spent an uneasy couple of weeks with Hetty and Bill. It was the end of the RCA term, and I hadn't enough money to stay on in London, even though Willy had offered to keep me luxuriously ensconced in Shepherd's Bush in return for some occasional nocturnal piecework. I had no option but to hang around impatiently in Oxford and borrow from Hetty on the strength of my future. Unshaven, unsmiling and chain-smoking, I sat one day at the family lunch table outlining my extremely important war work.

'Thank God,' my mother said loudly, as she applauded both the signal honour and the fact I was spared any physical engagement. For some reason I was far keener to hear Bill Geraghty demonstrate his grudging approbation. Committed to illustrating government propaganda sheets for the duration of the War, I felt obscurely compromised. I was convinced I must be blindly selling myself, but surely in my father's eyes I must be making a go of things.

I was rapidly disabused of this fantasy. Far from congratulating me, my father went one better and disclosed how he had pipped me to the post.

'Losty's, you know,' he boasted, messily wiping his mouth with a crimson handkerchief, 'are more than likely to be the ones who run off these propaganda squibs of yours.'

'Really?' I said startled. Not least because that noun 'squib' seemed far from accidental. I looked him sternly in the eye, just in case he was teasing.

'Losty told me we are one of a handful of printers selected from hundreds of tenders nationwide. The sums at stake are colossal apparently. Indeed it's quite conceivable I'll be the one to proofread your apprentice handiwork, George. Just imagine. Your eagle-eyed pop being the first to spot you've spelt "certain" as "curtain" and "defeat" with two "e"s . . .'

I scowled at his flagrantly competitive tone and said to Hetty, 'I'm a flawless speller and always have been. Dorryfield tested me on the spot as a routine procedure. He asked me to spell "diarrhoea", "haemorrhage" and "millennium" and said he was astonished that I got all three.'

Hetty smiled uneasily. 'But what preposterous words to fling at you. What on earth can diarr . . . can they have to do with demoralising the enemy?'

'Dorryfield says only one in a hundred thousand Britons can spell "millennium". They all assume one "n". It's derived from "annum" of course, but even those with a classical education get it wrong.'

My father was on his fourth glass of wine and in no mood to cede the table talk to a bumptious art student. He droned in a particularly unctuous voice: 'Or here's another predictable scenario. You or one of your myopic fellow bohemians might have gone and drawn Hitler's moustache unconvincingly short. Now should this deplorable facsimile go and land on my desk, I would have no option but to mark it up and return to source instanter. Let's face it, no perfidious Belgian or disgruntled alderman in Dresden is going to be lured away from Nazism by a drawing of someone who looks more like Tommy Handley than the invincible bloody Führer. Speaking as one who earns his bread by spotting minute but devastating errors of composition, I assure you it's this kind of zealous attention to nuance will make all the difference to our winning the war.'

Rather than fall upon my father and thus ruin Hetty's lunch, I rose in anger from the table.

'Most of the patriotic public,' he continued, a little moist about the eyes as far as I could see, 'are entirely ignorant of the crucial role of the proofreader. I tell you if I were Jack

Losty, I'd show a damn sight more farsighted deference to the likes of Bill Geraghty than those clients of his who send in their perennially illiterate copy. Half the time I need to rewrite from scratch all these restaurant menus penned by garlicky bloody dagos running their highway-robbery places down the High. Their solecisms you would not believe. "*Lamp* chop" is a common one. "M-o-t-h-w-a-t-t-e-r-i-n" is another. Also "r-o-m-p-s-t-e-c-k". Fancy not being able to spell a little thing like "rump". I ask you, Hetty.'

Hetty stiffened and held her hand over her wine glass. I left the house after announcing I was going for a very long walk down by Port Meadow. My mother looked at me worriedly as my father continued to catalogue the illiterate howlers of restaurateurs the length and breadth of the Cotswolds and South Midlands.

Just as I was leaving, Hetty appeared and whispered that it was probably only his jealousy. I grunted and told her that it didn't make his jibing any more palatable. The point was that even a blusterer like Bill must have known that a private interview with Sir Thomas Dorryfield had rather more cachet than the mundane confab he'd had with Jack Losty. But regardless of that, Hetty assured me, with a tender pat on the shoulder, your father deep down is incredibly proud of your artistic talent.

I doubted that very much as I walked past a string of moored boats and wondered what it would mean to experience another twentieth-century war. Rationing, blackouts, air-raid shelters and all the rest of it: it all seemed as remote as the tiny Hertfordshire hamlet where Sir Thomas orchestrated his propaganda strategy with his staff of handpicked Oxbridge graduates. But my stroll by Port Meadow seemed to work as a tonic and I was in a philosophic even expansive mood on my return. I decided I wouldn't, after all, start rowing with Bill, especially as I was dependent on him for the next few weeks. Hetty had left a note pinned to the hallstand, saying she was spending the afternoon with her friend

Miranda Summers over at Didcot. I paused en route to the kitchen and listened to my father mumbling away to someone inside the parlour. By the sound of it he must have been drinking continuously since lunchtime. I could also make out the clipped and stertorous responses of an old crony of his, Theodore Tennent. Tennent was a stout, lugubrious Banbury solicitor, a redoubtable old soak with a machine-gun way of speaking. Among other dubious feats he could empty an entire bottle of spirits without showing any signs of drunkenness. Only when he staggered to his feet and tottered sideways like a vaudeville turn was there any colourful evidence of cause and effect.

I was about to walk in on their little soirée and help myself to a whisky when I caught the tail end of one of Bill's remarks. Intrigued, I realised that it was me, his prodigal son no less, who was the subject of their mordant musings.

'What more can I say, Theodore?' Bill droned on after a boozy pause. 'Only that I gave George the very best of educations. To begin with that exclusive prep school over in Witney, run by two stout females but no less expensive for that. Next followed Lawless's arm-and-a-leg academy for the sons of brainy dons and the cream of Oxford gentlefolk. Frankly, somewhere along the lines of Dotheboys Hall would have been a wiser choice, in my opinion.'

'Huh?' grunted Tennent, manufacturing odd faint choking noises in between his words. 'Didn't exert himself unduly? Didn't pay back the paternal sacrifice?'

Bill sighed heavily. 'George never distinguished himself as a budding scholar, if that's what you mean. But of course there's a limit to how much even the most zealous parent might counter a pernicious natural indolence. So obvious was the latter that when he was a little lad I regularly used to test him on his French and German at the breakfast table, simply as a means of giving him a spurt ahead of the other chaps. For example, I'd shout out when he was least expecting it, just as the sausage or egg was halfway to his mouth, "Rightio, George. I want you to toss out all the Boche prepositions that take the dative case!" The kind of list that you or I could streel off while still in our infant skirts, Theo.'

There was an apparently contemplative silence from his friend. Then an extraordinary and absurd thing happened. As if to prove that he could succeed where I had long ago failed, the sixty-three-year-old Banbury solicitor shot back without a pause for breath: '*Aus, bei, mit, nach, zu, seit, von, gegenüber.* Meaning: out, at the home of, with, after, to, since, from, opposite. Any damn fool knows those things, Bill.'

My father applauded with a sniff. 'Not forgetting *ausser*, Theo. But George would look at me as if I were cuckoo and ask brainless things like, "What does '*Boche*' mean, Daddy?" Then I'd say to him, "Dammit haven't you read John Buchan and Mr Standfast, a great big lout of nine like you?"'

Tennent puffed patriotically, 'It means a blasted Jerry. Any fool knows that. Any nine year old who had read *Greenmantle* and Richard Hannay would know that.'

My father began poking away savagely at the fire before staggering back to his chair. Meanwhile Tennent was audibly repeating his dative list though continuing to omit '*ausser*'.

'So I would say to him, "Geegee, old chap, if you can't give me any of the damn datives, I'll settle instead for the prepositions that take the accusative". . .'

The old Banbury solicitor had an abundant and proud supply of them. '*Durch, ohne, für, gegen, wider, um,*' he rattled like a Tommy gun. 'Through, without, for, about, opposite, around.'

'Quite,' sighed my father in mournful agreement. 'But little George would still be staring at me blankly. Ultimately it would transpire that at nearly ten years old this idle young sprout didn't even know what a bloody preposition was!'

'Appalling,' denounced Theo Tennent. 'Absolutely appalling. Your hard-earned money would have been better spent on –'

'Too bloody saddening for words. Then I'd say, "George,

what the hell is that indulgent Miss Pettifer teaching you over at Witney? As far as I recall, at your age I was parsing Herodotus and doing verse composition in the epigrammatic style of Martial. Set down that sausage, lad, it doesn't matter if it gets cold, and listen to me attentively. The preposition, George, is one of the most important things you'll ever have to deal with. Without it . . ." and then I'd have to chuckle and be forced to put my hand to my mouth, Theo! "See what I mean, old boy? *Without*! Where would we be without 'without'. No 'without', no damn sense, George."'

'Of course not! Any bloody fool knows that.'

'All the rest you know, Theodore. Geraghty Junior slouched through his adolescence as a sulky and rebellious sort of specimen who spent a great deal of time doing Monsewer-in-a-Beret sketching down by Christ Church Meadow and Iffley village. Every pound of his pocket money squandered on silly bloody art books, most of them in German ironically enough. Kunstverlag editions imported by Blackwells I seem to remember. I caught him once poring over one while I was rooting for a Hausa Dictionary on the same bloody floor.'

Tennent sighed aghast. 'Dear dear. What an awful waste of money.'

'The final straw was when he categorically refused to take Oxford entrance papers. No amount of passionate petition from me would budge his ugly obstinacy. As a result of which, instead of distinguishing himself at dear old Magdalen like you and me, George is now ensconced at the Royal bloody College of *Lotus-Eating* . . .'

'Good Lord! Any fool knows –'

With a lachrymose hiccup, my father concluded: 'My son and only heir has elected to draw tomfool *satirical* cartoons as a way of spending his Biblical talents!'

Of course I was boiling with rage as I stood eavesdropping on this ludicrous P.G. Wodehouse pair. Yet I was also helplessly fascinated by their preposterous maunderings. I lingered there transfixed, waiting for the very worst they could offer. Theo Tennent earnestly resumed his *durch, ohne, für* roll call, but my patience was finally rewarded. At length I heard my father make a favourite sucking noise between two back molars, always a prelude to some outrageous declaration. Tonight he had decided to surpass himself. As if in search of some plausible physiological explanation of my delinquent nature, he regaled Theodore Tennent with a no-holds-barred account of the business of my conception . . .

'George ought to have been blessed with a decent enough genetic inheritance, you know. By rights he should have demonstrated my linguistic flair, or even Hetty's native common sense for that matter. Unfortunately, he exhibits neither. I've racked my brains for any feasible extenuation. In the end the only thing I can put it down to are the unusual circumstances of his conception.'

'Eh?' whistled Tennent impressed. 'But how the hell can you possibly pinpoint something like that?'

'Because I performed all the requisite sums, Theo, and was left in no doubt of it. The date in question was 21st June, Midsummer's Eve, 1919. It being the only time young maiden Hetty and I were to go the whole hog before our marriage three months later.'

I failed to catch the solicitor's response but my father's loud cackle suggested it was something obscene and possibly legalistic.

'As for the heightened amatory context, it was not just a hot and sultry Midsummer's Eve. Hetty and I were also footloose and rampant in remote Wiltshire countryside for a full three days. More to the point, prior to this first full consummation of ours, we had been drinking a deuce of a quantity of pungent home-made fruit wine. A turbid, not to say rancid sort of peach cordial that would probably have powered the Royal Enfield motorbike which Hetty and I had ridden down there to rural Wilts.'

'Ha,' snorted Theo. 'I'll bet.'

'Preceded now I think of it by several brimming mugfuls of some impressively astringent nettle brandy. In case you're wondering, all this preposterous hooch from the hedgerows was courtesy of a hospitable old couple who lived in a tiny hamlet called Bushel or Fizzle or Pizzle or something equally gentle upon the ears. You see being just kids neither of us had much money, so we were lodging with these two embarrassing and impoverished relatives of Hetty's, the kind you would never go near unless you wished a selfish favour of them. They were called her Aunty Maggie and her Uncle Setter . . .'

'Setter?' repeated Theo wonderingly. 'Are you sure?'

'Setter Phizacklea was his full name. An illiterate, more or less retarded tenant farmer for the nearby Pizzle or Fizzle estate. Damn queer Christian name eh, and old Setter looked disconcertingly like the eponymous dog breed. Enormous hairy ears he had, and enormous, dangling, dripping sort of tongue. His breath smelt more like the pedigree Galloways that he tended for the local Pizzle squire, but out in fruity and cordial West Wilts back in 1919, few of the yeomen gave a fig for oral hygiene. Beggars couldn't be choosers out in the remote sticks don't you know, Theo?'

'Ha,' assented Tennent.

'My future wife and I grew girt bibulous not say right amorous on our gallon of fruit wine. Especially once old Maggie and Setter had hobbled off to their blameless iron beds on the stroke of eight. It was their touching bucolic retirement hour, you understand. But Hetty and Bill, both nearing thirty, were still in possession of an ample pre-nuptial vigour. We decided that we would stay up and entertain ourselves here in our comfy country cottage until *at least* a quarter to nine . . . !'

'Hah!' guffawed Theo. 'I'll bet.'

'Ere long we found ourselves languorously euphoric in a billowing fug of peach and nettle fumes.'

'Hah! I'll bet!'

'And darn soon rutting furiously on the floor by the light of a full West Wiltshire moon!'

'I'll bet!'

'But listen, Theo, this is the really uncanny bit. There was a bloody *owl*, believe it or not, was sat there on the gate outside Setter Phizacklea's lonely little cottage. Doing a kind of unsolicited sentinel duty, if you follow me.'

'What? You –'

'Under that full moon on Midsummer's Eve, every one of its feathers was as clear as a bell as it gazed astounded upon Hetty and me.'

'An *owl*? Doing that?'

'It was parked there barely two yards from where we were thrashing. That impudent old owl was gawking in through the window at the sight of us naked inside.'

Theo gasped and complained of a strange shiver running up the length his spine.

'You sure that's what you saw? After all, with all that bloody fruit wi–'

'Neglecting to emit any owlish hoot, it stayed rooted to the spot, as peeping tom as you like. The whole time peering basilisk at me as I flailed and panted on top of fevered Hetty. I observed its piercing terrible gaze whenever I rose for a breath of air.'

Tennent had obviously trembled again and my father was helpfully filling his glass.

'Take this as read, Theo. I give no fool credence to the occult, the prophetic, the miraculous, to any of that. I pooh-pooh clairvoyance, telepathy, vaticination, hariolation, Julius Caesar's chickens' entrails and all that putrid tommy rot. Nevertheless, I sometimes think that wise old owl was sat there on Phizacklea's gate with a definite bloody purpose . . .'

'Oh? Meaning –'

'With some uncanny supernatural prescience common to its species, it obviously felt called to be the witness to an astonishing sight.'

By this stage Theo was losing the thread and muttered, 'But why? Why would a bloody owl give a damn about you and Hetty flogging away down on the floor?'

'Because the poor old critter simply couldn't believe its eyeballs! Its nictating membrane was frozen like a blessed icicle.'

'Eh?' sighed Tennent, and I pictured him with a face identical to the owl's.

'Prophetically speaking, sapient old Ollie foresaw the birth *not* of someone extraordinary . . .'

'Ah,' gurgled Theo. 'Got you now, Bill.'

'Old Ollie foresaw instead a pitiful albeit astonishing anticlimax.'

'Quite. Right enough.'

'Old Ollie foresaw the birth of our disappointing *George* . . .'

'Dear dear,' tsked Tennent with fierce sympathy. 'Oh dear dear dear.'

'Meaning,' growled my father and he paused to rattle his poker in the fire, 'that all the stunned owl saw heralded in the future was the birth of a rag-and-bone *artist*.'

'Doh,' grieved Theo, who had two rich sons, both of them experts in mercantile law.

'Worse still, of a damn fool squiggle-and-dash *cartoonist!*'

'Cartoons!' groaned Tennent from the depths of his being. 'As if we haven't all got trouble enough!'

My birth story was finished and a pregnant silence supervened. By which point I had decided to burst in on them, slap Bill Geraghty on both sides of his face, and challenge him to an immediate duel. But the silence didn't last, and I was very soon listening to their resonant contrapuntal snoring. I clenched my jaw and fumed as I realised they were drunk as lords and would be out stone cold for the rest of the afternoon.

* * *

That night I got drunk as a lord myself. Leaving the house I slammed the door as hard as I could, in half a mind to head straight for the station. I pounded vengefully down the Banbury Road, past the Tarkenters' villa, past the neat dim-lit houses of dons and doctors and one or two London brokers. I felt as angry at them and all they stood for as I did at my father's treachery. To jeer at me in front of Hetty was one thing, but to deride me to a ridiculous old lush like Tennent was quite unpardonable. No mention of my elevated war work, nor that Bill Geraghty would be acting in a purely mechanical and subsidiary role in the same endeavour. Reaching St Giles I realised that my lips were moving frantically in an imaginary argument. Alarmed and wondering how long I'd been talking to myself, I felt in my pockets and found all of two pounds fifteen shillings. I calculated how many pints it would take me to get drunk and scanned around for an inviting pub.

By eight o'clock I had deserted the sedate sleepiness of The Lamb and Flag and wandered down the dingy back-streets of Jericho. I was looking for some colour or at any rate the opposite of blighted suburban decorum. I was looking for the demi-monde, disrepute, borderline legality, life with some evidence of pungence. Perhaps what I was really craving was the equivalent of the Bijou Café, a place where people with life-and-death as opposed to pampered middle-class problems were attempting to make sense of their lives. At last I found a dingy little pub called The Farrier which had so much palpable atmosphere the weight of it threatened to choke its customers. The landlord, very emaci-ated and about fifty, had a blind left eye and a withered right arm. I stared at this gothic Dickensian character until he noticed my scrutiny and frowned. At once I blushed crimson and ordered a good malt as a placatory gesture. I even told him to have one himself, which he refused, though not all that gruffly.

The Farrier was a spectral twilight world of heavy-drinking

working men; of restless working girls with thick make-up and stifled expressions; of assorted Oxford oddities, some of them morose and peaceable, others just raucous exhibitionists. Immediately I sat down I was regaled by a malodorous middle-aged chap with a tangled beard who talked in a disconcerting word-salad. He began his jagged monologue with a comic expansiveness, pointing his thumbs at the rest of the customers and babbling, 'such paltry and beggarly commerce between distrait individuals'. As I was only twenty I smiled with a complacent tolerance, assuming that everyday life had obligingly turned into a Dostoievsky novel. But his directionless ramble suddenly metamorphosed into a humourless and malevolent paranoia. I winced as he started to growl and swear about all these 'harlots' and 'Philistines' insolently milling around him and 'stealing his air'. Before long he moved on into the smoky throng, kicking at barstools and denouncing all those detestable and wicked Jebusites, Amalekites and Perizzites.

'Hallo there . . . !'

A young man of about thirty plumped down at my table and beamingly claimed to recognise me. I had never seen him in my life, and his connoisseur's appraisal of my smart new jacket was accompanied by a famished stare at my unfinished whisky. He was clad in a tidy grey suit, had a modern American neckshave, and seemed altogether ordinary, until a shrill wild cackle seemed to erupt from the back of his bony skull. I stared at him worriedly and wondered if I should bolt for it. In the same instant, unable to contain himself, he picked up my whisky and downed it in one gulp. Apologising for a serious case of mistaken identity, he calmly shook hands and shot off in search of unfinished whiskies.

I was no drinker and was half cut by nine o'clock. I staggered into the gents, hovered at the urinals, and surveyed the lavatory doors. Two had shoes visible underneath, and the third stood wide open. That lavatory was occupied, however, and by a white-haired man with a flaming red complexion.

His shiny trousers were round his knees, his braces were trailing in the insanitary floor, and he was industriously wiping his backside with a pristine white handkerchief.

'No paper,' he complained, without the slightest embarrassment. He looked at me very angrily. 'Would you reckon that's scandalous?'

'Oh yes,' I said, as I raced for the door.

I tottered back to the smoke-filled bar. Dizzy from such a profusion of lunatics, I realised that the listlessness of The Lamb and Flag had its compensations. I was looking worriedly for the door when suddenly a mirage of a dozen extravagant individuals came hurtling through it. Like a squad of off-duty soldiers, they piled up haphazardly and noisily at the bar. I looked at the withered landlord who returned my stare and croaked just one word.

'Akters.'

Even a child would have known that the man hailed as Geoffrey with the broad-brimmed black hat could only have been an actor. Geoffrey had the girth and gravity of an elderly Orson Welles, though he looked no more than thirty. The rest were in their early twenties and as exuberant and clamorous as excited infants. From my whisky haze I assumed Geoffrey was the actor-manager-impresario, the rest his anarchic troupe. Later a woman called Giselle put me right and pointed to a boy called Eric sitting sulkily on a distant stool. Eric Glossop was only nineteen but it was he who ran the company on behalf of his incapacitated mother, Gloire. Giselle and I had fallen into lively conversation after a dramatic collision. She had bumped into me while attempting to transport four glasses of beer and had spilt a generous amount all over my startled crotch.

'Oh my!' she shouted with the widest blue eyes I'd ever seen. 'Oh you poor young man. *Look* where I've spilled it.'

Geoffrey examined my crotch and bellowed, 'Better buy the poor bugger a drink, Gis. Either that, or let him douse his pint across you.'

'But he hasn't got a pint.'

'Well bloody well buy him one!'

Giselle sported a sloping green beret and about a dozen cheap and glittering necklaces. She spoke very hurriedly, with an inspired artlessness that was lightly peppered with an attractive irony. Actors then as now were usually stereotyped as a bunch of fractious neurotics, backbiters and vainglorious egotists. But these ones, I decided, as I took in the appealing dilation of Giselle's lively turquoise eyes, were the opposite of all that. They seemed effervescently united in their precarious existence and even in their toleration of the hopelessly overloaded Eric. Giselle explained that his mother, Gloire, once a top-of-the-bill music-hall act, was now disabled by a mysterious neurasthenia. Eric seemed to have gladly inherited Gloire's hypochondria so that all the important administrative business had to be done by Geoffrey. Giselle also introduced Cherry who had black kohl daubed around her eyes and looked like a sly Siamese. Underneath her pantomime guise she turned out to be modest and kind as well as ebullient. A boy called Sammy, who had tight blond curls and was the double of Harpo Marx, offered me a cigarette. All of them apart from Eric, who had just had an explosive phone conversation with Gloire, crowded round me and gave me their attention. Giselle repeated that I was a student at the RCA, and that I had had my drawings in the *New Statesman*. Sammy and Cherry whistled, greatly impressed. Tonight, Cherry explained, they had been performing *The Miser* by Molière in an amateur operatic hall in Woodstock. There had been an audience of ten, five of whom had turned up assuming it was a religious lecture on the theme of avarice, but had stayed on glumly nonetheless.

Not much later it was closing time. Giselle clasped my hand and said they were about to go back to their digs on the Abingdon Road. It was partly that handclasp that inspired me but also I was radiant with the whisky. Reckless with Dutch courage and tantalised by her lovely smile, I realised

I had a far better idea. I downed my drink and pulled urgently at her coat.

'Come back to my place,' I begged her.

She said wonderingly, 'My my. You don't mince your words, young artist.'

'No, no! I mean all of you of, course. Please! Please be my guests. I've got a beautiful enormous house up the top end of Banbury Road. We've got an outsize electric fridge and it's always crammed with the loveliest snacks and tidbits. I've got an unequalled collection of jazz records. Duke Ellington, Jack Teagarden, Benny Goodman. My father has a drinks cupboard that's the envy of North Oxford. He drinks like a fish, you see, and he likes everyone else to do the same. He can speak fifty-five languages, Giselle. And so can all his cage birds.'

She gave me a spontaneous tweak on the nose and said I was in the wrong profession. I should have a stab at *The Miser* tomorrow night in Wantage Masonic Hall. But Geoffrey had wisely cocked his ears at my proposal and didn't wait for me to change my mind.

'How far's your place?' he asked.

'A mile and a half perhaps. Only a half hour's walk from Jericho.'

'Bugger that! Two taxis should do it. Will your old man fork out for it at the other end?'

'Of course he will! He loves young people! And as for loving *actors* . . .'

We arrived at half past midnight. Inside the taxi with Giselle, Sammy and Geoffrey, I was bombarded with an impromptu rendition of two long excerpts from *Timon of Athens*. It must be one of the bard's most vitriolic and abrasive creations, and certainly in the confines of a wartime taxi a trifle claustrophobic. Naturally Geoffrey played the raging, misanthropic Timon. Gesticulating violently in the passenger seat, he soon frightened the old driver out of his wits with the fury of his imprecations.

Whose procreation, residence and birth
Scarce is dividant, touch them with several fortunes . . .
The senator shall bear contempt hereditary
The beggar native honour.

Through my fog of booze the references to procreation
and contempt echoed all too painfully. I recalled Bill
Geraghty and Tennent guffawing at the image of the owl's
bemusement as it watched my conception. I seethed at their
mockery and quietly ground my teeth. Ranting and perse-
cuted Timon was a man after my own heart, and I decided
to read the whole play before I went to bed tonight.
Meanwhile in the comforting darkness I squeezed Giselle's
hand as she took on the part of Alcibiades' mistress, Phrynia.

'*This fell whore of thine*,' Geoffrey roared to Sammy/
Alcibiades, referring to the beret-wearing Phrynia, '*hath in
her more destruction than thy sword.*'

The driver dug the slavering actor with his elbow. 'Oy!
You watch your effing language.'

Giselle shot up in her seat and roared at Timon, '*Thy lips
rot off!*'

The old driver, assuming she was apostrophising him,
bellowed his outrage. He threatened to stop the car and kick
the young lady's backside. Luckily I could see that we were
only ten yards from the house. I shouted the number and he
pulled to an instant halt, delighted, he sneered, to be rid of
these chattering baboons who ought to be swinging up the
Banbury Road plane trees.

I led the way, hoping to find Bill sitting intent over a
Coptic grammar. No doubt he would be in the mood for
enjoying a bit of Duke Ellington at full volume. It would give
him a rest from all those tedious conjugations and declinings,
would it not? Would he decline for us a bit tonight, I asked
myself. Certainly he had never stopped conjugating in the
past twenty years. There was only the hall light on downstairs, and a pencil note from Hetty said they had gone to

bed. Please lock up, darling, finish off the salad in the fridge, love, and congratulations from us both on your wonderful career start.

'Hah,' I hiccupped sourly.

I took some change off the hallstand and went out to pay the taxi. Returning I tore up the note and invited my guests to follow me into the kitchen.

'Pile in there, no need to be shy! Come on, who wants a nice enormous sandwich? Or a plate of gourmet salad?'

Eric Glossop said mournfully, 'Gimme some gaw-may salad. But only if it has salad cream in it. It's the one thing that doesn't aggravate an acid stomach.'

'You know, I don't think we've got any, Eric. But hang on, I'm sure my dad has an enormous tin of Gentleman's Relish somewhere in these cupboards. It must be a bloody catering tin gone astray from the Officer's Mess at Sandhurst. Anyone for a bit of *patum peperium*?'

Giselle squeezed my arm and assured me I was her favourite London art student to date. Surprised, I asked how many she had known, and she looked vague as she said no more than six. Meanwhile the whole of the troupe, including bilious Eric, demanded doorstop sandwiches of Gentleman's Relish. They had all heard of the legendary substance, but none had ever sampled it. Giselle for one was full of the most extravagant expectations, assuming it would taste more or less like caviar.

She took a huge bite and spat it onto her plate.

'Ugh! You might have warned me it tastes like year-old bird shit.'

I patted her arm and suggested a drink to take away the taste. The rest of them took a gingerly bite, then put their sandwiches glumly on their plates. All except Geoffrey, still wearing his wide-brimmed hat, who insisted it was absolutely delicious. You needed to be a gentleman to appreciate Gentleman's Relish, he purred, and he was obviously the only one present. He paraded round picking up all ten sandwiches until he had assembled a foot-high pillar of GR. Guiltily I fished out the vast bowl of salad, enough for an army, and offered it round. Then I discovered a biscuit tin full of choice connoisseur cheeses: Stilton, Sage Derby, Cheddar with Chives. They were Bill's exclusive tidbits, bought with his own money and intended to accompany his modest collection of reserve ports. Delighted, I ferreted further, spilling lidless jars and bottles as I went. At last I found a bag of ham and some potted meat and a jar of pickled onions. I laid it all out on the table and invited my guests to demolish it wholesale.

It was all gone in about four minutes. I was thrilled to see that not a crumb of Bill's cheeses remained. I pointed in the direction of the sitting room: 'Music,' I cried. 'Duke Ellington. Jack Teagarden. Drinks all round!'

We straggled noisily into a room that was dwarfed by Stanforth's teak dresser and a vast mahogany cabinet. Some Dresden figurines were seen to start dancing on the latter as the lively herd made itself comfortable. Sammy with a guileless Harpo smirk fell upon my jazz collection. Cherry, whose kohl had begun to run, wound up the old record player. She turned and grinned like a ghostly ghoul, waving in all directions as if to reassure us of her harmless nature. Eric sat in a corner chewing away lugubriously at his salad. He complained to a chubby actress called Madge that the vinaigrette I'd lavished on it was truly torturing him. Giselle suddenly grabbed my arm and with her cornflower eyes at full dilation led me into a waltz. Geoffrey was chomping away through his fourth doorstop while snorting random snatches from *Timon*.

'*Be a whore still*. What's in this stuff, George? What's its principal ingredient? Anchovies? Really? *Give them diseases, leaving with thee their lust*. Pepper? *Season the slaves for tubs and baths*. Yeast? *Bring down rose-cheeked youth, to the tub-fast and the diet*. Right, eaten the whole bloody lot. Can I take back what's left in the tin?'

'Hang thee, monster!' Giselle shouted, as I nuzzled my nose hungrily into the fine hairs of her neck.

The record had finished. I made my way to the drinks cupboard and like a proud wizard brought out the connoisseur malts as well as the Bell's and the Beefeater. I lifted up the Cardhu, Jura and Islay bottles and gave their pretty little backsides a kiss. The bottles were all dimpled, with gently feminine curves, and I decided that that must somehow fuel my father's thirst for women as well as whisky. More than anything I was indignant I couldn't offer round his precious old ports which he kept under lock and key in case of burglary.

Instead of asking who wanted what, I poured a lavish selection of spirits and offered them to first takers. My guests drank indiscriminately and thirstily.

We were making such a noise, not even Bill, who slept like a log, would be able to ignore it. My mother was a light sleeper and would be bound to send him down soon to investigate. Sharp on the look out, I did not have to wait long. As I emptied the Cardhu bottle, I glimpsed the sloping bridge of a nose just visible behind the door. The door stayed a few inches ajar as the startled nose retreated. Bill, I realised, was either too furious or too thunderstruck to bowl in on us. In which case he would likely dawdle outside, trying to make auditory sense of this pagan ruckus. After about thirty seconds his curiosity got the better of him. He poked his face round and, aghast, withdrew immediately. In a trice he took in the monstrous vision of what he later described to Hetty as 'sybaritic bloody mountebanks'. He noted that the sybarites were sitting in a wasteland of lettuce leaves, fag ash, tipped whiskies, sandwich crusts. The heirloom Turkish rug that Stanforth had been given by a lady client in 1887 showed unmistakable signs of ground-in Gentleman's Relish. A Dresden figurine of a non-sybaritic eighteenth-century mountebank lay in shards in front of the cabinet.

But I was drunk and did not care. In any case, though he

mightn't have wrecked our home physically, Bill Geraghty had kept it in figurative disarray for as long as I could remember. What were a few mouldy antiques compared to the years that Hetty had spent stifling her unhappiness? His crimes, his family betrayals, were beyond number. For years he had preached his maudlin gospel of job security and had derided my childish world of fine art. With no deliberate forethought on my part I had just succeeded in brilliantly combining the two. Today, jealous as a schoolboy, he had derided even that. The didactic fable of the owl and the nettle brandy would be all round Banbury and environs by next week. I was just giving the old bugger some tit for tat.

It was the Gentleman's Relish on the rug that inspired me to a more fitting revenge. Given that Geoffrey was still licking it off his fingers, it was reasonable enough to bring it into general conversation. Bill, I confirmed, was still eavesdropping at the doorway. I could make out a few delicate coughs and sniffs, signalling his sensitive presence and his wish for an urgent interview.

I began to declaim in a parody of the old-fashioned thespian, august, bombastic and with gush: 'Did you know, folks, there's at least one place in this hallowed city where Gentleman's Relish is an indispensable postprandial accompaniment? Somewhere where it's consumed every night, rain or shine, Christmas Day and Boxing Day included?'

Eric asked what 'postprandial' meant and grumbled that his vinaigrette-induced heartburn was excruciating. Cherry swallowed about half a pint of Beefeater's, and suggested it must be the Randolph where the stuff was dished out at the end of every meal.

'Not at all,' I snorted. Then I pouted a Wildean moue, and spoke in a passable mimicry of Noël Coward. 'The place in question is *All Souls*.'

Cherry looked vacant rather than expectant, and it suddenly dawned on me that not everyone in the universe had heard of the venerable sanctuary. It was Sammy who hazarded that it was a very old Oxford college, but of a highly specialised nature which momentarily eluded him.

Donning an imaginary smoking jacket, I tinkled invisible piano keys: 'But you simply *must* have heard of it. It's generally agreed that the very biggest brains in the world reside there. Most of its dons do not teach or do anything as pitiably mundane, the only demands made on them are what they make on themselves. They sit there in their cloistered albeit sumptuous studies. Alone and with unstinting vigour, the only thing they're obliged to do, these enormously intelligent gentlemen, is . . . *lucubrate.*'

Only Geoffrey knew what that meant. He guffawed and in the angry voice of a taxi driver advised me to keep it clean.

Cherry, whose runny kohl was now blackening her lips, said, 'I don't believe a word of it. George is just making it up as a joke. I don't believe they stuff themselves with that beastly relish.'

I pouted indignantly, 'I swear that at All Souls they are in daily receipt of two remarkable comestibles. Or perhaps I mean combustibles? Firstly, Cherry, every evening, after dinner, these brainiest brains in the world are offered *two* different types of snuff.'

Giselle raised her glass despairingly. 'I don't believe a syllable either. You are incredibly drunk, you know. But your Coward take-off is excellent. You really ought to join us on the road if your cartooning ever grinds to a halt.'

'Thanks,' I gabbled, and I bowed so low I almost went hurtling into the grate. Giselle lurched protectively and grabbed my jacket tail. Once she'd pushed me more or less upright, I continued: 'After they've stowed away their eight-course dinner, the sated All Soulers are offered rough and smooth varieties of snuff from a silver salver. Really, I have all this first-hand from one who knows all the ritual better than he knows his own face. As soon as they've staggered into the lounge, a specially elected Fellow offers them this momentous agony of choice. Rough or smooth, old boy, smooth or rough, old chap, which do you prefer? A few minutes later, from a chased silver goblet, he proffers them a spoonful or two of Gentleman's Relish.'

My father was making agonised shuffling noises outside. I grinned to hear him so mortified by the mockery. There was such pleasing symmetry between my boyish drunkenness and that senile vaudeville of his with Theo Tennent. But tight as I was, I understood the painful irony. Much as Bill loved to scorn the place that had refused him entry, he loathed the idea of a mob of gypsies cackling at its sacred name.

Giselle was studying my performance with an intent professional eye. Buoyed by her attentiveness, I went on: 'Better than the comical nature of these eccentric tidbits is the ceremonial title given to the one who dishes out the snuffs and the Relish.'

They all looked blank, apart from Geoffrey, who, as if mightily challenged, scratched his chin with suave gravity. 'Tom Mix?'

'Nope,' I said, just as one might have addressed the one named.

'Mister Gentleman?'

'Certainly not!'

'Mister *Relish*?'

'Hardly.' Then quickly temporising, as I lurched to and fro by the drinks cabinet. 'Though very close. Rather close indeed with that one.'

'*Master* Relish,' said Sammy excitedly, as if he hoped to win a prize.

I gargled my whisky and looked at him admiringly. 'You're so close I'll have to tell you. The name of this Fellow is the *Master of the Screw*.'

Sammy's jaw sagged as he saw I must be fabricating, and the prize wasn't his. I could also make out Bill Geraghty's sheeplike moan of indignation. Luckily it was drowned by my audience who became clamorous with hysteria. Geoffrey repeated 'Master of the Screw' several times, then did taxi-driver tuttings and told me to keep things effin clean. Giselle smacked me on the shoulder, then grabbed my glass of Cardhu and mixed it with her gin.

I swayed across to Hetty's piano and slumped down on the stool. Incapable of even lifting the lid, I tinkled away in a little boy's pretence. Then I turned with a Cowardish smirk to my audience.

'I promise you it really is the time-honoured designation. Nowhere but Oxford could such a splendid tradition hold sway. Thanks to this Honorary Screwmaster, the twin elixirs of Relish and snuff sustain these intellectual colossi at their undiminished peaks of perfervid brilliance.'

Giselle looked at Geoffrey and said the sandwiches he'd guzzled already made him look a bit like Bertrand Russell. Geoffrey agreed and said he was ready to start lucubrating here and now, and he didn't give a damn what anybody thought. From my swaying stool I raised a warning finger.

'You may think I'm clowning, folks. But there's a desperately serious issue at stake! I can assure you I'm the last person in the world who'd mock a nightly intake of Gentleman's Relish. Let me tell you why, should I?'

I clasped a bit of lettuce that had been sticking to my trouser leg and brandished it solemnly.

'Very soon, you see, some of these All Souls men will end up being requisitioned for wartime intelligence. They were during the last war, of course. After all, if you're going to outwit the cunning Hun, you have to employ those acknowledged to be the cleverest in the land.' I paused and wrapped my knuckles upon a little oak table to demonstrate the strength of my conviction. 'It's no wild flight of fancy therefore to make the obvious causal connection. Just brood on this remarkable little paradox before you all fall asleep tonight. *Two pungent little helpings of Gentleman's Relish for the Fellows at All Souls will be* directly *responsible for us hammering the shit out of those Jerries!*'

After a second of silence there came a tortured moan, like

that of a wounded badger. Giselle cocked her ears in astonishment. I rose from the piano and tripped my way across,
as if about to ask her for a dance. I smirked at her reassuringly and said it was our cat.

With the same cat stuck in its pit of mortification, it
seemed such a shame to stop halfway. Especially now that
kohl-black Cherry was asking the obvious question.

'How on earth d'you know all this loony stuff about All
Souls? I thought you said you were a London art student.'

Impishly I flicked her cheek and my hand became sooted
with kohl. 'Because of my *father*.'

Madge, who had Eric sprawled across her lap, said, 'Will
he be working for intelligence too?'

I smirked and answered, 'My father's just a lowly proofreader. He really has nothing to do with All Souls.'

Even in my drunkenness I realised that it was the first time
I had ever derided my father's profession. I could picture him
reddening with surprised humiliation as he writhed behind
the door.

'But he's also a kind of unsung genius,' I said, with a
grudging judicial air. 'He speaks fifty-five languages. Some of
which he's taught to his pet cockatoos.'

'Blimey,' said Madge, shuffling in her chair as Eric nuzzled
into her folds like a nursing infant.

'And his mynahs and his cockatiels. If there'd been any
sort of justice, he'd have sailed into All Souls after his brilliant
years at Magdalen. But no, my dad made an inexpungible
error when it came to scholarly decorum. Reasonably enough,
tradition in All Souls counts for far more than a pair of
bulging frontal lobes. Even though he's a genius in anyone's
book, he blew it in five seconds in that All Souls' viva. By a
single crucial faux pas he changed his destiny for ever.'

Cherry wondered if he had refused a pinch of snuff. I
grinned and said she had almost hit the nail on the head.
Meanwhile a fretful ghost could be heard pacing the hallway,
as anguished as a young father attending a difficult birth.

'What in hell's that noise outside?' asked Geoffrey. 'What on earth's that queer sort of pacing?'

'It's George's ickle cat,' sighed Cherry. 'And it sounds like it needs an ickle widdle.'

Geoffrey snorted, 'A cat? A pacing cat?'

I said. 'No, it's our dog. He's a very intelligent old hound called Bill. His pedigree name is Old Twister. He's not in need of a pee, though, I promise. Being very old and very set in his ways, he just likes pacing up and down. An idiosyncrasy of canine old age. I believe old Bill probably *thinks* as he does his pacing.'

Giselle patted my sleepy countenance and said, 'What exactly did your pa do to ruin the All Souls show?'

'This,' I said.

I tipped my Cardhu on the carpet. Sammy and Madge were horrified. Cherry gaped, then adopted the Cossack spirit and tipped hers onto the grate. It whooshed into flame, and Geoffrey raced across to rescue her from spirituous immolation.

'Bloody hell,' growled Eric, raising himself from his substitute breast. 'Is it any wonder I get bloody heartburn?'

I said, 'My father didn't tip his drink deliberately. I did that on purpose, but he didn't. He was just young and vulnerable and clumsy. Nervous as hell, he spilt their priceless Madeira at the start of his viva. He didn't have a hope in buggery after that.'

As I rubbed the whisky into the carpet, I could hear his voice quite clearly inside my skull: *'I think that's quite enough, George. Don't you? No need to wholly destroy me in front of these pals of yours.'*

I shook my head as if I had an insect stuck inside my ear. I almost made a reply to that phantasmal voice. Yet I hadn't said all I needed to say. His full humiliation was yet to come.

'My father is what you would call a severely disappointed man. Fractious, addicted to booze . . .'

I gave a dipsomaniac hiccup to show my own sad legacy.

'An inveterate womaniser,' I added.

I paused for some response from beyond the door. When none was forthcoming, Cherry noticed where I was looking. 'Your dog's stopped groaning,' she said with concern.

'I suppose in medical terms my dad was a full-blown satyr. In biblical terms, he was addicted to concupiscence. My childhood was characterised by a mother always anxious and melancholy, always waiting for his explanations. But he was so bloody glib you see, always lying to the back of his teeth.'

No canine or feline movement from without, I noticed. I looked around the room for some signs of sympathy. Instead I saw Geoffrey, Giselle, Eric and Madge all nodding to confirm that their childhoods had been a variation on the same sad theme. I almost gasped. I felt so let down I even wondered if my father might have treacherously won the moral ground somehow. I ranted on doggedly.

'He speaks fifty-five languages. He's also had at least fifty-five mistresses.'

'Bloody hell,' said Glossop, as he allowed Madge to smooth his ears between the wedges of her bosoms.

Madge cautioned him, 'Now *that* would give you heart-burn.'

'But he sounds so wonderful,' Cherry cried in a melting voice. 'He really must be the most attractive man.'

I was baffled and dismayed by their total lack of con-demnation. They weren't remotely appalled by his lasciviousness or his lies. On the contrary Geoffrey was using his fingers to calculate the arithmetic consequences of all those mistresses. Fifty-five broken hearts, at least fifty-five marital fights, not to speak of all those loose morals and loose springs and loose ends . . .

'I want to see him,' Cherry said determinedly. The kohl all over her cheek made her look like an Alabama minstrel. 'Any chance of waking him up?'

I said sulkily, 'Not a bloody hope.'

They weren't waiting for the punchline of my vengeful

monologue, but I let them have it anyway.

'My father might have failed as a parent and in terms of his intellectual promise. He has fulfilled himself in one key role however . . .'

I looked around my audience but no one invited me to continue. Fatigue was starting to envelop the carnival atmosphere. Even Giselle looked moderately irritable. Even Geoffrey was starting to droop and grow listless.

'They might have succeeded in stopping him from getting into All Souls. They might have stolen his birthright just like Esau. I'm not saying a mess of pottage and a bottle of Madeira are anything like the same thing, but–'

One person at least could see what was coming next. Suddenly the door shot open as if on a loaded spring. My father made entrance clad in a faded beige dressing gown and his favourite Turkish slippers. Expecting to be confronted by his explosive outrage and a dangling horsewhip, I saw a pale elderly man come to a halt, stand still, and show the dire ravages of his years. Nonplussed, I swallowed my dregs of Jura, then pointed to this wan old dog that had sired me.

I bawled, 'Look! Here's my crazy father! Here's my crazy sex-mad father who is the *Master of the Screw*.'

There remains the swooning image of those speechless actors all embarrassed beyond words. And of my father staring with fright at the floor, rigid with an infinite shame.

Cherry cried bravely, 'Oh hello!' and she shook herself and ran across to shake his hand.

In my drunken state I thought that his shame was just for himself. But of course he was much more shamed by the vindictiveness of his only child.

'Fifty-five women,' I shouted, before something gigantic seemed to swallow me up. 'Fifty-five bloody languages! And he's a bloody liar in every bloody one of them! He is, I promise! Salute the great Bill Geraghty, the *Mast*–'

Then I went unconscious.

138

I never saw Giselle or any of them again. I suppose it must have been Bill who finally carried me up to bed. He would have been within his rights to drown me in the bathroom where I lingered to puke at monotonous length. Neither of us subsequently made the slightest reference to my late-night party nor to the theft of his Gentleman's Relish.

Eight

My wife's maiden name was Flitters and she did not enjoy being teased about it. Her father was the stockbroker Reggie Flitters, a company associate of Major A.S. Charne, another seasoned speculator and another north-country landowner. Reggie Flitters was part of that extended clan which owned ancient castellated farms and dozens of stone cottages all over Westmoreland, and when he wasn't in London, he liked to be up at his estate near Appleby. Major Charne, who was the father of the actress Frankie Charne, had a bigger estate near Penrith, and in his case there was grouse as well as pheasant shooting. The Major couldn't get enough of grouse shooting, and year after year he and Reggie would motor over Hartside and bag great quantities up in the wilds by Eals and Slaggyford. They drank surprisingly modestly when they celebrated their spoils in a dark and tiny pub called The Drove at the far end of the potholed road to Hanging Shaw. The landlord had been ordered to provide steaming tatie pot and unlimited beer for all the beaters and keepers. While they patted their dogs and laughed and shouted, Reggie and A.S. would continue to talk profitable shop in the ill-lit corner next to the bar. It was still paraffin lamps in the lonely North Pennines, and the dim light seemed oddly fitting as the two rich old men muttered and swapped gossip with that gentle imperturbable sonority that marks out those truly born to the manor.

Reggie was not pleased when twenty-year-old Jane Agatha announced her intention of marrying a satirical artist. He did not cut her off penniless but he told her she was a fool and that her whimsical, serendipitous, let's-see-what-happens-next attitude would be her eventual downfall. In his stony certitude he was rather less prescient than usual. Reggie had a reasonably subtle eye when it came to human foibles and was remarkably well read for a man of commerce and a club man. In any event Jane suffered no pecuniary downfall, she would always prosper with a variety of men and after her own unique lights. Even in old age she has no great regrets, beyond the finite availability of attractive young toy boys. Reggie Flitters insisted on meeting Jane's fiancé up at Charne's estate near Penrith. Also I was to accompany them the next day on the grouse shoot near Eals. When I told him I couldn't shoot, he said no matter, you can watch and see if the sport appeals to you. You can also teach me about the new journalism and about newspaper editors and the limits they permit when it comes to political cartoons. To my amazement, when we had our discussion about censorship, instead of a classic attack and defence between father-in-law and son-in-law, it turned out to be Reggie talking about Juvenal's Satires, A.S. interjecting balefully about London Asiatic rubber shares, and George Geraghty sat in silence wondering when the interrogation would start in earnest.

It never did. Jane and I married in 1941 in the Flitters' family church just north of Appleby. Frankie Charne at eighteen was an overgrown and ill-behaved bridesmaid, so volatile and extravagant she threatened to steal the show from the wedding couple. Bill and Hetty came up by train from Oxford and Bill took an instant liking to young Frankie. He compared her to a spluttering, incendiary Roman candle on first acquaintance. An hour later it occurred to him that she was not like a single tiger cub but like an entire damn jungleful, like the entire bloody Sundarban population. He never cared for daughter-in-law Jane because, he said to Hetty, who subsequently told me, her eyes and therefore thoughts were always moving in all directions like a blinking espionage merchant, like some mysterious Boche Fräulein out of Sapper. She almost seemed to pierce his skin with her frank and vivid gaze. Naturally his exuberant flirting with young Frankie did not escape her careful scrutiny. Bill likely believed his daughter-in-law saw him as a grubby old rake, whereas her verdict was that Bill was merely freakish in his persistence and his appetite. To that extent she saw her father-in-law as embarrassingly like herself, if more brazen and more innocent in his means of seduction. By contrast Jane and Hetty accepted each other without reservation. Hetty took to Jane's independence, her love of the theatre and theatre folk, and her overall pugnacity. Clearly this young girl would never be trampled on by her inoffensive son, and would never need to suffer any competition from over-endowed barmaids.

Frankie Charne was there right from the start of our marriage. As well as acting in farces and melodramas broadcast on the wireless, she managed to land decent if minor parts in what was left of wartime theatre. She had family and old connections as well as her natural talent, and what strings she couldn't pull herself were pulled for her by Jane Geraghty. The two of them also did a little volunteer work in some Putney legal offices that specialised in pensions for war widows. There were two elderly bachelors in the office, and two young men called Teddy Bennett and Sam Willis, both declared unfit for service because of chest conditions. Bennett was a self-taught jazz pianist, and Willis was a cabinet maker and woodcarver who sold his work in Bond Street galleries. Both avid theatre-goers, they would accompany Jane and Frankie to lunchtime reviews intended principally for off-duty servicemen. Frankie had landed one or two parts in these half-hour comedies, and Jane and the two consumptive young men would go along and watch their colleague excel in these cheery little entertainments. One day in a one-acter by Sandy Nichols, she played the part of a trembling housekeeper called Miss Flitters who was frightened of ghosts. The name of the part she had kept a surprise till the day itself, and afterwards Frankie revealed to

142

Teddy and Sam that Jane's maiden name was the same as the dizzy housekeeper's. Jane did her best to laugh as uproariously as the rest, but she came home that night looking vengeful.

I was mildly surprised by the intensity of her indignation. 'Did she also mention that your middle name was Agatha?'

'Yes she did! So I decided to tell them about Frankie's middle name. That definitely put the little toadstool in her rightful place. It set the two men chortling OK.'

'Why was that?' I asked. Uneasy about these poorly colleagues of hers, I felt guilty about my unreasonable anxiety. I had met neither in the flesh, so my imagination ran riot when she mentioned 'crazy old Sammy' and 'that wild young teaser Teddy'. At twenty-one I hadn't much clue about the unlikely things that can endear a woman to a man, still less about the inscrutable factors that can make for erotic attraction.

'It's *Chastity*. Quite incredible, isn't it? Francesca Chastity Charne. I asked her drunken mother at my wedding. Frankie always said it was Clare, but I never believed her for a minute. I wouldn't have believed her capable of blushing, but today she turned as puce as puce can turn.'

Meanwhile, I was busy designing Dorryfield's leaflets in a dingy suite of offices in Holborn. Illustrated with bilious caricatures of Hitler, Himmler, Goering and the rest, they were accompanied by those lightning punning captions that had been seen and endorsed by the War Office. They were printed in a dozen European languages and dropped into occupied countries at the rate of two a month. My specialist employment seemed no less compromising than it had two years earlier. Although I believed in fighting Fascism by all practical means, I was aware that the means weren't subtle, not at all artistic, and could be employed just as easily for the opposite ends. But of course the job paid very well, and as the Geraghty couple were quite incapable of the slightest economy, there was no real alternative at this stage.

If Jane's independence consisted of tripping off to theatricals with unattached males, my own liberties were initially less threatening. The theatrical world as I had glimpsed it was full of flippancy and hysteria, of effervescence and depression, of addictions and extravagance. My substitute for this fraught and insecure milieu, inadequate as it was, was the company of the painter Joseph Clifton . . .

I had got to know Joe after he came across one of my Mussolini caricatures in the *Herald*. He was reading it late at night in an appallingly unhygienic drinking hole in Kilburn, where he was swigging stout in the company of his very odd Aunty Biddy. As well as sinking one or two halves of Guinness, his aunt would be sporadically mumbling hymns and prayers in Ulster Gaelic. Biddy McMinahan was settled in London since 1900, while Joe was only recently from the Donegal Arans. His first tongue was Ulster Irish, which he told me one night was significantly different from Munster, Leinster and Connacht Irish; the personal pronouns, the *tha mujhs* and so on, were the principal variants as far as I recall. It took a single call to the *Herald* for him to learn the identity and telephone number of 'Jazz', and two days later we were boozing together in Kilburn and happily tearing the metropolitan art world to pieces.

Clifton was a phenomenally gifted landscape artist who despite his best efforts rapidly finished himself with drink. I always assumed it was the spiritual gulf between the remote Arans and the frantic metropolises of Dublin and London that unmanned him in the first instance. When Clifton was a boy the Arans were as spartan and unrelieved as desert Kazakhstan. His painterly obsession with death and the afterlife, with guilt and redemption and eternal punishment, undoubtedly reads like a standard Irish Catholic case study. But his painting also had that twilit, barren, monstrously melancholy quality that must have come from those lonely storm-battered shores. He was a great admirer of the novelist and revolutionary Liam O'Flaherty who was twenty years his senior. O'Flaherty was also from the Arans, but the Galway Arans in his case. Clifton read his Kafkaesque work of phantasmagoric bleakness, *Black Soul*, as regularly as he read his confirmation Bible.

His Aunt Biddy, who was eighty, had been born in a hamlet near Gweedore in mainland Donegal. The two together, especially in Clifton's London haunts, embodied the ultimate in mordant eccentricity. Biddy's nephew was often morose as well as odd, while she herself was simply odd. She claimed to have seen whole families, entire villages of fairies in her Donegal childhood, and to have talked with them about their customs, history and religion. She had met them back in the Eighties and Nineties and every single one was a good Irish Catholic. They all went to Mass in a miniature church quite close to Biddy's which was invisible to all but the sentient few who could see it. She was still very pious and attended Mass in Willesden at least four times a day. Biddy felt no particular unease about her pagan belief in the supernatural. She said there were no fairies visible in Willesden because fairies only flourished in the untainted countryside where people were naturally religious.

Biddy lived on her ground floor and Joseph had a couple of rooms above. One was a vast cold attic which served as his studio and the other a makeshift bedsit with a single bed, a gas ring, and a generous collection of books. In place of a bookshelf he had varnished planks supported by bricks, and the rest of his furniture was sombre, second-hand and dotted with paint. He had a very long green sofa that would have seated half of Willesden and on it he would rest for long periods while working at a drawing. He read his Bible every day, usually the Old Testament, though not out of Catholic piety. He read it for its poetry, its sinew, its potence, its beauty.

'*The thing that hath been it is that which shall be; and that which is done is that which shall be done, and there is no new thing under the sun,*' he read to me one night from Ecclesiastes.

It was a wet winter evening and below his studio Biddy was doing her weekly baking. Clifton had managed to place some drawings in a little gallery in Soho, and one of them had just been sold. He had received a cheque for ten guineas and a paragraph review of the exhibition in *The Times*, specifically singling out J.I. Clifton and his haunting sketches of the Donegal Arans. At once he had gone out and bought Aunt Biddy a sumptuous winter coat on the instalment plan. It was so glamorous she kept it on in the house, so loth she was to be parted from its newness. He had also bought himself two bottles of Powers, a box of de Reszke cigarettes, and a stack of pristine black volumes in the World Author series. Among these were Gorki and three writers new to me: Borodin, Golubov and Wanda Wassilewska. The last was a very topical Russian novel describing recent German atrocities in the Ukraine. Clifton recounted its plot, and told me he had wept as he read about the Nazi lieutenant bayoneting a little baby as he interrogated the partisan mother. Remarkably, once they'd recaptured the Ukrainian village, Stalin's Red Army comrades hadn't butchered any Nazis in revenge. Clifton had wept again at the pathos of that. Of course everyone loved Joe Stalin then, including us two painters, including even Frankie Charne and probably even Aunt Biddy.

He repeated that long verse from Ecclesiastes and said: 'What does that mean? It affects me the way it's written, it sounds true alright, but I don't really know what it means.'

'Nor do I,' I said. 'I can only guess. I can only guess the author means that everything, however wonderful or however terrible, has already happened before somewhere.'

'Like my ten-guinea cheque? A bit of fame preceded by a hell of a lot of waiting? A bit of money and then a hell of a lot of nothing?'

'I suppose so. And other more impersonal, more momentous events. I suppose it applies to this bloody awful war. For example what the Germans are doing in Wassilewska's

Ukraine. It has all happened hundreds of times before, in other lands, in other civilisations and in other centuries.'

There came a faint shout up the stairs. Biddy wished to know if we wanted some of her date cake. We didn't but we said we'd love to try it. She shuffled upstairs in a greasy pinny bearing a chipped plate with half a dozen slabs. She was wearing her fine new coat underneath the flour-spattered pinny. It was bright maroon and as stylish as a girl's. It looked very unusual on someone so old, especially with its patina of flour and stale fat. Biddy had her long grey hair done in braids and her face was as lined and scored as old ash bark. She murmured something in Ulster Gaelic and Joe replied to her in Ulster English. She countered at great length in sibilant Irish, then resumed her habit of talking to herself. Her speech was liquid and pensive and very strange. Joseph said it was prayers and proverbs and bits of random reproof she was muttering to herself. She could speak sensible English after a fashion but never used the unwieldy tongue to her nephew. As she jabbered away and occasionally smiled at me I decided I had never seen anyone odder in my life. Only my father Bill Geraghty seemed anywhere on the same scale.

I returned to find Jane and Frankie drinking and arguing about a current *Othello* in the West End. Interspersed with denunciations of the casting and the set and the direction, they were competing in waspishness when it came to some of the audience. That thirty-year-old monstrosity Celia Bellingham who dressed like a spangled Mata Hari and frightened anyone who didn't know her. She had a drugs problem, cocaine of all things, and so much money from her boozer banker father she threw nightlong champagne-cum-charades parties three or four times a month. Jack Temple, the sixty-year-old sculptor who despite his age was still wonderfully handsome and whose conversation still dominated any gathering. It wasn't the content of what he said at all, it was the understated, piquant delivery and the generous light in those lovely blue eyes. Of course nearly all the young men were away fighting, so the old ones left behind were thrown into anomalous relief. For lack of competition and for the first time ever, men over forty-five became serious objects of interest. It really was astonishing, Jane and Frankie both agreed, how many of the old men still had full heads of hair, and how a fine bone structure or a deep and resonant voice could compensate for the creaky joints and the hesitant reflexes.

Frankie added drily, 'The young ones are usually servicemen in transit and hence rather predatory. Unless they've been invalided out and therefore not serious players. It's not easy dealing with either category, I find.'

I stared at this young woman who spoke with such airy assurance. 'Is that how you see Bennett and Willis in Putney? Your two colleagues with TB?'

They exchanged glances which could have meant anything or nothing. Watching Jane and her best friend I realised I didn't remotely comprehend either in any practical or imaginative sense. How could anyone know what it was like to be beneath the teasing mask of my playful wife? Or more to the point, beyond the strictly guarded frontiers of her body? Every month when she had her period, she became bloated, sardonic and withdrawn. She would customarily order me around like a pitiful minion. This was her body chemistry encouraging her natural temperament, but under her goadings I could not make the distinction. She was a spoiled woman who could also be impulsively generous with her affection and her time. One day she might be lying peevishly on a sofa, quibbling and snapping at every sentence I uttered; the next, she would be springing to her feet and suggesting a day out at Brighton and with every indication that I, her meek young husband, was all she'd ever need to be happy.

Listening to her and Frankie satirising their friends, I suddenly thought of Clifton's Aunt Biddy. She lived only a few miles from us and inhabited not so much a different existence as a separate physical universe. She was of the same British Isles as our British Isles, but she spoke a language that might as well have been Chinese for all it signified. Her English, scant and hesitant as it was, was expressed in a stage Irish syntax. *I'm after doing. I'm after going. I'm after dropping off to sleep.* She was completely remote from her Willesden milieu, a linguistic and sociological relic, waiting each day for Joe to take a break from his work and talk to her in her own tongue. She believed in supernatural creatures and had seen them with her child's eyes. Biddy McMinahan was poignantly comical. Everything she did was comical. She wore her prized overcoat underneath her rancid pinny, because she simply couldn't bear to neglect the only treasure she possessed.

Who was it she reminded me of? Who else was so unselfconsciously comical and so guilelessly absurd?

'My father,' I suddenly exclaimed.

The two of them looked at me bemused. Jane also flinched as she thought perhaps I'd seen Bill waving and grinning at the window, dropping in for a surprise visit. As she saw it, my father was entertaining enough on home ground, but debilitating to have as a guest. Strange, embarrassed late-middle-aged women sometimes turned up at our door months after he'd been to see us. He had met them wandering round the Tate or the British Museum, and had soon struck up affable and sympathetic conversation. Before they knew it they found themselves having afternoon tea and a stroll with this kindly, very intelligent stranger. Two hours later Bill had gone back to the divorcee's or widow's or soldier's wife's flat, just to help her fight against the tragedies of transience and painful solitude. After their tender act of defiance, Bill had faithfully promised to keep in regular touch. He had even given them his married son's address, as a discreet poste restante, and as proof of good faith that he would renew acquaintance the next time he was down.

'What about your father?' Jane asked quickly. 'Is he about to ring our bell?'

'No,' I shrugged. 'No, I'm only speaking my thoughts aloud. It's to do with just having listened to one of the oddest people I've ever met. It reminded me that the thing about my father is objectively he is very funny.'

Jane said warily, 'Are you sure he's really so hilarious? Didn't we once agree his amusingness is best enjoyed from a distance?'

'I've just been to see Joe Clifton,' I said. 'I spent a few minutes chatting to his Aunty Biddy who must be one of the queerest people alive. She's Irish-speaking, she talks to herself non-stop, she believes in the fairy world, she only leaves the house for Mass, she wears her best overcoat indoors . . .'

Jane sniffed. 'Your father is peculiar, but not in that way. He doesn't usually dress bizarrely. Though given his inveterate habit of you know what, I suppose one day he might need to adopt some sort of camouflage.'

I decided to play the devil's advocate. 'But he teaches his cage birds to chat to each other in Hittite and Elamite and Akkadian. He hid his father's ashes in a wardrobe for year after year. He speaks all those obscure languages, but he's happiest with barmaids who can barely speak the King's English. D'you know anybody else who does things like that?'

Bill's daughter-in-law said prosaically, 'He's also the most obsessive philanderer since Casanova. If that's the correct analogy. Was Casanova married, do you know?'

Frankie contributed in a kinder tone, 'He's a dear old, dear old sweet. Even if his hands go everywhere like a stage magician's.'

'But he is a *character*,' I emphasised. 'Like Aunty Biddy he is larger than life. Bill Geraghty is very odd and she is very odd, but self-evidently they never actually see themselves as odd. They see themselves just as themselves. That blindness allows them to give the world some heightened colour as a result. They give it the colour of extraordinary anecdote, I suppose.'

I found myself hesitating to say more. And I swallowed the obvious conclusion. Which was that Bill and Biddy, for all the nonsensical things they did, were rather more acceptable, arguably much more human, than the ones who never made fools of themselves. Jane, Frankie and I all lacked that gift, that special grace of human innocence. We were only in our twenties but the only folly we were capable of was the folly of self-protective actors. We were all destined to go severely astray and suffer for our deeds, but the world was never going to see us as funny, nor for that matter as seriously tragic.

My father came down to London a fortnight later. He was staying the weekend and on the Saturday evening Jane suggested that we take him to the opera. She had secured some expensive tickets for *Fidelio*, but possibly on account of its name and the implied association, he decided to give it a miss. In any case, fond of classical music as he was, he detested all opera and lieder on principle.

He whispered to me in the hallway, 'Vibrating bloody divas with crimson faces and pneumatic chests, hooting and bellowing, "*Is he here? Is he there? Is he any-bloody-where? Woe is me and my accursed blasted fate.*" I ask you, is that reckoned to be fit entertainment for sophisticated adults in 1942, George? When we're going through a bloody war to end all wars, after all?'

He didn't state it as baldly as that to his daughter-in-law. He shook her cool hand and kissed her very gingerly, this over-intelligent young thing who frightened him.

'Thank you, my dear, but I've been galloping round too many galleries and exhibitions all day. What I'm most in need of is a quiet scotch and perhaps a bit of a read. I managed to get myself an Ossetic grammar in that book shop in Bloomsbury and I'm keen to mug-up the morphology before I nod off.'

'Acetic?' echoed Jane, as sharp as any vinegar. 'Is mugging-up Acetic as good as listening to Beethoven?'

I butted in pacifically, 'What is Ossetic, Dad? I mean where is it? Who is it?'

'The language of the Ossetes,' my father burbled back gratefully. 'A Caucasian minority within the borders of Soviet Georgia. Excellent philological correspondences with Iranian dialects, Avestan, Pahlavi, Middle Iranian and so forth. Just the blasted ticket when my blistered feet are killing me, George.'

Jane said smartly, 'Isn't Joe Stalin a son of Georgia? Oh well, your Acetics must be a fine old race in that case. Even dear old Ludwig can't hold a candle to Uncle 'Joe and his pals.'

Bill made a quiet rejoinder about not trusting that mousta-chioed rogue as far as the lavatory door. As he himself presented the consummate image of a sleek rogue in posses-sion of a sly moustache, Jane couldn't restrain a smile. She sniffed a little, forgave his hypocrisy, and decided she would take along the two chaps from the office instead. It was agreed I must stay here with my father, not leave him all on his own. My father blinked affably, and made no protests. But a pretty young woman with two young men as escorts, I could see him thinking. Don't say my son the charcoal johnny is allowing himself to be made a fool of after only eighteen months of marriage?

'Willis and Bennett both have TB,' I explained, giving them both resentful looks. 'That's why they're doing their pension work in Putney.'

I also said in terse eye language that as infidelity was his own hobby he had no real grounds for worrying about its victims. After Jane had made two phone calls and set off to the opera, father and son retired to the sitting room and confided over a bottle of whisky. The Ossetic grammar didn't leave Bill's luggage, as his real reason for staying in was that he was so drained by recent events. Given that he would be dead in three years time, it was fortunate in those last years we didn't bother to conceal much from each other. That night I told him that Jane could be bloody moody, and Bill grunted and murmured that a chap needed to lay down some ground rules for a young wife. He spoke measuredly, even chastely, about his other women 'friends'. He also coyly divulged that Hetty had 'some very decent men pals' down in Reading, Thame and Wantage.

'I'm in hiding, George, to a certain extent,' he suddenly disclosed with a shudder. He didn't look particularly embarrassed, but he certainly looked hunted.

'From someone's angry husband?' I asked, remembering Hetty's frying-pan fracas with Barrie Thorne.

'Not at all. And don't look too panicked, boy. I haven't given this lady friend of mine your address, thank God. I had rather an idea about this one, so I told her a little white lie. I gave her the home address of the Curthwaite Professor of Moral Philosophy at All Souls. But dammit, she spotted me today in a little café in Bloomsbury and came imprecating and beseeching at my table. At first I panicked and talked nonsense and said I didn't recall knowing her. At which she went completely cuckoo and struck me on the ear with a pepper cruet, and showered me with the foulest unladylike language. She has a . . . she has a . . .'

He seemed quite unable to go on, and I had no idea how to finish his sentence. I thought he was trying to say she had a facial wart or venereal disease or a speech stammer, but I kept such guesses to myself.

Bill recounted how he had met her. A few months ago, shopping in Bloomsbury, he had purchased a tin of *Baby's Bottom* from a pretty tobacconist's assistant. Mildred was her name and she was dark-eyed with flouncing, flirty, jet-black curls and vivid rather cheeky lips. She was twenty-four, he added blithely, and I could not contain myself. I gasped. Why, I demanded, should any girl end up making a date with a man twice her age? My father looked very offended and said as far as he knew his looks hadn't significantly faded in the past quarter century. Perhaps, he conceded, the comical name of his tobacco had helped the ice to melt across the age and culture gaps. He had deliberately slurred the second half of the *BB*, so that Mildred had been obliged to giggle and repeat it. After that it was all child's play, so to speak.

And it was true. He was still a handsome, charismatic and magnetic sort of man. That treacherous kindness in his eyes couldn't help but draw you towards him. Even if you resisted him, you couldn't offend the easy kindness in a face that was so full of its own fictions. The gas and nonsense he talked was always quaint and touching in its way. He was a one-man pantomime who could charm a child, and if anyone can do that they can charm the entire human race . . .

Mildred was single and shared a flat with a girlfriend in Highgate. Her parents were divorced and her father was a window cleaner and Somme veteran, now conscripted to bellow at recruits down in Aldershot. Bill found that altogether charming, the patriotism and the window cleaning. Dammit, what'd we do without clean windows? No clear view out into the outside world, what? No head held high before the nosy neighbours if the windows weren't as clean as a new pin. Kiss, kiss, kiss, on Mildred's cheeky little mouth. On their first date he ignited a brimming bowlful of *Baby's Bottom*, patted Mildred on hers, and the two of them climbed chortling onto a bus to the West End.

Their assignation had been delightful. A Will Hay comedy at the cinema, a decent if extortionate restaurant, an arousingly empty flat back in Highgate as Mildred's flatmate Myfanwy was away visiting relatives in Mumbles. Myfanwy Jones had relatives scattered all over the principality, including an elderly uncle and aunt who farmed near Penrhyndeudraeth, Merioneth. The uncle and aunt stepped improbably into Bill's story, as they owned a small caravan that lay along the edge of a mountain lake. After three or four perfect Saturdays together, Mildred, at Myfanwy's prompting, suggested the pair of them might enjoy a romantic few days by renting Uncle Pender's lakeside caravan.

A Welsh weekend with a tobacconist's assistant had obviously seized on Bill's imagination. Bill had told Hetty he was going to look up an old college chum living close to Porthmadog. Dickson Toll-Gravey he was called, a brilliant Sinologist and Japanologist who had been stricken with a wasting disease contracted in the Sinkiang desert, and had been obliged to retire to the family home in Wales. Bill would go and push him about in his bath chair, massage his withered arms and emaciated legs, no doubt. They would swap notes on Mediaeval Korean and Manchurian bawdy farces, and the Magdalen personalities of 1910. It was a timely act of charity on Bill's part, but anything for a distressed old Magdalen chum. Hetty had packed him off without protest, and had planned a jam-packed weekend of her own. Bill had to take four trains to get to Penrhyndeudraeth, where in the station café he had met his cheeky Mildred. In consultation with Myfanwy, they'd decided that for the purposes of fooling Uncle Pender and Aunty Megan, Mildred was to pose as his daughter, i.e. that Bill was a window-cleaning Somme veteran called Reg Perrick. Bill the mimetic linguist could easily enough transform himself into a Pygmalion Cockney. And the unworldly uncle and aunt would be as likely to spot a false London accent as notice that Bill's beautiful suits were rather unusual trophies for a window cleaner.

Like some stanchless Celtic bard, he continued his strange epic under the dim light of our table lamp: 'Pender and Megan, having taken one startled look, began vilifying us in gruff conspiratorial Welsh. Of course I couldn't allow them to see I understood every slanderous word. They addressed us in doleful surly English, but had the gall to comment derisively in *sotto voce* Welsh. They thought I was a Cockney illiterate called Reg, you see. No one would anticipate an urban window cleaner knowing the Welsh for a word as unWelsh as 'bull walrus'. I can tell you I was damn incensed to hear it applied to me by the hideous farmer's wife. She had a fine sea-lionish tash herself, plus a few thick bristles on her chin. Truthfully, George, when we first went in, in the weak light of the kitchen I thought she was the husband of the dreary old pair. In fact I addressed Aunty Megan as 'mister', then changed it smartly to '*mysterious* change in the weather, all this drizzle'. They also insulted Mildred with a word I have only ever come across in the old *cynghanedd* martial epics. It approximates with Ben Jonson's use of the term 'punk'. Mildred had laid on the rouge and the puce lipstick a trifle thickly, and in Old Testament Welsh Pender said to his whiskery missus that she 'bore semblance to Behemoth's dam'. They were miserable teetotal Methodists, needless to add, saying a ten-minute grace every time they slurped a cup of tea. We explained that as daughter and father we were taking a little holiday to refresh ourselves from constant tending to Mildred's sick mother, Mrs Elsie Perrick. She was languishing with TB in Highgate and being looked after by their niece Myfanwy for the weekend. Myfanwy didn't dare to tell her puritan relatives she lived independently in a London flat, so she claimed to be the lodger of the Perrick family. Of course we would have gone straight to our love nest, but we had to present ourselves to this repulsive couple in order to get the key. Mildred was also supposed to go for milk and eggs on the Saturday and Sunday mornings . . .'

Supposed to, but never did. The weekend turned out to be short and dramatic. When Bill strode outside to Pender's dry earth closet and took down his trousers, he observed that either Uncle Pender's or Aunty Megan's dentures were watching him in an unnerving manner. They were sitting in a glass of murky water on an old painted cupboard. Next to them were some sheets of torn newspaper intended as lavatory paper. My father wiped his backside on *News from the Districts* as described in Welsh in the Voice of Merioneth. Before which he took an inquisitive glance at it. A recent talk to the Penrhyndeudraeth WI had been on 'Coping with the Very Different Ways of Londoner Evacuees', given by the village postmaster, Preacher Dafydd Evans. Bill stared at those horrible dentures which were floating up and down very slowly, hallucinatingly, like something foetal or fossiled. Like a sunken battleship perhaps, or a water-boatman insect slipping and slithering in a viscous liquid. He felt a sudden chill at the strangeness of where he was and who he was. At fifty-three he was having a dirty weekend with a woman just out of nappies in the mountain fastnesses of North Wales. Which might as well have been Toll-Gravey's bloody Sinkiang for all it had in common with Oxford or London. He knew fifty-nine languages by now, and when he had managed Ossetic it would be sixty. He had slept with about sixty women perhaps in his fifty-three years. He told me this without undue boasting over his third whisky in my Belsize Park flat, as if there were nothing to be lost by his innocent candour.

There was a plaque hung over Pender's toilet door. What it said in Welsh was, *Ye shall know them by their deeds.* For some reason instead of inspiring spiritual terror it reminded Bill that he had brought along his fishing rod to Wales. For camouflage, he'd assured Mildred, so that I look like a real dad having some innocent sport, not your bold lover enjoying the sport that lovers enjoy. Back in the farmhouse he asked Pender about the fishing, and the old man growled there was a little rowing boat he could use next to the caravan. There were plenty of trout over there in the mountain lake. For cooking there was a stove powered by methylated spirits. There were a couple of oil lamps in the caravan. As it was summer, they shouldn't need the paraffin stove, he added threateningly. But he kept a very little paraffin here in the farmhouse if they found it too chill for their city tastes.

'What a bloody old shitter,' said Mildred coarsely as the two of them walked the half mile to the caravan. It had stopped drizzling and the sun had come out. The mountain lake was dappled with silver. Bill's heart rose as he saw the myriad flies dancing over that lonely water. The little tarn was melancholy and grave but it was very beautiful. My father did not see much rugged and powerful countryside near Oxford, of course. It was at least twenty years since Bill Geraghty had done any fishing. Lord, how his heart tugged to be out there right this minute with his rod and his flies and his hip flask and his idle thoughts.

They entered the caravan, which was tidy if spartan. Like the lavatory it contained exhortatory plaques in Welsh. They located the oil lamps and the matches and the spirit stove. Bill dumped their luggage on the two bunks and Mildred stubbed her neat little foot and swore. She stooped down and pulled out two huge chamber pots both with messages engraved on them in Welsh. Mildred guffawed and insisted they must be rude peek-a-boo verses about bottoms, but Bill sighed and said no, they were all about blinking humility and blessed abasement.

Mildred began to disrobe immediately. Bill salivated and started to remove his handsome countryman's tweed. Mildred was soon down to her suspenders and brassière. She was so ripe and so plump, he told me approvingly, she had sweet silvered thighs like magnificent young birch trunks. She had a pendulous and peerless little behind you would have gone and blinking died for, George. She had . . .

Unfortunately their bunk was sited in full view of the lake. In fact they had half drawn the curtains lest Pender should have a stroke observing father and daughter naked together. Then of course, it had to happen. Suddenly, just as Bill was about to remove his jacket, he saw a young trout leap out of the water and flex its burnished back like a gilded fairy prince.

After which there was little more to be said.

'Would you excuse me?' he murmured in a queer voice.

'Does oo need to have a wee-wee, Billy?'

Who knows what he thought he needed as he lifted his old fishing rod in its faded green case. Before departing, he rummaged in his luggage and took out what Mildred didn't notice was a hip flask. As a precaution, he also grabbed his raincoat from the peg next to the door.

'Where the hell are you off?' asked Mildred with narrowed eyes.

He snorted, 'I've just seen a blasted fox out there! It's heading for Pender's allotment and his hens. I'm off to chase it with this rod, and then I'll be back for some rampant dalliance, I promise.'

He sidled off, as if in a hypnotic dream. Mildred looked at the cupboard clock and noted it was ten past seven. Aroused and then frustrated, she remained impatient and tense. It might have been May, but the night was very cold, so she sat huddled in a blanket awaiting 'Reg Perrick's' return . . .

Time passed in the usual way it does on Welsh mountains. Time kept on passing and passing. After what seemed as long as a *cywydd* epic, it got to eight o'clock. Swathed in a horse blanket on the first evening of her first real adventure with her first educated gentleman, Mildred was consumed by anger. Before long the anger was molten rage. God, such a bloody fool she felt! Such a bloody old pisser was old Bill, with his cigars, his pipe, his toff manners, his always so charming and bright. By ten past eight her rage was murderous hatred. Where the hell had the slippery bastard *gone*? Was this supposed to be his cowardly way of saying goodbye after a frantic three-week fling? To leave her on her own in a freezing bloody caravan in the middle of the Welsh bloody hills?

'Oh!' she moaned, feeling a burning, inconceivable loneliness.

She looked outside. She shuddered to see it was raining torrentially. The downpour was of the relentless clattering kind which battered on the caravan roof like a deafening volley of stones. It sounded almost like cannon artillery. It rattled on and on and on, like a dream of endless torture . . .

It grew dusk. Mildred rose and shivered and went to the window. She peered hopefully but saw nothing of Bill. Ironically he was only just out of view, obscured by some alders that skirted the shore. He and his boat were out there on the lake in the gathering darkness. Had she stepped outside in the monsoon and walked a hundred yards, Mildred would have seen his little torch shining oh so tinily and eerily in the middle of the blanketed tarn.

Bill was bobbing gently on the tarn, oblivious of the deluge. He was fishing, he was perfectly alone, he was perfectly happy. Mildred was bone dry inside the caravan and she was perfectly wretched. The little caravan's roof was being rammed and battered by the terrible Welsh elements. The shop assistant who had only once left London in her twenty-four years suddenly felt as frightened as an abandoned child. She started to weep. Before long her sniffing had turned into frantic sobs.

But she tired very quickly of her misery. Her young pride and natural gumption were far too strong to indulge it. She stirred and gave herself a shake and rose from the bunk. Her blanket slipped and left her naked and she was frozen stiff. Retrieving it, she approached the door and shuffled on the table for the matches. It wasn't quite dark, there was a sliver of moon, and she exulted when she saw them.

She struck one, turned, then screamed in terror. Her matchbox dropped to the floor . . .

She could see the face of a mountain *witch*. The witch was staring at Mildred with frowning, quite lunatic intentness! A mad demoness was watching her in the infernal setting of

160

this cramped and rain-hammered shack . . .

'Agh!' she shrieked.

It was Mildred's own reflection. It was her tear-stained make-up and ragged curls she'd sighted in the mirror by the stove. The match had illumined her with a deathly radiance, as if she was playing a part in a mummers' play for Halloween.

She picked up the matches. Wincing at that deathly spectre in the mirror, she reached on the shelf for a paraffin lamp. As a London girl she had never encountered one of these loathsome museum objects. She stared at it hostilely and wondered how it worked. There was a massive upright wick inside a large glass shade. She lifted the glass and set it on the bed. Then she applied a match to the wick. It flared a little, but there was no paraffin in the base and it went out. Mildred groaned and lit it again. It went out again. Mildred gasped. She staggered across to the caravan door and bolted it. Against Lord knows what ravishing spectres of the night.

Of course she should have stumbled out into the rain and shouted for my father. But in a lightless caravan she had few means of orientation. She couldn't remember how far it was to the lake, and was frightened she would fall in and drown. In any case she was convinced Bill had slipped down to the village and was wrapped in the arms of a monoglot Merioneth barmaid weighing twenty-three stones. It was probably his profession. He was a professional lush, a travelling ponce. He was a bigamist. He probably had a thousand aliases and a record for criminal deception. He said he was called Bill Padstow but he could be Wild Bill Hickox in reality.

In the end she fell asleep. She put down the useless lamp and wrapped herself in a couple of blankets. They were Methodist blankets; rough and hairy and penitential, and they made her feel dreadfully unloved. She fell into a doze at first and had a mad dream in which Uncle Pender was sailing a toy boat that was actually his dentures inside a full chamber pot. He was telling her that the man with the tash and the slick tongue was a queer one. Pender said he was sailing his dentures in piddle because it made them a better fit. An hour later she awoke in the pitch dark, not knowing where she was. She saw the dim confines of the caravan and thought she might be in an evil underground cave. She sniffled and bubbled with an infant's misery. Then nodded off again.

She woke again at dawn. The light was breaking and the sparrows were twittering away like queer little ghosts. There was also a rhythmic thudding sound which inspired her to imagine a frightening domestic scenario. It was the angry rapping of window cleaner Reg upon the kitchen table as he berated his daughter Mildred for carrying on with a dirty old man like Bill. Why he's the same bloody age as me, she could hear him rant, as he reached for the regimental belt he wore for his Aldershot duties. Mildred stirred inside her blankets and made an uneasy ascent to the world of sense. The thudding noise continued unabated, then stopped. She looked over at the window and in the dim light beheld a second dreadful sight.

'Agh!' she shrieked in incalculable panic. 'Agh . . . !'

She began to dance around the caravan floor in a crazed hysteria. A vile thing had its face pressed against the window! Its nose was flattened into a squamous leech, the lips bloated like those of a drowned man. The eyes stared wildly. The hair was matted and as rank as that of a gorgon with its hissing snakes. The monster was moving its filthy lips and muttering. Leering, it brought up its weblike fist and rattled on the glass with a sickening violence.

This ghoul appeared to be copiously whiskered. It lurched back from the window and became a recognisable simulacrum of a man. As well as being a man, it was also a drowned rat. Sometimes this drowned rat was called Bill Padstow, and sometimes it preferred the name Reg Perrick.

'Popsy!' it hooted through the window.

'You!' she hissed. 'You!'

'Open the bloody door, old thing.'

'*You!*' she stormed, and she shook her fist. 'You you you . . . !'

'I'm as dripping as a slimy bag of eels. Get out of that roll of sackcloth and open the damn door, will you? Sharpish, cmon, cmon, do you want me to get my bloody death? I'll get these togs off and dry myself and be there at your pearly breast in a jiff.' He braked his aqueous babble and scrutinised her rather critically. 'Hm. Must say, old gal, you don't look particularly tasty with all that seedy green rheum in your eyes. Perhaps a quick splash at Uncle Pender's pump over there . . . ?'

She screamed, 'You *bastard*! You bloody old bastard! How *dare* you go terrifying me to death?'

The sodden Gorgon was altogether nonplussed. Like a music-hall comic, it blinked and searched around for the guilty party. 'Done what? Who on earth are you talking to? Is old Pender on the horizon?'

Mildred lit a cigarette and stabbed it in the air like a baton of justice. 'What the shitting hell are you playing at pressing your terrible face at the window?'

'What the sh . . . what the hell d'you *think* I –'

'I nearly died of shock! D'you understand? I nearly *died* of nervous shock! You looked worse than any House of Bloody Horrors. You . . . you madman! Where the bloody hell have you been, you bloody old cheat? You wicked old sod! You evil old crock. Hah! Old alright! You look at least a hundred years old, all drenched and sopping and lines across your old face. You look old enough to be my bloody grandad!'

At last it penetrated that she was mad with him and with no one else. It wasn't a case of her maidenish vapours or her monthlies. Apparently the truth was he had been out on that lake for some eight or nine hours . . .

'Come, come,' he cajoled with a leer. 'Oh my sweet ickle tiddly ducksie woo!'

She brandished her sharp nails and bared her teeth at him. 'Bugger off! You're not getting in here, you bloody old bastard. Not after leaving me all on my own all bloody night.'

Like a wet old mongrel, my father was obliged to shake himself dry. He wagged his finger and shouted through the glass: 'You damn trollop! Is this my reward for staying up all night to catch our breakfast? Take a look at these, will you?'

He held up two minuscule, emaciated trout. They had looked massive, even monstrous in the dark, but in the light they looked more like joke sardines.

Mildred became hysterical and began to cackle madly.

'Stick em up your arse!' she jeered.

'Eh?' he said hoarsely, cupping a dripping earhole. 'Come again, Billy's wayward little popsy-woo?'

'Shove em up your bloody arse!'

For good measure, she forced some saliva and pretended to spit a nasty bolus in his face. Then added: 'So its tail sticks out behind, and you can swim all the way back to Oxford. You dirty shark! You dirty, dirty, dirty bloody *shark* . . .'

They took separate trains back to England. Bill told Hetty that Dickson Toll-Gravey had suffered a stroke in his bathchair on the Saturday morning. His relatives had soon descended and Bill with tactful discretion had decided to make himself scarce. One month later Mildred had accosted my father in his favourite Bloomsbury café. What she had to tell him today was that she was expecting his baby. As Bill confided man to man, it was all a bit of a bind . . .

Nine

My ex-wife arrived for lunch yesterday, as did my daughter Sally and my grandchild Maria. Jane was en route to Edinburgh to visit an eighty-year-old friend called Margot doing an emphatically mature degree in Contemporary Media Studies. Jane said she thought Margot's college was called the Spanking New University of Caledonia, a conjecture I thought just possible. Sally and Maria were also scheduled to visit Sally's in-laws, a frail if bilious couple called the Tripp-Pevises who had decided to grace the Isle of Skye in their monied dotage. Within five minutes of arrival Jane had started a fight with me about nothing in particular. My carefully prepared Greek-style banquet was digested in a strained and dyspeptic atmosphere, broken only by Maria's glum admission that she wanted Wall's sausages rather than these laboriously hand-minced *loukanikos*.

Sally admonished her and squeezed my hand as I bridled at Jane's far less acceptable criticism. She had just declared that my *skordhalia* was inadequately garlicked and compared it unfavourably with that of her favourite taverna in Salisbury.

'Ah,' I sniped at her sourly. 'You have a horde of Greek Cypriots twanging their bouzoukis down there in Salisbury? And me thinking they were all *Turkish* Cypriots in cosmopolitan Wilts?'

Sally heaped Maria's *loukanikos* onto her own plate and covered them lavishly with *skordhalia*. 'It's absolutely delicious. And a great deal more ambitious than anything I cook.'

My gentle, serious daughter, who is a Richmond music teacher, loves my sixteenth-century smallholding. She is entranced by its remoteness and unkempt beauty, not to speak of the reiver-warfare associations. She cites its purchase as an example of my original taste and the fact that wherever I go and whatever I do I always behave differently from the crowd. Jane chortles at this fey daughterly loyalty and accuses me of reclusive misanthropy and the perpetual striking of poses and postures. Now that I have rheumatism in both legs, she insists that my body is punishing me with the painful physical posture that I deserve.

Sally and Maria stay here every Easter and alternating Christmases, but the last time I saw Jane was a decade ago. In January of 1982 there was a terrible cold snap, and she rang me at five one morning to assure me she was halfway through a nervous breakdown, as well as starting a bout of bronchial pneumonia. Grudgingly I drove up from London to offer her moral support, and found her squatting underneath a spurting lavatory pipe, bawling at the ponytailed plumber for allowing things to reach this 'Respighi's bloody Fountains of Rome stage'. The plumbing sorted, she berated me for taking so long to get there, and within half an hour was happily airing grievances she'd apparently been nursing since 1941. *Inter alia* these included the hesitant way that I positioned my vegetables upon my fork, the unacceptably pungent odour I'd always left in our Belsize Park lavatory, the fatuous habit I had of bogus yawning whenever I was nervous in anyone's company. The Wilts plumber watched my berating with great relief, and went so far as to charge nothing for his emergency services.

Stomping out of her sodden cottage, I swore I would only be happy if there was a ten-hour drive between us. A month later an estate agent rang with news of a four-bedroom North Cumbrian smallhold on offer for the crazy sum of fourteen thousand pounds. It had been on the market for over a year, as the north-east uplands in those days were considered too distant from Carlisle to be commutable. A decade on, it's worth ten times what I paid for it. These days Home Counties inroaders will blithely commute thirty miles from the Scots side, and even venture down from the antarctic hamlets of Bewcastle and Bailey. I don't commute, of course, I just stay at home and draw. When I tire of drawing, I go and sit at my computer and pretend that I'm writing a brilliant, pioneering work on the history of satirical art. Life mightn't be exactly the way I would wish it, but I definitely have no intention of leaving this place before I die.

'What are you up to these days?' Jane asked, as she chewed away martyrishly at her square of baklava. 'And why the hell do you bury yourself so far from London?'

I told her I was attempting to write an encyclopaedic study of satirical art and satirical artists, and that peace and quiet were essential for the mammoth task. I lied that I had a commission from a major art publisher and a handsome advance to boot. I made no mention of that ignominious Grosz broadcast, but was on tenterhooks just in case she'd heard it.

'I think you'll end up getting odder and odder, living in a hole like this. Retiring into the desert is only for hairshirt ascetics, not for selfish, grumpy types like you. It would do you the world of good to get back into the thick of things.'

I grunted. Far from being the sour old hermit my wife describes to her friends, I'm far more sociable stuck at Mallsburn than I've ever been. I have got to know a few talented painters, some barely in their twenties, as well as one or two boozy farmers of anarchic middle age. I go to all the touring theatre that visits Roadhead, and clap louder than I ever did in London. Last week I saw a flawless adaptation of *Don Quixote* done by actors of genius in that furthest-flung outpost this side of Anatolia. Inside these four walls, I am as industrious as anyone could be. I draw and work at the computer at least five hours a day. I subscribe to several literary and art magazines and strive to keep abreast of current affairs. I don't bother with the Carlisle cinema, but I watch anything worth watching on the TV. With my

Videoplus video I tape all foreign films and watch them optionally upstairs or below. It might seem absurdly expensive rather than terribly ingenious, but with my rheumatism I have one of everything on each floor. Two videos, two radios, two tellies, two hi-fi systems, LPs and CDs in both upstairs and downstairs lounges. A young Dumfries painter and drinking partner called Elliott says my place reminds him of the Dolmabahce palace in Istanbul. There in the interests of grandiose geometrical symmetry everything has its mirrored double, whether it be costly French ormolu clocks or fabulously jewelled caskets wrought by Levantine master craftsmen.

Yesterday's gathering was particularly strained as Jane wasn't drinking. Unfortunately the only wine I'd thought to provide for my Greek lunch was five bottles of supermarket retsina. By an oversight which Jane reckoned was deliberate there was nothing else to drink in the house. After the three-hundred mile drive I offered her a glass of Kourtaki and assuming it was some sort of riesling she thirstily gulped it down. A look of hysterical amazement swept across her face. She spat it into the sink and turned on me with pained disgust.

'Why spoil me with a glass of Harpic, George? Or is it maybe Dettol?'

I told her stiffly, 'It's Greek retsina of course. To go with a Greek bloody lunch.'

'You are so bloody *juvenile*, George! Why at your age go in for Zal-has-freshness-with-a-zing, the pine cleaner at £3.50 a bottle from Gretna Kwik-Save? You could have got a decent little claret for the same price.'

'To annoy you, unsweetness,' I snapped. 'That is why, my assertive if astringent ex-wife, Jane. Let's phrase it as a grammatical conundrum, shall we? To piss you in which direction? To piss you in the direction "off".'

Sally stood tensely by the door as we bickered away like senile chaffinches. Maria, who is the very image of Jane and mortifies her by always calling her 'Nanna', stared dispassionately at the spectacle. Perhaps it reminded her of what it was like before her father left her mother. My former son-in-law is called, incredibly, Terry Tripp-Pevis. Poor Sally had always sweltered under her double-barrelled marital surname, its leisurely assonance ironically at odds with the impatient unpleasantness of her stockbroker husband. I could certainly never stand my self-aggrandising son-in-law, The Brick/The Stone/The Sarcophagus as I called him behind his broad, uncomprehending back.

After coffee and when Sally and Maria had gone out for a walk, I said to Jane: 'I suppose it's true that we ruined our daughter's childhood with our affairs and our constant arguments. Perhaps she thinks it'll upset Maria when she sees us squabbling.'

Jane snorted. 'Hardly. No one in recorded history has ever been upset by their grandparents rowing.'

'But mightn't she get upset by her mother getting upset?'

'She would if Sally did get upset. But nowadays our daughter just thinks of us as a pair of boring old prizefighters. Like a couple of Punch and Judy puppets, though with subtler vocabularies when it comes to aggression.'

'I'm glad you are so blasé. I really think Sally hates us rowing.'

'Sally is a forty-year-old woman with her own messy marriage behind her. She has far more important concerns than the behaviour of her bonkers old parents. If anything she's impressed, even envious, that I still have a bustling sex life, while sorry for you who so obviously don't.'

I gasped, 'What the hell would you know about my sex life?'

She answered airily, 'Because I am a mature intelligent woman, and to a sad extent I know you inside out. An unsavoury sight, I assure you. To see you inverted like a grubby grey sock. Or do I mean "everted"? I'm telling you, boy, you'll never meet a woman more sharp and shrewd

169

than I am. If I couldn't recognise the signs of sexual starvation at my age, I'd be a prudish anachronism, a dried-up old school ma'am.'

Hurrying to join Sally and Maria, I rammed on my wellies. 'Far be it from you to be an anachronism.'

'Too damn right. I have a toy boy of thirty called Edward.'

'Oh shut up,' I said, kicking my gumboot against the armchair. 'I really don't need to know.'

'Oh but you do,' she trilled. 'You do, you do! Euphoric copulatory ecstasy twice a day and five times on Saturdays. Nothing at all unfortunately on Sunday, when he gives himself up to amateur-league football.'

'Or his attractive young wife,' I said spitefully. 'Or another of his dozen sagging dowagers.'

Jane was half startled and I couldn't resist a vindictive chuckle. The banal probability had never occurred to her. It seemed laughable, this selective naivety of hers, but was all in keeping with our early marriage. No consideration of any third party had previously overburdened her. The last time the pains of an innocent victim had made any impression on her imagination was when she was a little girl of ten. On Christmas Eve 1930 she had spied her father Reggie weeping over her mother's infidelity with his Marxist younger brother, Tom. In a single brutal cameo she had perceived the overpowering hurt that 'A One' can inflict upon 'An Other', simply by following his instincts. Cause and effect being more or less indivisible from a small child's point of view, she had resolved to arm herself against all that confusion. At once she had bathed her ten-year-old's tears in hysterical mirth. Later, as a cynical teenager, she would boast that she trusted neither marriage nor Marxism, both pious tyrannies cowardly denying the obvious nature of human frailty.

Sally and Maria left at three but Jane lingered on another hour. Without embarrassment she commenced a full inspection of the house, making brisk inventories as she strode into every room to size up all my acquisitions. When I explained the logic of having two of everything, that it reduced the struggling up and down the stairs, she laughed with derision and anxiety. To mask her confusion, she tutted at the dust in my bedroom and the incredible quantity of fluff on the carpet. As she descended to the kitchen, I noted the stiffness of her own movements, that her erstwhile agility was no longer. I wondered briefly if toyboy Edward was as ruffled by the sight as I was.

Having finished her stocktaking, she kissed me goodbye and stepped back to take stock of the man himself. I could see her thinking, George might have two of every gadget, but there's only one of him, God help him. And as a gadget I doubt whether they'd keep him in the Dolmabahce palace. Perhaps that realisation explained a sudden moisture in her eyes which she quickly averted. It was a reluctant emotion but it was there. I took note that her cheekbones were still as fine as ever, her skin still clear and smooth, her voice as resonant with the old assurance.

'I'm still fond of you,' she confessed, and I flinched as she did. My eyes began to itch like the devil.

'Me too,' I said grimly. 'Perhaps.'

She said hurriedly, giving herself a swift shake, 'Actually I don't think so after all. I think it's more I'm concerned for you than eternally fond. I'm only fond of you when I'm miles off in Wiltshire and can picture you from a distance and feel tenderly nostalgic.'

I answered stiffly, 'Very well. There are grains of remnant love and tender reminiscence somewhere in the overall picture. Once we're together, right enough, it's all friction and accusation and worse. We were just twenty-one when we married, which probably explains a lot.'

'Not everything,' she said with unusual sincerity. 'Not all, but quite a lot.' She turned at the door and addressed me solemnly. 'Take care, George.'

I looked at her balefully. 'You know what? I really hate that brainless valediction, Jane. As far as I can see, half the

British population concludes a conversation with that idiotic rider, "Take care". What the hell do they mean with that moronic funereal formula? Don't keep smoking High Tar fags? Don't end up talking to yourself? Don't at any price dabble with the occult? Don't go and have an affair with someone who's a Roman Catholic?'

'Very well,' she shot back with pugnacity. '*Don't* take care, you nasty old bugger. Don't take care, whatever you do. Just see where it gets you!'

Clambering into her car and vainly scanning the empty countryside for a signpost screaming 'Edinburgh', she heard me say: 'Sorry. That was uncalled for and unpleasant.'

My voice was lost on the wind. But Jane's parting words weren't.

'Go out and get yourself a woman as soon as possible. Get yourself a woman or you'll go queer, by which I mean crackers rather than gay. Buying two of everything is only the start of it, believe me, George. It's the oldest story in the world.'

Later, as I washed the plates from my Greek banquet, I felt the sadness that came from parting with my remnants of a family. Even Jane's barbs seemed to lose their sting, and I saw her in her kindest aspect as an unabashed and independent person who refused to dance to anyone's tune. I regarded her as a unique, intriguing and dramatic character, while mourning the fact that I was nowhere in the drama of her life. The only way to accept her as she was, was to survey her from a distanced bird's-eye view, unpossessively, tolerantly, forgivingly. But to take such a sage and disinterested stance was damn near impossible in the case of one like Jane. The very act of sexual congress with someone, indeed with anyone, inevitably creates an enduring spiritual adhesion. That irreversible equation even applied to one-night flings and the farcical affair that I had enjoyed with Frankie Charne in the Fifties. I was still, if I thought about it, comically jealous of Frankie's numerous lovers, even though it was forty years since she and I had last been in harness . . .

Two things happened then, and it was difficult to know which came first. I had focused on one of my favourite pictures of Joe Clifton's, a little still life done in gentle water-colours. It showed some irises in a blue vase upon which the flickering sunlight danced both white and blue. The picture always seemed to exude the chromatic equivalent of aromatic dill or other gentle herbs. Fittingly it had ended up hanging adjacent to my massive herb and spice rack. Joe had painted it in his declining years in the summer of '52, and it was one of the few that showed the confidence of his earliest work. For a week or so he'd been granted a mysterious access to his virgin talent, and he'd even reduced his drinking to make the most of it. Its technical brilliance and supernal tenderness, a defiant affirmation of painterly kind-ness and vulnerable reverence, had combined to make his final testament. Ironically, each time I looked at it, I saw Joe's open wounds, those invisible sores that were the conduits of his sensitivity and his genius. He needed his booze to soothe his sores, but he needed too much of the stuff too soon. He needed also to –

Suddenly a motorbike sped past and the exhaust back-fired. This road was so quiet I jumped out of my skin and dropped the plate I was drying. It smashed to smithereens so I jumped again and realised my nerves must be strung at some inordinate pitch. My eyes focused on Clifton's painting and immediately like some textbook *déjà vu* I was back in the London art world just after the War. The decorous tepidity of dinner party intercourse and the demonstrative unruliness of a major new talent were instantly connected by these two simultaneous noises: the bang from the Suzuki and the dropping of a china plate . . .

Clifton had celebrated his acceptance by the metropolitan art world by deciding to make himself completely unacceptable.

This headstrong instinct would soon accelerate his ultimate eclipse and eventually lead him to a terminal obscurity. Of course Esmond Jell on his own hadn't been responsible for his five-year descent into minor commissions, ill-paid magazine illustration, and the final ignominy of doing public-house signs in exchange for drink. But once the grand old man had decided to ignore him, all the lesser critical fry became self-conscious about their premature and incontinent approval. Jell, who was in his mid-sixties, was both florid and barbed, and an expert at making everyone uneasy. The best-paid art critic of the day, he wrote for *The Times* and *New Statesman* and numerous specialist journals. A good review from Jell in *The Times* could transform a young artist's career, and the only reward Jell sought was a humble acqui-escence of the favour done. Joe was not the one for smiling gratitude, and his behaviour at Jell's party outdid everything Joyce Cary could attribute to his disgraceful hero Gulley Jimson. Jell postponed his revenge but in 1951 refused to recommend him for a commission from the Festival of Britain. It was worth four hundred guineas, enough to survive on in London for a year. Ironically this Irish-speaking republican had been approached by the Festival committee to paint a picture with the theme 'The Positive Spirit of the British Way of Life in 1951'. Clifton was desperate for income in 1951 and would have accepted a commission to build art-deco sandcastles on Bognor Regis beach if he'd been asked. Afterwards I learnt that Jell, seconded onto a sub-committee, had argued against Joe not just on the grounds of merit but because of his antagonistic politics.

'Believe me,' Jell had exhorted from underneath his wistful silver locks, 'I'm not criticising his virulent and at times violent republicanism. That's his own private affair entirely. I've no doubt he had scores of ancestors died in the potato famine, and maybe he was beaten on a daily basis for talking Irish in the Aran schoolyard. I simply can't see how any artist who has reached an indifferent peak some time ago can suddenly decide to produce a pictorial advertisement for a colonial power he despises. Given how rancorous he is about the English art world, he's unlikely to attempt a laudatory tableau of anything British. It's a bit like asking Mr Nehru or Mr Jinnah to write some encomium to the undying moral superiority of the old Raj. It's my frank suspicion that Joe Clifton will simply take the money and run.'

Jane's Ministry of Ag man, Timothy Constant, had a sculptor sister on the same sub-committee, which is how I got to know this. I was also present at the infamous party where Clifton made his lasting mark upon the cream of the London art crowd. As well as several ageing critics, all quaintly attired in their crumpled cravats or patterned bow ties, there were two old gallery proprietors, Imogen Stilgoe and Magenta Mahony. These wrinkled beldames both used jewelled cigarette holders supposedly presented on the same day by Picasso (both claimed to have had carnal relations with him when on a buying trip to Paris in the Thirties). Imogen was seventy and had a ginger cat Pablo which accompanied her everywhere. I once saw her with it in Hampstead on what I thought must be a lead, until she explained that she'd trained it to walk three paces in front like a dog. Pablo was sprawled on Imogen's huge lap purring appreciatively when Clifton commenced his monumental performance. Most cats would have been terrified, but as Imogen said, there was nothing Pablo liked better than a night at the theatre, or preferably opera. Last week she had taken him to see a rehash performance of an Arnold Bennett play, and next week they were off to see *Lucia di Lammermoor*.

Clifton and I had received beautifully embossed invitations for the dinner party, and when I telephoned Jell's number, was informed that we young Turks were the only artists invited. The rest would be either critics or patrons, and it was an indication of the remarkable promise we showed that no other 'bumbling artisans or lacklustre apprentices', as Jell put it, would be present to lower the tone.

'It ought to be an amusing crowd,' he went on sonorously. 'Magenta and Imogen are both completely bonkers, it goes without saying. You know about Imogen's dog disguised as a cat, I suppose? She lets it sip wine out of her glass which perhaps explains its permanent stupor and its uncanny resemblance to its tipsy mistress. Magenta at random moments will fall into a profound trance and begin to mutter she is undergoing astral projection or other out-of-the-body experiences. Siddall who writes his column for the *Telegraph* is a reasonably sweet old boy but he dribbles his soup and is tediously obsessed with postboxes.'

Uneasy at the thinly veiled malice, I said, 'Sorry?'

'Postboxes. It's the queerest thing. He has an album he takes with him everywhere, replete with labelled photographs of postboxes from all corners of the British Isles. No one but hawk-eyed Siddall would bother to take a second look at these dreary monoliths. However Siddall's photos demonstrate an extraordinary variation: tall ones, squat ones, curlicued ones, mouth up top, mouth down below etc. His most treasured example is egg-shaped and built into a dovecot in a farmyard in Peebleshire. He takes a holiday cottage up that way just so that he can go and stare at it for day after day. You'll also meet a young chap, Broadstairs, who's always blushing, and with very good reason, because of a pained conscience. He writes his inchoate waffle for *Acumen*, his only knowledge of artistic matters being cribbed from a study of the back issues of the *Burlington*. Once I recall discussing the matter of Late Tintoretto and he seriously thought I was talking about an ice-cream parlour called Les Tintanetto's on the Finchley Road . . .'

The evening of the party did not bode well. Clifton and I stopped off at a pub, as despite our outward truculence we were both uneasy at a sudden access of patronage. We realised we were going to be among important connoisseurs and potential buyers of our work, and whilst disdaining any ready-made connections were hoping against hope that we would come away secure for life.

We were also bizarrely encumbered. We were not a simple twosome but a complex threesome. Clifton had invited along his Aunt Biddy without forewarning Esmond Jell. I had warned him her uninvited presence might embarrass both Biddy and Jell, but he said if they were going to be eccentric with their bloody cats and postboxes, he had every right to bring along his harmless aunt. Biddy had done her bit by dressing up in her maroon coat, still her best but starting to show signs of wear. It was stained with blue splashes of washing starch and had gaping tears on the sleeves. Neither she nor her nephew seemed discomfited by her mendicant appearance. Our progress to Jell's was incredibly laboured. She was a slow walker and the last time she'd travelled across London was in the Twenties in a horsedrawn cab. We took the tube to Pimlico and she grimaced and clung to our arms with terror at this business of descending into the dark earth and then flying through it in a roaring chariot. At one point she went so rigid Clifton lifted her up like a dummy and carried her the last few steps. During that fireman's lift, she muttered Ulster Irish prayers and beseeched him to turn round and take them home in a taxi. She would never have made it home by herself of course. Unperturbed by her absolute dependence, her nephew said he would get her to Jell's and back, no matter what, even if he had to carry her on his shoulders.

In the pub we asked for a milk stout and two double Paddies. Clifton took a heavy snort from his snuff tin and offered me some. I refused but Biddy in her shattered state accepted a pinch. Clifton had to give her a demonstration, and with a single wild snort her eyes dilated and she threw a minor fit. Joe finished his whiskey and sighed with content-ment. His exhalation unlodged a ball of hard snuff which shot from his nostril and bounced cleverly into an ashtray. It sat among a sea of fag stumps looking like a rabbit dottle.

Biddy gazed at it impressed and then prodded her nose to encourage the same phenomenon.

'Here's to not kow-towing,' said Clifton, setting two more whiskeys on the table. 'Here's to letting them know that subversive talents have a frightening penchant for genuine sedition.'

I said, slurred: 'Meaning what? *Fin-de-siècle* excess? Should we embrace those old ladies Magenta and Thingummy Stilgoe who have their exclusive galleries? Should we become their devoted troubadours and avail ourselves of their cheque books?'

Jane was with Timothy Constant that night and as of the last twelve months had been boasting rather than hiding her love affairs. Canoodling with bohemian dowagers, pimping for ready money, seemed an amiable enough fantasy on my part, something that would punish Jane roundly for her betrayal.

'No. Bugger that. Just not eating out of their hands. They can be privileged to patronise us pecuniarily, but they needn't bloody well patronise us literally.'

The adverbs came out as 'pakyunly' and 'littally', but I knew what he meant. He rose unsteadily and headed for the Gents and I sat there with Biddy wondering what on earth Jell would do with her. As if to confirm my fears, she suddenly put down her stout, raised her eyes meekly to heaven, and began to emit a piercing lament. She might have been howling quite quietly but it was with a shrillness that amplified itself to a peak of discordance. She sounded like a stricken ewe that had been caught on barbed wire whilst looking for a missing lamb. I blushed and looked about to see who was watching. I had often heard her croonings at Joe's place but this was more like a hallucinatory message from the outer spheres, Biddy being the two-way trans-former. Doubtless she and Magenta Mahony would get on wonderfully, both adepts at hypnotic transfixity accompanied by dolorous effusions. The couple at the next table made brief acknowledgement but were far from startled. It was central London and just after the War, so no one seemed to care that an old woman full of stout was groaning an Irish spiritual.

We reached Jell's house just as she was finishing her Gweedore psalm. We were right outside and I was busy checking the number when my foot stepped in something soft. There was an enormous quantity, and it squelched and spread as if I'd stamped on a gallon of treacle. I looked at the pavement and saw that I'd stood in one of those bird's-nest configurations of newly expelled dog shit. At least four large turds had been plaited in a whorled heap, as if the brainless hound had been striving to imitate the building expertise of a robin.

'Buggeration!' I said, half choking. I turned to Clifton who I saw with horror looked an awful sight. He had shaved before coming out but had nicked the side of his face. Instead of leaving well alone, he had been picking at the scab ever since and streaks of blood were smeared all over his cheeks. His tie for some reason was looped round his left ear, after the manner of a petrol-pump hose. Maybe he intended using it as a handy sponge for his scab? Unable to restrain myself, I grabbed at his sleeve.

'Here we are, hoping to make a turning point and establish ourselves somehow! My wife spends every penny I earn, so like you I'm desperate for a helping hand. Now you turn up here all smeared with blood and snuff, looking like you've rolled in a midden or an ash heap! Your aunt meanwhile is caterwauling like one of the damned. Anyone might take her for a drunk, and her coat is torn in a hundred places. To cap all, I've stood in enough dog shit to fertilise a field or two of Irish cabbages. We've come to a swanky dinner party reeking of whiskey and shite and looking like a bunch of gypsy potters . . .'

Esmond Jell must have caught the last of my oration as he opened the door to investigate the wailing. He blinked in terror and was about to slam it on the passing derelicts. Luckily I'd managed to scrape most of the shit off while I'd ranted away at Clifton. Before Jell could threaten to ring the police and have us put in charge, I stumbled with outstretched hand into the streetlight.

'Mr Jell? George Geraghty! We met once at the RCA a long time ago. I'm sure you won't remember. I don't believe you've met Joseph Clifton . . .'

Jell shuddered at this six-foot bull of a man with a stained and bloodied cheek and a tie wrapped round his ear. Even more disturbing was the old madwoman wrapped in a torn maroon quilt, her eyes wider than tablespoons as she droned at some outlandish dirge. She resembled one of those deranged old thespians sometimes found in charitable asylums, still obsessively muttering the lines of *Hamlet* or *Macbeth*. But what could be her connection with these two young men?

'This is Miss Biddy McMinahan, Clifton's aunt.'

Jell gulped. 'His aunt? You mean that you've met her out here by accident?'

I blushed in the darkness. 'I'm afraid she's with us. She's part of our party. Joe thought that she'd benefit from seeing you because . . . because she's so interested in art. I hope . . . we hope . . . that you don't mind.'

Motionless in the doorway, Jell surveyed us at length. I could more or less imagine what was going through his mind. Was this weird trio likely to be entertainingly colourful or downright odious? Would we make for ripe future anecdote or just make bloody nuisances of ourselves and spoil his evening totally?

Rubbing his chin dubiously he said, 'I'm sure we can find an extra place at the table. I'm certainly intrigued to hear that his aunt is an art enthusiast. May I ask who your favourite contemporary painter is, Miss McMinahan?'

Joe scowled at the lordly tone. Biddy ignored the eminent critic and kept her eyes raised as she continued her penitential song.

'Joe's her favourite artist,' I said quickly. 'And she's Irish-speaking, Mr Jell. Miss McMinahan knows very little English; she's a virtual monoglot. So it's best to talk to her through Joseph. His first tongue is also Ulster Gaelic.'

His glistening tonsure inclined at a careful angle, Jell led us through to the guests. We were an hour late and they were sitting down to dinner. They turned in slow motion as Biddy resumed her wailing, and there was an incredulity which the host did nothing to dispel. Instead Jell smiled to observe both the biddable old friends and the brash young newcomers being put on the spot. Imogen and Magenta, who had sampled the anarchic milieus of Twenties Berlin and Thirties Paris, might have been assumed to be impervious to shock. But their lined old jaws dropped open as this tattered old mummer made her procession into their midst.

'Foowara, foowara, shoowara,' she intoned in a piercing banshee descant.

Jell noticed some of the party murmuring approval at the picturesque arrivals. He smiled and informed Magenta that the old lady's devotionals were being sung in a dialect of Ulster Irish. The gallery owner tapped her drooping cigarette holder and made reverent reference to Yeats and Lady Gregory. She told Clifton she'd once had afternoon tea with Yeats during which the great man had seemed very dull as well as hopelessly abstracted. The morning after there had been coffee with Lady Gregory who had been sheer vivacity in comparison. Imogen then chipped in that she had once sunk nightcap port with John Millington Synge in a grim old hotel in Galway, but that Synge unlike Yeats had had more than a bit of go in him.

'Is that a fact?' said Clifton politely. 'Do you know, I've never met anyone famous in my life? I wonder why that is?'

I kicked him lightly. 'Except for tonight, that is. We know we're in among a lot of eminent people here.'

Jell threw him a doubtful glance. Broadstairs, the critic

who knew nothing about art, agreed that he'd never met any world-class celebrities either. Imogen in a weary tone boasted that she'd met more famous people than she cared to remember, but that the finest person in the world was her milkman, an amateur fortune teller and an expert at fruit-bush grafting. Biddy was still singing as I guided her like a blindwoman to the table. Jell's maid had set a place for the uninvited guest, but before she'd pulled her chair out her nephew had finished half his soup. As if auditioning for the part of Abel Magwitch, he flung himself down and shovelled it in like a famished convict. Impressed by such an atavist, Imogen plumped down beside him and told him loudly he was a bloody good painter.

'Thank you,' he said, blushing like a shy young coun-tryman.

'Not at all. Obvious to anyone with a pair of bloody eyes.'

Clifton racked his brains to think of something nice to say about Imogen. He noticed her fat little cat being fed alternate spoonfuls of his mistress's soup. Joe decided to mimic Imogen's formula and told her that 'your wee man, wee Pablo' was 'a bloody good wee cat'. Any beast, he said judi-cially, that would drink red-hot mock-turtle soup off a silver spoon was worth the time of day. Then vaguely aware that his own soup was all over his face, he removed the petrol-pump tie from his ear and used it as a handy serviette.

Imogen said staunchly, 'I like very much the undisguised passion in your island landscapes. I admire the sombre fury, the naked torment, the saturnine bleakness.'

As if she were talking about somebody else, Clifton said: 'Is that a fact?'

'Does that sound impertinent coming from the mouth of a disagreeable old Englishwoman?'

Clifton demurred, 'No, no. Not at all, ma'am.' He patted Imogen's varicose knee with a reassuring smile, as if she'd been another Aunt Biddy. Then he offered Pablo the dregs of his soup, but Pablo turned away.

Meanwhile Biddy had stopped her ululations and was mopping her soup up with relish.

'A courageous rawness,' Imogen continued with an envious glance at his guzzling, slurping aunt. 'A willingness to expose oneself to the pusillanimous public gaze. That is not the fashion in contemporary English painting.'

Esmond Jell interposed drily, 'It's probably because Joseph Clifton happens to be Irish, Madgie. Though unlike your afternoon-tea acquaintance Yeats he's no pampered landowner sat sequestered in a majestic demesne. Mr Geraghty tells me Mr Clifton is from the poorest part of the Donegal Gaeltacht. He is an Irish-speaker like his aunt, Miss McMinahan. I believe he must be the first truly native Celt I've ever met.'

They all turned to examine Joe in his disarray and tacitly confirmed the accuracy of 'truly native'. I looked at our host to see if his choice of terms was deliberately insulting. But no, he simply didn't hesitate too much before opening his twitching mouth. Clifton had a purplish discoloration around his neck, always a sign of brewing indignation. I was relieved to see old Biddy getting stuck into her turtle soup, obviously ravenous after her groaning. It was strange that a single milk stout and a pinch of Old Jack Riley had tipped her into that half-hour trance. Talking of trances, as if to relieve Biddy from the exhaustion of supernatural communication, Magenta put down her spoon and drifted off into a soporific stupor. She slumped there as vacant and immobile as a Kirghiz shaman and I wondered why no one seemed startled by her behaviour. A good ten minutes later she blinked her way back to life. She stared at me hard and said that, desperately in need of recuperation after a very hard day, she'd allowed herself to drift back to her Parliament Hill parlour. She had just enjoyed a gramophone recording of some deliciously plangent études by Frédéric Chopin. Had she not left Esmond's table for a restorative few minutes, she would definitely have been out of sorts for the rest of the evening.

'You mean you left the table in your imagination?' I said with a blush. I had no belief in occult powers, but was genuinely curious about the credulity of others.

'Not at all,' she said, bridling at such literal-mindedness. 'I commanded my spirit to depart posthaste from my body. So off it dashed to Parliament Hill which is where I had ordered it to go. My non-corporeal self then decided of its own volition to put the Chopin on. It then lay down on the chaise-longue and allowed its aural energies to revitalise. Perfectly straightforward, no hocus-pocus involved. It's a skill that can be learnt like anything else, like playing the flute or the fiddle. Once, you see, back in 1899, I had lunch with that hulking great clergyman's son John Cowper Powys, and he showed me the simple trick. He assured me that on several occasions he'd sent his extracorporeal self across London to retrieve an umbrella or a hat he'd left at a friend's . . .'

Imogen put her many-ringed finger on my arm and leaned across to impart something else.

'I once had William Gerhardie, that dandified young author, to one of my gallery previews, and Willy had the same fascination. He was forever spouting about out-of-the-body experiences, especially to attractive girls and admiring newspaper proprietors. He also attempted to fascinate me and was outrageously flirtatious throughout his demonstration. But I told him that I do not care for men as a rule. There is only one man in the world I have ever cared for. Willy was no match for Señor Picasso, I can assure you, Mr Geraghty.'

Ten

The next course was halibut. Post-war austerity being what it was, this focused everyone's attention and Imogen's only subsequent trance came from her beatific experience of the fish. The potatoes were roasted in heavy cream and garlic, and Biddy and her nephew licked their knives so as not to miss a single speck. Pablo sat aloof and mournful as Imogen forgot to share either fish or cream. Only Siddall of the *Telegraph* would make the occasional cheerful remark. He described to Broadstairs a three-foot-long postbox built in the side of a chimney stack in Ostwaldtwistle, and lamented the fact there wasn't a single decent hotel or even guest house in the bloody town. Broadstairs, whose familiarity with northern geography was on a par with his knowledge of cosmopolitan art, asked him where exactly Oswaldtwistle was in Cornwall.

With the sweet, Jell tried to get these two Young Turks to earn their gourmet dinners. In a jousting donnish manner he tried to push Clifton and Geraghty to offer their ideological manifestos. I obliged by sitting up straight and telling them that my cartoons were intended to jolt the complacent British public, nothing more nor less. Siddall frowned and fingered his postbox album. Broadstairs grinned a good-natured approval. Jell assumed a magisterial trenchance and asked me whether the shock factor alone was a proper artistic means.

'Of course not,' I said, more brusquely than I'd intended. I found the great man's permanently distracted air supremely frustrating. It was obvious that he found himself the only really interesting person at his party.

A doleful fiftyish man called Summers, a senior lecturer at the Royal Academy, suddenly decided to speak. 'So what else have you, Geraghty, apart from this shock effect of yours?'

I looked at him carefully. Summers had a large brown mole on one cheek and was sat uneasily next to Biddy. 'To put it another way, how do you explain your ubiquity as well as notoriety? Every damn paper I open has one of your cartoons in it.'

I replied as calmly as I could, 'I think people are affected one way or the other by the anger in my work.'

'Anger?' pouted Summers, as if to a precocious infant.

'Yes. Moral anger. As well as political anger.'

I was trying to communicate that in all sincerity I was as keen as anyone to understand my own artistic motives.

Jell said in a needling yet indifferent tone, 'Righteous anger perhaps?'

I shrugged as I felt my neck stiffen. 'If you say so, Mr Jell.'

Imogen Stilgoe suddenly decided to open her mouth. I was aware she still hadn't pardoned me for doubting her extracorporeal doppelgänger.

'How d'you know,' she demanded, 'that you're not being desperately *self*-righteous?'

I put down my dessert spoon and did my best to fight my corner. 'I don't know it with any certainty. I only have a sense of right and wrong, just like everyone else. If I read about some imperialist massacre in the Middle East, or some gross act of oppression against African tribes in our Colonies, or about the hanging of a possibly innocent man at Worm-wood Scrubs . . . then I feel a sense of outrage. The outrage is moral outrage or some would call it righteous outrage. A great many other people feel the same indignation after all. In my case it happens to express itself through drawing.'

Clifton, who'd appeared to be dozing for the last ten minutes, stepped in on my behalf. For a moment he appeared quite as sober as a high-court judge: 'If his anger was faked, he wouldn't be as successful as he is. Bogus righteousness wouldn't give this feller the huge following that he has.'

Esmond Jell promptly decided to draw out the silent 'native'. 'In the old days angry prophets were often stoned for their beliefs. The public took great exception to the vehemence of their attacks.'

Clifton stared at his thimbleful of dessert wine, but didn't rise to the bait. He asked Jell gruffly if he had anything substantial to drink.

'What?' sniffed the critic with his legendary insouciance. 'Oh you'll find plenty of everything in the drawing room. Let's act on your helpful prompting. Why don't we have our coffee. You can all reach up for brandy, and Magenta can raid the cigar box and Imogen can offer Pablo a little crème-de-menthe in her saucer . . .'

Crammed with antiques, the drawing room had an atmosphere part languorous, part sober as a London club. The silk curtains were a delicate bird's-egg blue and would have enchanted a young bride of twenty. The heavy mahogany and walnut furniture could have been an octogenarian banker's. The really striking thing was the total absence of paintings. The oak bookshelves groaned with splendid first editions on painting and sculpture, but England's best-known art critic hadn't a single picture hanging on his walls. I looked for a lone print, an antique cameo, even a calendar or a framed photograph of Jell at Balliol. Nothing. Was it just an allergic reaction to his critical labours that he wished to exclude all reminders from his leisure hours?

Then I noticed something I might have expected in the parlour of a tweedy vicar or a sentimental don. In the far corner was a vast walnut dresser incorporating half a dozen shelves. Arrayed on each were three or four exquisite antique plates. Surprised, even touched, I walked across to take a closer look. In fact I spent so long admiring them Esmond Jell eventually joined me. Restraining a pink-faced pleasure, he offered more brandy from the decanter.

I said shyly, 'I'm really impressed by your plate collection, Mr Jell. I've not seen anything as grand outside of a museum. My father used to collect Dresden figurines but they're nowhere in this league. I don't know much about it, but this is Worcester, isn't it?'

My admiration was real but I sounded perhaps like a toadying supplicant for the great man's favours. I waited for Jell's scorn, but he dropped his guard and became almost warm. He allowed himself a smile and a tiny blush of modesty, and confessed that collecting antique plates was his one little vice.

'I don't usually boast about it, Geraghty. Collectors of anything tend to be an unalluring species, don't you find? I've no wish to be bracketed in the same category as Siddall and his eggshaped postbox. But yes it's a Worcester Basket, a very fine example. There's this lovely crimson scroll band and the flowers and leaves are superbly done. About two hundred years old and in near flawless condition . . .'

That evening served me well as my unfeigned interest in Jell's pottery kept me in his good books till he died in 1968. He couldn't wait to point out the Copeland cabinet plate that dated from 1859 and had been part of the dessert service ordered by the Prince of Wales. Jell said it was worth about the same as the Worcester Basket and possibly twice as much as the Minton adjacent. The latter was in the style of Christopher Dresser with a rich blue border and a design of bent corn stalks. There was also a Wemyss Gordon which was about sixty years old, and Jell chuckled when I complained that the gooseberries were painted red rather than green. The most valuable piece, oddly enough, was from the 1920s, a pottery charger made by Carter, Stabler and Adams. Its painter had the unforgettable name Nellie Bishton, and the central motif was a nymph identified as 'Leipzig Girl'.

When Biddy came waddling across, nephew in tow, I wondered if she'd come to admire the same little nymph.

'I doubt it,' said Clifton, grabbing the decanter and pouring himself a brimming glass. It slopped a quantity on the Afghan carpet and Jell winced.

'Does your relative want more brandy?' he snapped.

Clifton said, 'No, but I'll swallow her ration for her while I'm here. I daren't give her more drink in case she starts a singing fit. She was stuck in one once for a day and a night, and I nearly rang the Fire Brigade to put her out. No, sir, she's asked me to make a humble supplication, as to whether you'd kindly put on your fine Cossor wireless for her. My aunt says at half past nine they have her favourite programme on the Home Service.'

Even Jell couldn't hide his stupefaction. 'She wants me to put my wireless on for her? I see. I must say my guests as a rule don't squat in a corner attentive to a BBC broadcast. Logically they would choose to keep themselves at home in the first place. You'll recall, Mr Clifton, that your aunt wasn't on my original guest list. Which reminds me. I've still to hear you translate her considered reflections upon twentieth-century art?'

Jell waited for his embarrassment, but Clifton smiled a kindly indulgence. Which emphasised the deplorably obvious, namely that Jell was the bad-mannered one, not this rough Irishman educated in an island hedge school. Supportive evidence was there in the shape of anxious-looking Biddy. What reasonable host would refuse to placate her, simply by the twiddling of a bakelite knob?

'May I ask the nature of the broadcast she's so keen on?'

Nephew and aunt conversed in Irish, and amongst those squelching aspirants I heard the incongruous euphony of the English 'Walter Leadbetter'.

'Walter Leadbetter,' said Clifton.

'Eh?' started Jell. 'Walter Who? I've never heard of the man. Is he one of those ghastly mewling clergymen given to hour-long exhortations?' Something occurred to him and he turned on me suspiciously. 'Geraghty, I thought you said

Miss McMinahan barely speaks our language? How is she supposed to understand a wireless programme in English?'

Blushing, I burbled, 'But she doesn't need to in the case of Walter Leadbetter. Have you really not heard of him, Mr Jell? I'd have thought it impossible. His Jumping Thumping Dance Band has been all the rage since the end of the War. Why, he's mentioned in the same breath as Joe Loss, Cyril Stapleton, Ted Heath and . . .'

Jell raised his eyebrows woefully. 'My wireless is permanently tuned to the Third, I'm glad to say. I can assure you, Geraghty, I would sooner listen to my washbasin emptying than to a jumping thum . . . to a popular dance band.'

He shuddered as Imogen and Magenta glided our way with inquisitive and hostile looks at their host. They had observed the monoglot mystic Miss McMinahan becoming very agitated and beseeching, and were conscious that old 'Jelly' was being typically obdurate about something. The 'native' nephew turned to his two old admirers and by sign language indicated he had made a humble petition which was being refused. Jell stared at this palaver with disgust. Frowning at the smirking old women, he indicated a stoic acquiescence.

'Very well, go ahead then, Clifton. Don't let me spoil your aunt's party, even if she ends up spoiling mine. Provided you have the volume on reasonably low, you can settle her in this chair and she may listen to Walter Leadbitter . . .'

'Better,' corrected Biddy, to everyone's amazement.

Jell strode to the far end of the room where he began a neck-twitching denunciation to Summers of the Academy. He stole a brief, tormented glance at Clifton who was assaulting the wireless dials with one hand and clutching the decanter with the other. I smiled sheepishly at Jell and shoved him out of the way. In two seconds I had it tuned to the Home Service. The Jumping Thumpers was the name of the singers accompanying the dance band, and they were halfway through a gusty rendition of 'My Old Man Said Follow the

Van'. Biddy was reclined in a deep armchair in a state of beaming rapture. She was so tiny and the armchair so plush that she sank like a plum into a dish of custard and her legs rose up from the ground. She appeared semi-levitated. Once again, she was mystically entranced, though this particular trance indicated certain profane characteristics. Her crimson brogues, which matched the torn coat, tapped up and down with the uncontrollable force of a pair of magic clogs. Magenta and Imogen had come across to investigate and, both being hard of hearing, were bent over the wireless as they tried to catch the dying strains of the Jumping Thumpers.

'That's jolly good,' said Magenta and she shoved Pablo's right ear against the speaker so that he could enjoy the same thing. Pablo yawned and flexed his paws against the mahogany casing of the custom-built wireless. A deep and horrible scratch appeared. Magenta inspected it critically before murmuring that Jelly should get himself a tougher wireless instead of spending all his money on silly bloody plates. She stared witheringly at his dresser and blurted: 'He has those wretched Worcesters and Wemysses up there valued at over five hundred pounds. Personally, I wouldn't give a fiver for the lot. Flowers and scrolls, flowers and blasted scrolls! Interlinked roundels, you should hear him maundering about those. That's always been old Jelly's problem. I've always maintained he needs a woman to give him backbone, though there's fat chance of that. Ah, but I adore this infectious music. There's one thing I find puzzling though. What do they mean by "the old cop linnets". I always thought I knew all the common song birds.'

After some thought I said, 'It's "the old couple in it".'

'Eh? Why must Imogen and I stoop over this radio like two termagants who've lost their ear trumpets. Can't the volume be turned up?'

I raised it a fraction and said that our host didn't want to disturb his other guests, that it was a special concession to Miss McMinahan. Magenta grunted and pushed Pablo's other ear against the speaker, and he yawned and made a second mutilation of the mahogany.

'Dear dear,' cooed his mistress. 'What flim-flam rubbish. He paid forty-five guineas for this wireless, it was custom built you know. I would send it back if I were Jelly and get a decent gramophone instead. Tell me, is it possible to buy this excellent dance music on record, Mr Geraghty?'

I assured her it was, and I repeated 'Jumping Thumpers' several times before she had it down accurately in her notebook. When the music stopped, both gallery owners became childishly crestfallen. They brightened only when Leadbetter came to the studio microphone and announced the next number.

'Ladies and Gents, I would ask you please to sit back in your armchairs . . .'

Biddy shuffled into the depths of her chair so that the brogues were on a fault line with her chin.

' . . . and enjoy our newest number. We've only played it once on this show, but the volume of fanmail has assured that it will go into our "must hear" repertoire. As I explained last week, it's a song that Billy "Mr Magic" McCumiskey of the Jumping Thumpers has penned. We all think that William (as his wife begs us call him!) has mined pure gold with this cute little melody. Of course the words themselves, Mr Magic frankly admits, mightn't make an awful lot of sense. But as Mr Jim Bellarby of Whitehaven, Cumberland puts it in a letter I'm holding in front of me in the studio, after two awful world wars a little bit of harmless nonsense doesn't go amiss when it comes to cheering up the man in the street! The tune is called "Wibbidy Wab, Wibbidy Wob". Hold on to your hats, and here we go. Ah one, two, ah . . .'

Biddy repeated the title excitedly to Joe, rendering it phonetically as '*bhopatha tha, bhipatha thu*'. Clifton drained his brandy and replied at length in Gaelic. The gist of it he translated in a drunken slur for the benefit of Imogen and Magenta.

'I told my aunt she's the one has the right idea, hurling and tapping away there to Walter Leadbetter. After all this is supposed to be a party, not a funeral. Isn't it true we're all supposed to be *artists* here in one shape or another?'

Imogen puffed, 'Of course we are.'

'Of course,' echoed Magenta.

Pablo miaowed.

'You two with your beautiful galleries, your beautiful cat, your beautiful dalliances, forgive me, with Picasso and Yeats and J.M. Synge. And didn't you say with Lady Gregory? Gathered here in this room, folk like us are the cutting edge, the new iconoclasts, ain't we? So what the hell, I ask myself, are we doing sat in the corner all terrified of having ourselves a good time. We ought to be having a *Fleadh*, a musical *Feis*. "Wibbidy Wab" is about to come on the wireless and we ought to be giving a kick and a hoot and a bit of a shout . . .'

He hulked across to the Cossor and turned it to dance-hall volume. Esmond Jell looked as if someone had shoved a firework up his backside. Siddall clutched his postbox album and appeared as if ready to flee. Lifting a minuscule glass of port, he drained it in one gulp.

Wibbidy Wab, Wibbidy Wob
Life's what you make it
So make a good job!
Wibbidy Wob, Wibbidy Wab
Don't try to fake it
Take all you can grab!

Transfixed by the gnomic resonance of the lyrics, Clifton obeyed the Thumpers' command. Without consulting Magenta Mahony he began to fling her in staggering hiccoughing ellipses around Jell's Afghan carpet. Siddall and Jell watched with arms tight against their sides, just in case Magenta proved too old for these centripetal tossings. After about the tenth ellipse, she put down her brandy and urged him to hold his blinking horses. Snoring Pablo was put on her partner's vast shoulder and Picasso's fag holder in her mouth at the ideal forty-five degrees. Then she meekly surrendered to the magic of the Jumping Thumpers.

'Wibbidy Wab!' roared Clifton, as he spun her in a cascading e-circle.

'Whippity what?' said Magenta with a grave expression. She tottered into his outflung arms and lingered panting before being spun again into orbit. 'Wippity something. You know, Picasso and his crowd thought prancing the moonlit tango or thumping guitars and performing flamenco, ola señor, were the be-all and end-all? One day I decided to show his gang in the Montmartre café how to put themselves nicely in groups of eight and practise something much more wholesome, much less Iberian, much less fanatical. I had them all nicely marshalled, cheerfully clapping their hands and doing a round of "The Lancers". That was followed by "Strip the Willow", "The Dashing White Sergeant" and . . .'

As 'Wibbidy Wab' continued, Clifton employed Magenta and Imogen as simultaneous partners, twirling them to and fro like a pair of yoyos in staggered sequence. This was exhilarating for both dancers and spectators, but a sudden crisis seemed all too likely. Before long the weakening effects of all those sybaritic years in Paris and Dublin became apparent, and both old women demonstrated a nasty purple-ish congestion around the face and neck. With cupped hands I bawled in Clifton's ear that they seemed short of oxygen and were about to have seizures. He craned his neck at these two wrinkled puppets on strings, and immediately let go of both. Imogen rolled backwards into a delicate octagonal card table and ended sprawled across it. Under her tonnage, it started to crack and splinter. Catapulted Magenta was about to macerate Aunt Biddy under her leaden girth, had I not lunged and grabbed the back of her skirt in the nick of time.

Joe seemed seriously aggrieved as he removed snoring Pablo from his shoulder. The cat had slept serenely through the dance and didn't wake as he laid him gently down. Clifton then took off his jacket and tossed it roughly on the floor. Complaining that there were no other female partners, he informed me moodily he would have to go it alone. Unless perhaps, throwing me a whimsically mordant look, I fancied a twirl with him myself?

'Like hell,' I snapped. 'Haven't you noticed that Jell is really furious? Look at his colour, he's as purple as that gash on your cheek. Can't you see you're turning this party into a bloody circus? He won't forgive you, you know. He won't do anything for you, unless you make some amends right away. Why not turn the wireless down and just concentrate on your brandy?'

Clifton leered and categorised me as a tame apologist for an arrogant fool: 'I'm supposed to be a rude "native" according to your man over there, Praxiteles's ugly twin brother. Jell's a world expert on art and every other branch of the liberal humanities, so he should bloody well know. He goes and proudly announces I'm the first truly aboriginal specimen of a Celt he's ever met. That explains all this embarrassing behaviour, eh, George? How can I, a primeval island savage, do without my ritual dancing and my ritual drunkenness? It's my ur-Celtic bloody savage's instinct, after all. You watch me, George Geraghty. I'll show that silver-haired get how a truly "primitive" artist behaves.'

What happened next was terrifying, entirely without precedent in any Pimlico drawing room of 1947. Without preamble Joe Clifton removed his tie, his cufflinks and his cheap old flannel shirt. In doing so he revealed a chest as ferociously hirsute as an adult chimpanzee's.

I begged him, 'Please put it back on! Don't go barechested in Pimlico. It's just not done in these parts.'

Clifton scratched vigorously in the Amazonian forests of his body hair. For added effect, he stopped to linger over an imaginary louse or maggot extracted with thumb and forefinger. He cracked it with the deftness of an expert nit-nurse. I groaned. Joe Clifton cackled and started removing his shoes and socks. Imogen watched his partial striptease enchantedly, then asked: a) was his munificent chest hair real, genuinely copper, or dyed with some sort of henna?, and b) could she and Magenta have another go at the Aran Island Morris Dance?

Jell's brain was racing in all directions as this Donegal drunk swaggered his repulsive torso. Should a sensible host take the impetuous step of dashing over to remonstrate? Was it more prudent to employ George Geraghty as bear-tamer? He caught my eye and telepathised a peremptory message. You, Geraghty, are selected to be tonight's zoo attendant and will be held personally responsible for any more of this lunatic's tricks!

'It's because he's so hot,' I shouted hoarsely above the din. All eyes turned as I listened to the puny reverberance of my words. 'He's stripped off because he was roasted with all the dancing. It was a reel from the Arans and he only did it to entertain Miss Mahony and Miss Stilgoe. And Miss McMinahan of course for nostalgia's sake. But he's decided to stop it and quieten down. Haven't you, Clifton?'

The savage assumed a mien of grovelling acquiescence. But just as I was about to turn off the wireless, he held up a minatory hand.

'Have I shite!' he cried, tossing a size-twelve shoe into the air. 'I have only shiting well started . . .'

Clifton stripped off his scuffed and crumpled trousers. I began to feel faint. Esmond Jell turned green and looked to anyone for any explanation. He stumbled backwards into the arms of worried Siddall. Magenta nodded at Joe's disrobing with a stern approval, as if a Bohemian connoisseur of male torsos, dangling appendages, and anything else designed to make one's blood race.

Clifton's underwear might once have been white, but was now grey and grimy and an oddly marbled yellow about the orifice areas.

'I say,' commented Imogen. 'Isn't he a very big sort of chap!'

No one believed their eyes as he took off his last bit of clothing. Clifton stood there beaming drunk and ballock naked. His manhood, as Imogen had divined through his skimpy linen, proved to be the size of a carthorse's. It was as fat as a prize rhubarb stem and as long as a compact tea tray.

'I say,' repeated Imogen. 'Someone ought to do something about a thing like that. Someone ought to sketch it. Look at how it moves so, Magenta. Someone ought to write a feature on it surely.'

'It's a dear,' murmured Magenta. 'I mean he's a dear. I mean, they both are such dears.'

Biddy, who might have been stricken on the grounds of outraged Catholic piety, stared indifferently at her naked nephew. No doubt she had bathed him when he was a child and saw him now as merely an overgrown water baby. Her expression simply confirmed the ineffable innocence of her Gweedore soul.

Esmond Jell was shocked to his metropolitan core. Confirming Magenta's soubriquet, he was bristling like a silver jelly. He was also gasping something to Siddall who in turn was beckoning to me.

'Boy!' Siddall mouthed, as if this was a New York hotel and I was an idle bell-hop. 'Boy! Over here! Now! Over here!'

I decided to play deaf and stay where I was. Biddy had begun singing along with Walter Leadbetter, ignoring her naked nephew. The same individual had begun a repetitive circular marathon in front of the wireless, a bit like a small boy anxious to time himself over a hundred laps. His radial capering had a diameter of some four yards and at each 'Wibbidy Wab!' and 'Wibbidy Wob!' he would take a tetanic leap into the air. By the laws of physics his outsize penis would flap in the opposite direction, and when this happened Magenta's left eyelash would jump in percussive sympathy.

'*Don't try to fake it*,' boomed forth at deafening volume. Billy 'Mr Magic' McCumiskey was providing an uproarious solo. '*Take all you can grab*.'

Clifton assented. 'Take *all* you can grab! Do you hear me? Take all you bloody can.'

As he pranced in the air, he struck his palm across his naked thigh. I winced at the huge weal, but anaesthetised by brandy Joe felt less than nothing.

The Donegal painter made a dozen of these skirling circumambulations before growing tired of their repetitive nature. His spectators, especially doting Magenta, were manifesting signs of dizziness. They found that their necks were imitating his pinball trajectories, and they blinked in surprise at the harsh reflected glare from his blindingly white backside. The rest of him was as ruddy and rough as a seafarer, but his bum was as anaemic as a virgin's pallor.

If Clifton had stopped at that point, he might even have been forgiven. Apart from the cracked table and the brandy on the carpet there was no irreparable damage, and his child of nature gambolling might have furnished Jell with extravagant anecdotes for months. There was something arguably Wagnerian and Rabelaisian, not to say totemic, primitive and vulpine, about this extraordinary Irishman. He was a frighteningly simple, frighteningly brilliant painter, who was nonetheless frighteningly complex and frightfully unpredictable in his frightening behaviour. But Clifton had yet to exact full vengeance for being called a 'native' and for having his old aunty greeted with patronage. Our host needed far sterner punishment if he was to feel any real repentance in his bones. And if Esmond Jell had the gall to show him any more unction, then . . .

'Mr Geraghty,' Siddall roared above the wireless. 'Esmond tells me to tell you would you tell your friend to put his clothes on and stop acting like a savage baboon! It's simply outrageous, downright obscene to do what he's doing in the presence of two elderly women. Esmond has just mentioned the word police in my hearing and . . .'

Magenta turned on Jelly's lap dog scathingly. 'But we're in a private house aren't we, Siddall? There are no minors here who might be affronted or corrupted by the sight of his unusual what-shall-I-call-it?'

'Phallus,' supplied Imogen crisply. 'His divine omphallos, Madgie.'

Magenta wagged her hand dismissively. 'Painters spend half their time leering at lady models in the buff. Why shouldn't gallery owners and art critics see a bit of bare flesh too? We're obliged often enough to wade through books about the tedious social customs and political intrigues in Mantegna's and Velazquez's day. Well why not see what it was like for Rembrandt or Michelangelo to be a yard away from a shimmering splendid naked male? Answer: jolly good fun and jolly educational . . .'

'*Wibbidy Wob! Wibbidy Wab!*' responded the Thumpers.

The obscene baboon was panting heavily from his gyrations. Digesting the simian epithets, Clifton flashed Siddall a leer. With three quarters of the brandy decanter inside him, he had shrunken eyes, loose face muscles, and was muttering in an arguably monkeyish way. The *Telegraph* critic trembled at such extreme abandonment and retreated behind Jell. Jell whispered something in his ear, but Siddall shook his head and pointed to strapping Broadstairs. The Acumen man was muscular and heavy and possibly could execute a rugger tackle on this imbecile.

'*Take all you can grab,*' bawled Mr Magic. '*Don't try to fake it. Take all you can grab.*'

'I bloody well will,' snarled the native. 'So I will, so I will, so I will.'

Then he muttered what sounded like a Gaelic proverb to Biddy who was still enjoying his bare-arse capering as a harmless variation on a Donegal church treat. Encouraged by that, the caperer grabbed a little footstool adjacent to the wireless. He lifted it and set it beside the walnut dresser. As his hands groped blindly for the shelves, Esmond Jell gave a gasp of horror. Employing his paws, arms and hairy chest, Clifton was accommodating every single one of those priceless antique plates. Imogen, whose nose happened to be about six inches from his quivering backside, found her lips moving in a palpating moue. We could all observe the colossal effort she was making to stop herself planting a tender buttock kiss.

'No!' groaned Jell in a petrified falsetto. 'Don't you dare, you Irish bastard! Put those plates back, you savage!'

'Jelly!' gasped Imogen as the hallucinatory beauty of the sensuous Irish buttocks were displaced by the bleary ugliness of a peevish English fizzog. 'What an appalling way to talk to one of your guests!'

Clifton had some twenty plates balanced below his hairy nipples. He looked like an eccentric barrow boy who had opted to push his household wares via a devastating sales gimmick. 'Savage is it? Savage by nature and savage by deed, you'll find.'

Joe leapt off the footstool. Surveying his audience he winked a spurious reassurance. The tower of pottery started to totter but didn't fall, as he began to skip a wild conga to the rhythm of the Jumping Thumpers.

'*Wibbidy Wab! Wibbidy Wob!*'

From the top of the pile he took the Wemyss Gordon with its matchless design of rosy gooseberries. Hooting with triumph he smacked it on his thigh just as if he'd stunned a Donegal trout. Then, seemingly as an afterthought, he flung it with all his might against the wall.

This plate-smasher was the man Esmond Jell had hailed as the most accomplished Irish painter for two decades . . .

Crack!

The word 'smithereen' is an Irish one. The Wemyss Gordon broke into innumerable smithereens. Esmond Jell's heart was heard to break alongside.

'My God!' sobbed Jell. 'This is killing me, I swear it's

destroying me what he's doing! Someone please knock him to the floor, will you. You, Broadstairs, you stop him. If you can get all those plates off him intact, I promise I'll give you fifty guineas in cash. I don't care if you have to cripple him, but stop what he's doing at all costs.'

Broadstairs glanced with awe at the prancing Maori and didn't hesitate: 'Ah no. No I don't think I shall actually, Esmond. Naked or not, I should say he's one of the biggest chaps I've ever seen.'

Jell clenched his fists and mimed a feeble blow at him. 'You preposterous coward! You're built like a bricklayer and you're shaking in your blasted shoes. Words fail me, Broadstairs. Just as they have always failed you in your appalling art criticism. A bloody bricklayer could write a lot more cogently. It's an embarrassing joke your reviewing, are you aware of that?'

Not particularly sheepishly, Broadstairs answered. 'Yes, Esmond. I couldn't agree more.'

A Worcester basket shattered the wall . . .

'*Take all you can grab!*' shrieked Magic McCumiskey.

Heaps of plates swaying pendulum-wise, Clifton continued his conga as in a Chaplin film. Like a Chaplin waiter he fought as they lurched and slithered but stayed magically next to his chest. It was as if his shamanistic nakedness was lending him miraculous powers. He seized a second basket and cracked it across his left buttock before tossing it at the wall. Scrolls and roundels shattered like so many shattered hearts. Esmond Jell gave a scream, then started to weep. Between sobs he urged Siddall to tell Geraghty to tell Clifton something he'd duly honour, no matter what. If the vandal would stop his destruction, Jell would not only forget the whole thing, he would write Joe a cheque for two hundred pounds . . .

Clifton sneered, 'Tell him I can't be bought! Tell Siddall to tell the wee pimp his money has even less power than his criticism. Just tell him I won't be bought at *any* price.'

He put his hand to his mouth and gave a silent war cry. He pranced his right foot like a fearless Comanche brave. He jabbed his left foot like a hen exploring for worms. Every time the Thumpers finished a chorus of 'Wibbidy Wab', he walloped a plate on his thigh and flung it to its death against the wall. Clifton laughed very solemnly at his dance of destruction. He tittered not vindictively but as an impersonal acknowledgement of the comedy of temporal fragility. Nothing ever lasted, nothing was really solid, everything had to pass away. Whether prized if piffling antiques in the case of Jell, or looks and sex and dignity in the case of Imogen and Magenta, or even the heterogeneity of the modern hence bastardised postbox in the case of mournful Siddall. Who knows, perhaps he also foresaw the impermanence of his own talent, as the booze eventually stripped away his sense and finally his sanity.

Crack. Smash! Crack. Smash!

It took about twenty minutes to smash Jell's twenty plates. I wouldn't have believed a grown man would take hysterics, but Esmond Jell threw himself on his back, thrashed his legs in the air, and began gasping like an infant with a choking fit. Jelly's plates had been valued at over five hundred pounds, a reasonable annual income in 1947. The unreplaceable Copeland was the last to go. The ten chorus version of 'Wibbidy Wab' had reached its finale, just as Clifton had come to his. He was free of plates, and he flung up his hands with the relief of dropping these pointless encumbrances. He was a devout and naked anchorite whereas the rest of us were worshippers of mammon and . . . so-called precious objects.

His tree-trunk thighs were tattooed with impressed plate patterns. The Afghan carpet, on which our host was gasping and thrashing, was a sea of broken pottery. It was only that that stopped Joe doing anything worse. When the music ended and Walter Leadbetter coughed into his microphone, Clifton staggered and stood on a sharp piece of Copeland.

His foot trickled blood as I walked towards him bearing his unsavoury underpants. Clifton grunted and fashioned them into a filthy if effective tourniquet. Imogen Stilgoe absently fingered his perspiring stomach, and told him he reminded her of someone extraordinary she had once met in Cannes in the Nineties. But for the life of her she couldn't think who.

Eleven

My father, with a puzzled expression, had just finished telling me Mildred was carrying his baby . . .

The last time he had seen her was on Penrhyndeudraeth station where she was heading furiously for Highgate and he was bound sheepishly for Oxford. He had changed back into his travelling suit, his hair still damp from the night on the lake. In his left hand he had a leather bag containing his silver trophies, the two little trout with their gentle, hopeful faces. Bill hoped they would last all the way to Oxford where he would pass them off as presents from Toll-Gravey's housekeeper. It was such torment to see Mildred looking so agonisingly fetching as she waited for the train in her black and witchlike suit. And that ferocious anger of hers was also inexplicably captivating.

Hetty never got properly enraged, he confided to a startled son, she ticked him off sometimes but she never resorted to full-blooded explosions. Mildred, by contrast, had thrown things, some dangerous, inside Pender's caravan. She had winged his left ear with a jet-propelled glass ashtray. Scowling in the strong sunlight on the Welsh platform, he felt the raw cut and winced. Not content with the ashtray she had stamped on his foot, the one with the corn, creating unbelievable pain. Finally when he had stooped to the ground to pack his bags she had lifted her foot and booted him up that sensitive area where the arse divides. He had humiliated her by his desertion and then terrified her by his return, and her anger knew no bounds. What should have been a thousand and one nights of love turned out to be freezing her behind off, alone under a horsehair blanket in a pitch-dark gypsy caravan. Bill begged a thousand pardons and blamed the lure of the lake, a magic spell that had taken him back to the wildness and poetry of his Tennysonian youth. Then padding after her to the telephone box where she rang for a taxi, he attempted crude bribery. He would fork out for a decent hotel in Penrhynbloodydeudraeth and stand her a five-course dinner this evening. Quail's eggs dammit. Venison in port. Hare in port. Chicken in port. Smoked bloody salmon in bloody port. He was bemused when she didn't answer, much less flutter at the prospect. He insisted that last night's caddish forgetfulness was comically out of character, completely unlike his usually spotless etiquette. Mildred snorted and said that was the problem. Any middle-aged bloke who could forget all about a ripe and willing young woman for ten hours was beyond the pale by any definition. He must be good and bonkers. Anyone who could sit alone on a Welsh lake all night in a monsoon must be dangerously bloody mental.

He made a last attempt, as the London connection came in. He fished out his tin of *Baby's Bottom* and waved it as a sentimental tribute to the tender, silly joy of their first weeks of romance. A faint pulse of something flickered across the stoniness of Mildred's resentment. She hesitated and then with an ambiguous expression crooked her little finger and invited him across for intimate dialogue. Bill breathed great relief. What a timely brainwave! Easiest way past the barbed-wire entanglement better known as a woman's emotional bloody repertoire was to tease her with a romantic memory in the form of a visual aid. A picture postcard, a snapshot, a handkerchief, a bottle of her favourite scent. Or in this case a memento of their first-ever erotic transaction in that Bloomsbury baccy shop. A tin of tobacco so supernally smooth, the only thing to rival it was the texture of a baby's bum.

Mildred crooked her finger again and indicated she would like to whisper something very important. My father bristled with pleasure and walked across with a placatory smirk. Penitently he presented his wounded earhole, and Mildred reached up to convey something by way of feminine repentance, contrition, forgiveness and perhaps a little token of her recrudescent love.

It happened with astonishing speed after that. The guard blew his whistle. As if that were a prearranged signal, Mildred promptly spat some of her outrage, a gob of saliva, inside my father's ear. She also lifted back her delicate hand and dealt him a colossal clout most tellingly across that portion of his lug that had been damaged by the glass ash tray.

'Bloody *hell*!'

My father leapt and staggered and turned purple with pain. He was also purple because the station was thronging and at least half of Penrhyndeudreth was busy enjoying this Buster Keaton vaudeville.

'You bloody damn . . . vicious damn . . . *doxy*!'

Doxy? Was that supposed to be orthodoxy or heterodoxy, I asked. Bill Geraghty grunted. Mildred had beamed at his insult and bowed to the incredulous onlookers. As they'd averted their faces, she had leapt onto the departing train and had vanished out of his life until today.

'She's pregnant?' I asked, trying to sound sanguine but feeling as alarmed as he was.

'As gravid as any twenty-four year old can be.'

'Oh.'

'Oh alright. Two months gone, George. She provided me with the exact date, time of day, plus the precise geographical location of young Pongo's conception. In a worryingly truthful manner unfortunately. Mildred has something of a canny photographic memory, most unusual for one of her social class. I stared her hard in the face but knew she wasn't just seeking vengeance over the Welsh fiasco. No chance she's fibbing, worse luck.'

'Or that young Pong . . . or that it's someone else's?'

'Before meeting me, she'd been without a boyfriend for over a year. And no, she's simply not the type. She's no unprincipled flibbertigibbet, despite her love of blazing rouge and garish make-up generally. For all her temper, rough tongue and crude working-class outlook, she has a lot of basic decency in her make-up I should say.'

Father and son stared into space as they polished off the rest of the whisky. The more it went down, the more philosophic we became.

'I'll have a brother,' I said witlessly. 'Or a sister, of course, it might well be one of those. I always wanted one, you know. And now, at twenty-two, I've gone and got one.'

Bill looked at me dubiously. 'You can keep in touch, if you care to, with your . . . your ah half-brother or half-sister. Seeing you two . . . offspring . . . will both be living here in London it's maybe not a mad idea. As for me, I imagine I'll let sleeping dogs lie. I'll pay her an allowance, adequate maintenance right enough, but I can't seriously imagine involving myself with the child. Too bloody tearing, too painfully upsetting, George. Either you have a child in toto or you don't. You can't have one on some loan arrangement like a library book.'

'No,' I said worriedly. 'No, I don't suppose you can.'

'Supposing,' he urged me intently, 'you hadn't been lavished with unstinting affection by myself and Hetty, and you'd not had our sunny doting faces at the tea table every night of your life, wouldn't it have left you as an adult feeling desperately unsure of yourself?'

I said unaccusingly, 'But you weren't at the tea table every night. You were always working late at Abingdon, getting involved with –'

'Fff,' he grumbled at my tedious nit-picking. 'I was always there *with* you, George, in the most crucial sense. I never showed signs of leaving home or deserting my responsibilities. The house was rock-solid stable, the family that we were was always as sound as a pound.'

I added quietly, 'My mother almost ran off with Greer's friend, Hass the poet. Did you know that?'

For five seconds he looked grave, even stunned. In his nebulous imaginings he had perhaps sensed some mysterious, impalpable threat, but had never dared acknowledge it. He erupted with a vicious cackle: 'That *fin-de-siècle* Oscar Wilde with his dangling pair of eyeglasses! That nancy poetaster! That sibilant and susurrating pansy! Hetty almo–'

I shuffled at his outburst. 'It was only your bereavement that stopped her. When you lost Mrs White you were such an emotional wreck, she stayed on just to take care of you. But she was seriously considering having you examined by a doctor. Don't you realise that the death of the budgerigar was all that stopped her eloping with Hass?'

'Eh?'

And a shudder went through him as the hallucinatory darkness was breached and a dazzling unworldly light peeped through. It illumined an irreversible passage of time and a meaning to his existence so overwhelmingly strange that Bill Geraghty promptly decided he would never ever look in that direction again.

Three months passed. As the War dragged on and the propaganda work continued, as my wife and I spent ever more evenings apart, I consoled myself with the tender little phantom of my baby brother. I would have been just as happy with the notion of a baby sister, but like my father I always saw this accident of his virility as inescapably male. Without trying, I kept imagining a vulnerable little foetus struggling through its vital embryological stages. Words like 'amnion' and 'placenta' floated unanchored in my imagination, and they left me with a gentle echo of things classical, Hellenic and perfect. I rarely stopped to consider the extreme unlikelihood of Mildred allowing me anywhere near the baby, especially if my father had nothing to do with his own child. For that matter, the compound 'half-brother' had nothing very impressive about it; it sounded half-cocked, half-formed, half-born. That being the case I left out the half and thought of Mildred's baby as my full-blood brother. I became painfully impatient for the latest news of her condition. Bill said that he was keeping in regular touch with her by telephone and one-way letter, so I grew inordinately anxious for his next London visit.

He turned up at the start of the New Year, smiling like an insatiable mongrel. Staring at my calendar, I promptly panicked that Mildred might have had the baby prematurely.

I asked, 'How is he?'

I had already informed Jane about her father-in-law's folly, and she'd been typically uncritical. Tonight she was absent at the premiere of a Priestley play in which Frankie Charne was playing a principal role.

'How is who?' asked Bill, removing his handsome tailored raincoat. For a man of fifty-three he looked resoundingly in his prime. I glanced in the hallway mirror at the reflected image of father and son. By his side and with the uncertain tenor of my marriage, I looked a rather wan and unimpressive quantity. At my age, I thought, it was lamentable that I should be so perpetually lethargic, not to say as pale-faced as a consumptive.

'My brother.'

'What?' he said, looking worried. He studied me carefully, as if for signs of fever or hallucination. 'What the hell d'you mean by that riddle, old boy?'

'My brother! The one you callously refer to as young Pongo!'

Bill looked blank. Blanker than blank. I was stunned. Seemingly he hadn't a clue what I was talking about. I fumed and clenched my twitching fists. I felt incredibly angry at this master of obliviousness, this expert at selective amnesia.

I shouted, 'Mildred's baby, for God's sake!'

'Who's Mildred?'

'Grr!'

'Bah, only joking! Cool down a bit, George, or you'll have

some sort of haemorrhage.'

I shuddered at that particular noun in that particular context.

'How's Mildred's baby? There's nothing wrong is there?'

He smirked. 'On the contrary. Things couldn't be righter. I'm off the blasted hook. In fact I've been off it so long, I'd forgotten I'd ever been on it.'

I felt my heart sink and my limbs grow weak. My face perspired and my teeth felt loose in my head. I suspected a backstreet abortion and even those vile words 'hook' and 'haemorrhage' seemed to confirm something bloody and horrible.

'What the hell's happened?' I shouted.

To his astonishment I grabbed his arm and locked it with all the strength in my fists. Of course all I was doing was trying to fix him to one spot, attempting to ballast my vaporous, chattering father, fighting to stop him being spirited away from his paternal responsibilities and very possibly my physical vengeance.

'What have you done to her?'

'Eh? Why the bloody hell are you playing tag with my arm, George? Childish bear hugs are one thing but –'

'I'll strangle you if you've hurt her! Or hurt him.'

'Hurt what?'

'Hurt Mildred! Hurt the . . .'

'I hurt Mildred only as much as I had to. Dammit, people do get hurt in this thing called love. Read Shakespeare, read Stendhal, read Kalidasa, read old George Eliot if you want it all in black and white. Read anyone who's ever followed the painful passions of the heart. Then try to talk and think like a man, instead of like a bloody old maid.'

I bawled, 'What's happened to the baby! Did you have it aborted?'

Bill Geraghty shuddered and looked at me with disgust. 'How dare you think that of your poor old dad! Me let a bonny young girl bleed to death, maybe die of septibloodycaemia in a filthy London back street? Do I look like that kind of crook?'

His moustache had turned slick from all the drizzle outside. He looked as criminally dubious as the day was long.

'OK, I'm sorry. She's had a miscarriage, then?'

'Miscarriage, my arse!'

I scrutinised his bland expression and then had the most painful foreboding of all. It occurred to me that he might have made the whole thing up. Maybe there never was any Mildred. Maybe he spent all his weekends down here in town daydreaming about salacious adventures with enticing twenty-four year olds. Could he really have stayed out all night on a Merioneth lake? It was the first I'd heard of his passion for fishing. I said as much in a flood of contemptuous passion and my father blinked amazed as it came hurtling out. Tweaking the drizzle from his tash he reached into his pocket and pulled out a wallet. He eased out two quaint little items. One was a tiny snapshot of a very pretty young woman about the same age as me. The other was the printed card of a tobacconist's in Bloomsbury.

'OK,' I said forlornly. 'I believe that Mildred exists. But what the hell's happened to my brother?'

'You never had one, George. Mildred was never actually with child.'

I stormed like a maniac. 'What! You mean that she lied? She made the whole thing up? Then why did you believe her in the first place, you bloody old fool?'

He made no swift reply and allowed me to hear the echo of that most grave of insults. According to Scripture, neither one's brother nor one's father should one ever call a fool. With weary forbearance, he answered: 'She didn't lie. She genuinely thought she was having a baby. Her how's-your-thingumee, her blessed menstruation, had stopped alright. But the pregnancy was a phantom. It was virtual rather than real, boy. It was a ghost pregnancy, partly brought on by

211

her natural fecundity, partly by her wishful thinking. She's young, you see, hence bubbling with incendiary hormones. Those full young breasts and sizzling, blazing loins of hers were yearning with a maternal intensity sufficient to bring on a spurious pregnancy. Crikey, George, she was even flipping lactating when it was all in her tiny mind.'

I said dazed, 'A ghost pregnancy?'

'Some simulacrum! Phewee!'

I said in a grotesquely deflated voice, 'I . . . how is she now?'

I felt stunned, and hoped and prayed that Bill would leave our house as soon as possible. Because, of course, I felt nothing less than bereaved. Extravagant as it sounds, I felt like the victim of a backstreet abortion myself. For several months I had had a brother who was a little baby, a tiny egg, a minute sentient creature. In my mind this fragile little thing had bravely swum the sea of creation. Yet all 'it' had been was my fond imagination, which was to say Mildred's ghost. It had never been there at all. I realised how painfully broody I was becoming for a child, how desperate to become a young father. Yet it was to be a biblical period, a full seven years, before our daughter Sally was born. Jane wanted to have a child just as impatiently, but it was as late as 1950 before she conceived. She assumed, as I did, she was incapable of conception. And doubtless that was a considerable part of the bitterness, the levity and the heartlessness that she paraded all the way through the War.

Shrugging off Mildred and her phantom child, my father refused to acknowledge that his fingers had been burnt. At fifty-three years old one might have assumed that his adventures would have become more sedentary, if not of the imaginary kind. At the very least he might have found himself a woman a good deal closer to home. Far from it. Patently the glittering capital offered more choice, more surprise, more spice than sober Oxford and its satellite towns. His terminal Nemesis wasn't far off, but of course he didn't know that. Certainly his next love affair ought to have shaken some sense into him, instead of whetting his fallen appetite for more. It involved not only the metropolis, it also involved the long arm of the law. My father, W.G. Geraghty, was interrogated in my presence by the police after being accused of attempted murder . . .

I realise now that this wasn't the climax to his adventurer's career, nor even the anticlimax, but the anti-anticlimax. Hetty knew nothing about the bizarre incident until after his death, and even seemed resentful I'd disclosed it. As it happened, the 'victim' turned out to have a criminal record so extensive, the charge against the assassin was always going to be problematic. The incident itself was so improbable, the detective ridiculed the statements of both victim and accused. Only the victim's mother, she who was screaming blue murder, was lent an initial credibility. She said my father had tried to stab her son in cold blood. As both son and Bill hotly denied this melodramatic slander, the detective was forced to turn to me for some cogent explanation of my father's dubious mental state.

The wounded man was possibly as mad as my father. His name was Lenny Risley and he was a barrow boy, a fruit and vegetable seller from Rotherhithe in the East End. He and Bill Geraghty wouldn't normally have been such boon companions, but as of the last three months they had spent considerable closeted time together. Risley was an ugly, barrel-shaped man of about forty-five, whose red and pitted complexion was in keeping with his temper. According to my father, he always walked around in vest and braces whatever the weather, snow and frost included. The braces, absurdly, were never completely attached to his trousers, but always a half or a quarter buttoned. Bill saw this as an example of Lenny's infantile retardation, and looking at the fruitseller in the East End terrace (the baffling cause of the attempted homicide in the first place) I would not have disagreed. Hanging on the wall was a picture of Risley's father, a London docker long dead. According to Lenny's sister, Coco, Wesley Risley, legendary greyhound man and bottomless drinker, had 'butched Leonard good an proper' when he was a boy, hammering him on a daily basis for nothing at all. Lenny was surprisingly proud of his father's unprovoked cruelty, regularly boasting to my father about it. I looked at Wesley's photograph and marvelled at this impeccable reproduction of Cro-Magnon man. So prognathous was the jaw, so rhomboidal the skull, it looked as if he had been encouraged to pose for his portrait in a museum of palaeontology.

Wesley's widow Elsie was screaming for justice. She had a large red mole on her chin and a nervous tic affecting her elongated neck. She swore that the toff, this one's dad, him with the tash of a music-hall masher, had tried to kill her Lenny with a kitchen fork. In point of fact the fork had impaled Lenny's left arm, and the detective took note of the red puncture marks before asking him to roll down his sleeves. My father disputed Elsie's garbled account and said with a shudder that Lenny had forced him to aim it at Lenny's skull. For reasons of his own, he had tried to manoeuvre my father's hand round the fork and force him against his will to ram it into Risley's forehead, or possibly temple.

'What the hell for?' asked Detective Rollo, a thin young man with extraordinarily slim hands. He wore a large brown trilby obviously intended to add years and gravity, but which looked disconcertingly like a pantomime hat. Rollo's companion was a sixty-year-old constable, mute throughout, who gave occasional ironic glances at the headgear.

'Onner,' croaked Lenny.

'Eh?'

'Affair of bleedin onner, guv.'

Rollo examined the real heart of the matter, Coco Risley. Coco was a barmaid in her early thirties and was Lenny's impudent kid sister. Her pub in Rotherhithe was a notorious den of illegal gambling, of which Lenny was a central arbiter. His childhood thumpings might have made him dense in some ways, but his mental arithmetic and computation skills were those of a genius. Card games were played there for high stakes, and in the backyard there were regular cock-fights and even dogfights. This criminal's sister had been visiting a married friend in Finchley, which was where she and Bill Geraghty had bumped into each other in the vicinity of a chestnut stall. After some carefully calibrated banter, Bill had smirkingly paid for her chestnuts, having scented the tantalisingly dangerous as well as the tartishly alluring. The fact she was called Coco was an aphrodisiac in itself. Later I asked if that was her real name, and he said he had no idea. Nor did he look amused when I said the only other Coco I knew of was a pedigree bull terrier.

'Whose honour?' asked Rollo. 'Your sister's honour? Is that what this is about?'

Lenny was most contemptuous. 'Nah. My bleedin onner. My onnerin a bet. If I don't go an onner it, my name ain't worth nothin in Rotherhithe.'

Rollo said his name wasn't worth anything anyway, if all the rumours were true. Elsie Risley shrieked at the gratuitous impudence and said that slimy old toff had tried to kill her Lenny for a very good reason. So that he could get his grasping hands on the family house here, and boot Elsie and Coco out of it. Or more likely, she added plaintively, kick her, the unwanted old widow, out, and maintain young Coco as his fancy woman.

Rollo said, 'Why would he want to live in Rotherhithe? He's says that he's a proofreader from Oxford. He wouldn't want to live in a nole like this, even assumin he's in love with your Coco.'

Lenny interrupted impatiently. He had no interest what-ever in Bill's allegiances to his sister. It was his personal honour that was at stake. He had wanted to die honourably, and they wouldn't bleedin let him. It was too late now to take the right remedy. Or was it, he wondered longingly? My father shot up his hands and squawked, Lenny, for God's sake old boy, no need to commit blasted *seppuku*, just because of a poor run at pontoon. Rollo sighed at this incongruous Sicilian bandit stuff and forced the chivalric barrow boy to go through it in sequence. But at all costs leave out all this daft palaver about East End *honour*, which seemed to be leading them all up the garden path.

Leaving the chestnut stall, Coco had given my father the name of her pub and had invited him to come along any evening for a 'drinky-pinky' and a 'good old knees-up'. Bill was stimulated by the artless terminology, at the graphic colloquialism of 'knees up', and the appropriate improvisatory parallels. He turned up at the pub a week later, moderately nervous in his cheapest suit and, even though he rarely gambled, holding a racing paper. It was his subtle means of introduction. Coco smiled her recognition from the bar and seemed genuinely pleased to see him. After a cursory glance, the wordless patrons of The Bull decided he was some boozer toff with a geegee habit and resumed their games of cards. Obviously the toff was choosing to plumb the abyss as quickly as possible by heading straight to its lowest depths here. Thereafter they politely ignored him.

Bill was introduced to Lenny who examined him without comment. He bought him a drink immediately and set about praising his sister. Afterwards he watched Lenny playing at pontoon and noted outstanding skill in the way of bluffing and timely 'twisting'. Lenny squinted at him in an odd manner before returning to his game. Coco came over and said she could see right away that Lenny really liked him. Bill was surprised, as he'd detected no signs of amity. Coco explained how Lenny often bared his teeth at new acquaintances, telling them to 'bleedin well shut up' and 'bleedin piss off, so that he could have a meditative think about them. After the introduction, he would normally retire to The Bull's function room, lie down on the old sofa, and take mental stock of the newcomer. In Bill's case all that was dispensed with. Lenny obviously liked Bill to distraction.

One night a week over a three-month period, Bill and Coco pursued the following pattern. Bill would lounge in The Bull drinking and chatting with Coco, and every hour or so buy her brother a double whisky. The brother was immersed in various card games and rarely left The Bull until dawn. Come midnight Bill escorted Coco back to her terrace where Elsie Risley was fast asleep and where they were assured of privacy for two or three hours. Bill and Coco would swiftly disrobe in the back parlour, but conduct their business in the pitch dark, just in case. Come two o'clock, a pre-booked taxi would arrive for Bill and he'd be driven back to his Chelsea hotel.

All this had been proceeding without complication until last night. By some quirk Lenny had grown capriciously bored with his nightly routine and decided he needed a change. He'd lifted himself from the card table and yawned rudely in the faces of his friends. Lenny possessed six gold teeth, the only ones in his enormous mouth. These friends, my father explained to Rollo, were an intriguing crew. One, called Tilling, was impressively mutilated in the nostril area. Another, Pendennis, had an uncontrollable shake of the neck as well as an occasional ungovernable violence. The rogue neck had come about via an unrehearsed petrol explosion, when in trying to oust an insolent rival in the gambling business, Pendennis had accidentally set himself on fire.

By Lenny's own admission, he had made certain carefully chosen remarks to his sister's manfriend. They confirmed his suspicion that Bill Geraghty knew quite a lot about card games and gambling. In fact Bill had learned all about Aryan dice games via Vedic Sanskrit, about games of chance in an Arabic treatise on maths, about card games in an Old

Provençal manuscript rootled through in the Bodleian. His scholarly fascination had already demonstrated its practical side, when, shortly before I began at the RCA, my father had started a lunchtime card game in an Abingdon pub. A separate ladies' league had had Bill as both unpaid coach and zealous social secretary. Once poker and rummy had been mastered by the two Abingdon groups, pontoon and five-card brag schools were quick to follow on.

Lenny abandoned Tilling and Pendennis and walked back to the terrace with Coco and the 'ole puff weeder', as he referred to my father. There was no imputation of unmanliness, Bill stressed, it was simply his Rotherhithe elisions and lispings. Back at the house, Bill and Coco imagined he would go straight to bed, but instead he asked this mystery man from Oxford if he would care to take a hand at pontoon.

'Ten bob a stake?' glinted Lenny. 'You've played pontoon, eh, I expect? Or maybe you'd prefer freecard brag or poker?'

Bill offered a glassy smile. He was certainly torn. He had carefully observed Lenny's pontoon, and while skilled at bluffing, Risley had tell-tale rapid-eye blinks and minuscule adjustments of the knees of his trousers. He did those every time he bluffed but Lenny's hideous simian oppos, Tilling and Pendennis, never twigged. Bill, who liked his little luxuries and never spurned a windfall, decided he'd risk winning a fiver from Risley. If he won it, he'd refuse to play further. Should Lenny turn ugly at that, he would simply return the fiver and say he didn't believe in mixing comradeship with gambling.

He hadn't reckoned with Lenny's sword-sharp sense of honour. Risley and Bill alternated as bankers, as despite her objections, Lenny refused to let his sister play. She was worried already by this unusual tournament and wondered if it wasn't some prelude to a punitive attack on her new man. Lenny said that he refused on principle to play cards with females, especially those also members of his family. Coco snorted at his ludicrous misogyny and tried to force the issue.

Lenny raised a single threatening finger and promised to wallop her with his spare pair of braces if she tried to argue the toss.

'Wimmin need discipline,' he grunted at Bill. 'An not just the young ones. If I forget to wallop the old lady she ends up not respectin me.'

'Your mother?' asked Bill discomfited. 'You, ah, sometimes thrash her with your braces, do you?'

Coco said drily, 'Lenny thinks she misses the old man knockin her about. But Lenny don't know anything about anything.'

Bill quivered at the sight of Lenny's fists which were on an enviable par with docker Wesley's. Three of his fingers had black letters tattooed on them. They seemed to spell H-O-G. What on earth could that mean? Acknowledgement of his unstemmable appetites? Existential self-evaluation? A lifelong love of breakfast bacon?

Bill played skilfully and easily won the first game. Lenny Risley looked at his self-deprecating opponent with strong fascination. Without comment he pushed two ten bobs over to his sister's unusual beau.

After some frowning, he asked in a hollow tone, 'Where the hell you played before?'

Bill flushed and beamed his humblest smile: 'Eh? No, no, that was an exceptional fluke. It's very rarely I play any cards, old boy. The very odd occasion in a pub, with a few bumbling old colleagues from work.'

He also won the next game. Lenny coughed and handed over the pack to the smirking fancy man. My father had seen the barrow boy dealing from both ends and took revenge by apeing an apprentice's stupidity. He fumbled the pack and deftly shifted an ace as he reshuffled.

Bill Geraghty won ten consecutive games in all. Lenny passed no comment throughout this marathon flogging. Ramrod tense on the sofa, Coco Risley seemed to be both tittering and groaning at Bill's prowess. Bill held up his hand to brother and sister, and refused to play any more, especially as this winning streak was an outrageous fluke. He was just a cack-handed amateur, a Christmas-party whist player, and he insisted that kindly old Lenny was letting him win every time.

Lenny said stiffly, 'No, I ain't. I ain't letting you do anything. Including not letting you stop at playing cards . . .'

Coco shot up and insisted Bill had a taxi for Chelsea coming at two. Lenny waved her back to the table and said they had a good hour till then. In any case, they could easily up the stakes and hurry things if need be. Bill Geraghty's five pounds winnings matched by one of Lenny Risley's fivers . . .

By a quarter past one they had played another five games and Bill had won twenty-five pounds. He was flushed both red and white as he envisaged easy wealth and personal destruction dancing hand in hand tonight. Frightened by his own genius, he said that he must stop playing immediately and/or hand back Lenny his winnings.

The barrow boy might have been a cardsharp but he brooked no charity. Like a solemn plutocrat he waved a bulging wallet and counted out his cash. Unknown to Bill it was his entire personal fortune. It amounted to one hundred and ten pounds. Rollo gazed at the sum sitting there in my father's hands and frowned uncomprehending at the sight. Two hours earlier Lenny had tossed down five fivers before handing the pack to Bill.

Bill had sweated and quivered as he cleaned him out of his pony. Lenny took back the pack and threw down fifty quid against Bill's accumulated fifty. He drew recklessly from the bottom of the deck, but my father easily trounced him with a five-card trick.

'Stop it, you bleedin idiot!' Coco shouted at her suicidal brother. 'For God's sake, stop *forcing* him to clean you out of everythin you got!'

Bill seconded as much with an anxious squeak. Dizzy at his spectacular success, he was terrified by what it might mean. Perhaps, astonishingly, this was how he should be making a living? In his hand was two months' salary, all from playing a card game with an imbecile in an idle hour.

He said, 'Let's call it a day, old man. Let's just sleep on it, shall we.'

Risley croaked, 'Nothin doing! Here. Take the lot. I'm chucking down all of it, do or die. All of yours against all of mine.'

Lenny wagered his last thirty-five pounds. Bill the banker trounced him with a monumental seven-card trick. Lenny started to laugh, though he was far from amused. He was now completely penniless. He didn't even possess a bank account. Because of his personal honour, he never borrowed off family, and indeed never needed to borrow. He always won at everything he played, and if anyone played the loan shark or domestic banker, it was he. Faced with bankruptcy, he simply didn't know what to do. He possessed not a single useful possession he could gamble.

Unless . . .

'Come on,' he urged with great excitement. 'You put your two hundred down. An I'll bet . . .'

'What?' Coco threw at her brainless sibling. 'Your hat? Your coat? Your bleedin teeth?'

Her brother announced sternly, 'This *arse* . . .'

Putting a finger in his ear, Bill turned pale, then philosophical. 'I really don't want *that* from you, old man. Thank you but ah . . .'

'This arse?' echoed his sister, outraged. 'Our arse? You ain't touchin anyone's arse, Lenny. You loony tick! This blinkin arse belongs to Mum, not you.'

Lenny protested, 'She's leavin it to me, Coke. She's leavin the bleedin arse to me, she promised me she was. She's leavin all her insurances to you, but the arse an everything in it is goin to me.'

At last my father cracked the code. 'You mean you intend to wager your mother's house?'

'Yis!' the barrow boy boasted.

'Old boy, put yourself in my position. I have a perfectly adequate place up in Oxford. Now if I –'

He rose, whistling hopefully, but Lenny grabbed his jacket and yanked him into his seat. Ordering him to whack his two hundred on the table, he gestured Bill to deal the cards. Risley's cumbersome stake couldn't be put there of course, but on a piece of paper he managed to scrawl an infant's version of an ugly little house with some smoke billowing out of the chimney.

Bill did his level best to lose the game, but their separate cheatings confounded each other to my father's advantage. Bill paid twenty-ones and showed seventeen, while Lenny turned up a king and a five . . .

'Right,' said Coco's brother, with philosophy. 'This arse is your arse now.'

Bill looked across to Coco and grimaced. Her family home was his to do with as he liked? He attempted to comfort his troubled girlfriend. He gave her an encouraging smile, and said the first thing he wanted to do was donate his win as a present to the Risleys. Lenny glowered horribly and indicated such a breach of convention was impossible. Why, he would sooner die, he would sooner kill all three of them than suffer the shame of welching on a bet! It was a matter of honour, of Lenny Risley's honour, and all that that signified in his part of the East End.

'My onner,' he sighed, with the conviction of a Rotherhithe Lancelot.

Coco sobbed and said Lenny was a bloody cockeyed cretin who couldn't even tie his galluses. Her brother blushed and insisted it was his untarnished reputation that mattered. Bill Geraghty coughed and murmured that they might talk about the ownership and the blessed title deeds on his next visit. Meanwhile, if they didn't mind, he would very much like to leave the table. His opponent grinned with scorn. That, snorted Lenny, was quite impossible.

'Keep on playin,' he ordered. 'An stick to the bleeding game.'

Bill said, 'No thank you, Lenny. Sorry to spoil the show as I am. You see, I've won your house, old boy, and I don't need the whole blessed street.'

Picking his teeth, Lenny said, 'You ain't about to win the bleeding street. You just lay down the arse and the two hundred, and I'll bet . . . somethin else.'

My father prompted, 'Ye . . . es. Meaning what perhaps?'

'His brains,' said Coco tearfully. 'He'll bet his enormous brains against your arse and your money.'

Her sibling glinted with a daredevil gleam. 'No I won't. But you'll never guess what I *am* going to bet. Never in a million years.'

'Your braces?' asked Bill queasily.

The grim silence of the small hours had slowly descended on the table. Lenny mutely examined his nails and playfully protracted the torture.

'What?' demanded Coco. 'Just tell us what the ell.'

The barrow boy answered, 'My *life!*'

'Eh?'

'I'll bet my *life* against this puff weeder's money and his arse.'

Bill squeaked, after a considerable pause. 'Oh? Oh indeed?'

'My life against your arse and your lolly!'

Rank horror and incredulity did battle, and my father began to shake. 'Your *life* against my ar . . . your . . . my . . . house?'

'Exactly,' said Lenny proudly. 'That's exactly what I mean.'

Coco screamed. My father attempted to scream but found himself unable. Faint stirrings came from above as Elsie Risley woke at Coco's wailing. Stone sober by now, Bill attempted to avert a horrible fate by making a run for it. With nightmare apprehension he could see how all his sinful ways, those artless infidelities, that unrepentant deceitfulness, had led him at last to this dreadful charnel house. If he won the next game, this barrow boy with the chivalric code of a Moorish vizier would demand that he take his life. He would force him to be a bloody murderer! My father stared slyly up at the ceiling. Tensing his fists, he raced for the door. He got as far as the sofa before Lenny grabbed him by the hand and dragged him back to the table.

'I don't feel well,' Bill muttered, as grey as those ashes in the Risley fireplace. 'In fact I feel rather blinking ill.'

Lenny loomed across the table and addressed him with a timely pun.

'*Your money or my life.*'

Coco screamed again. Lenny Risley was banker again. Bill Geraghty shook like a lily again. When it came to say 'twist', he actually said 'toast'. He exerted every muscle to lose the game, but when he tried to drop an ace Lenny forced it back into his palm.

'Pay twenty-ones,' intoned the fruitseller grimly.

Bill clutched the ace and the jack as if they were anthrax. It was pontoon itself. Lenny displayed his sentence of execution, his two tens, with the peevish glumness of an indignant shopper.

'My God,' choked my father, 'Coco . . .' he whispered. 'Ring the police.'

Their house had no phone but to seal things further Risley bolted the door. Bill's legs became like putty and his skin turned tight as a drum. With a whimper, he collapsed next to Coco. He took her small hand as she wailed her desperation. Lenny was manfully preparing himself by baring a chest tattooed with a snarling greyhound and a panting mastiff. In his fist he brandished the cutlery drawer he'd found in the kitchen. In there was a motley array of meat skewers, bread-knives, potato mashers, spoons, forks and carving knives.

'Choose your weapon,' he said to Bill.

Eyeing a saltspoon hopefully, my father said, 'Ag . . .'

Risley appraised the cutlery with a connoisseurial air. 'This meat skewer might be the quickest, guv . . .'

Bill said with chattering teeth. 'Bugger me! Oh bugger me, bugger me, bugger me!'

'Gawd,' screamed Coco.

Lenny pointed his finger impetuously. 'Come ere an bleedin kill me!'

'No, old boy! Not blinking likely! No blasted need! No blessed point!'

'Course there's a point! You won the game and you deserve the bleedin stake! Hurry up for Gawdsake. I ain't got all night, an your taxi's comin soon.'

My father counselled him with every jot of his elusive sincerity: 'Bugger off, you demented damn simpleton! You appalling decerebrated imbecile!'

Lenny was comprehensively mystified, as if he could only have mistaken him for Coco.

'Simpleton? What the ell d'you mean? I'm talkin about my reputation.'

'I mean . . . no . . . I'm sorry, I don't mean that. I mean . . .' Then it was as if my father suddenly awoke from the dream of an artless, senile fool. He turned on sobbing Coco with an evil suspicion. 'What a bloody fool I am! Aren't I? Exactly how much money do you two con trick merchants want from me? Isn't that what this Russian roulette charade's in aid of? I should have known it was an idiotic trick . . . a bloody extortion bid two bandits have dreamt up to rob me of my last penny!'

Coco gaped her obvious innocence. Bill scrutinised the East End pair for outward confirmation of an inward criminal guilt. But even as he blustered on, he knew it wasn't so. They really didn't want his money. Neither of them were interested in naked fraud. Lenny Risley really was an East End Don Quixote, even if he was a dog-fighter, a cock-fighter and a crook. He believed in sticking to his bond, even if it meant his death. Coco was recoiling from Bill now he'd made his appalling accusation. Meanwhile the barrow boy was painfully restless at this superfluous debate. Clutching his knife drawer as if it were a school trophy, he grunted: 'Ere. Take your pick of one of these bleeders.'

Bill waved away the drawer, as if it were an inferior brand of cigarette. 'No, old boy . . .'

Lenny rapped his knuckles hard on Bill's refractory head. 'Do as I says! Kill me like you been told! Ram it in as hard as you can.'

Bill folded his arms and shook with delirium tremens. He shivered and whimpered, but refused to unknit them to kill Lenny. The barrow boy nodded dolefully, as if at a mutinous schoolboy. Seizing Bill's arm, he extracted his hand and forced it towards the meat skewer. With a tally-ho snort, he plunged it at his naked breast. Halfway through its brief trajectory, my father rammed a kneecap in Lenny's groin. Risley roared, like an ox convulsing in a slaughterhouse. His balls, so he claimed, had been turned to powder by the blow. The meat skewer fell with a clatter to the floor . . .

'Gor!' from Lenny. 'Gor, you bleedin little bastard.'

His knackers cruelly aflame, the fruitseller tried to get Bill's fingers round a carving knife. Instead, eyes shut in agony, he closed the fingers round a piffling fork. It was the type you would use to spear an errant pickle. He squeezed my father's fist, then rammed the little fork towards his massive skull.

Bill had no alternative but to knee him once more in the ballocks. The pickle fork hence failed in its assault. Side-shunted from an unmissable target, the barrow boy cleverly impaled himself in the arm.

'Bugger!' said Lenny furiously. He looked at the idiotic pickle fork dancing just below his shoulder. 'Wot the ell you do that for? That's no good at all, mate.'

Bill gasped, 'I'll do anything you say. But for heaven's sake let go of my wrist.'

Lenny complained, 'This is all gonna put me to some bleedin inconvenience. I'll need a bleedin tetanus prick seein you've made a balls of finishin me off.'

Then a *deus ex machina* in the shape of warty Elsie Risley came hurtling on the scene. She gasped at the sight of bare-chested Lenny, tattoos dancing wildly on his copious folds of belly fat. She hadn't her specs, but could see he was gripping the toff by his skinny old neck. A diabolic implement was hanging ghoulishly from her little boy's arm.

She wasted no time and ran to wake the neighbours. It was obvious what had happened. She had seen her little lad writhing and shouting on account of a vicious knife wound. It's only, Coco screamed after her, Lenny's stupid knackers what's in agony! Mrs Risley paid no attention to her callous younger child. She slammed the front door and went battering on the one opposite.

Once the statements had been taken, an embarrassed silence descended upon the gathering. Something authoritative was to be expected of the boy detective at this point. Rollo tipped the brim of his sombrero-trilby and stared at Bill Geraghty accusingly. Having watched plentiful movie scenes of rough interrogation portrayed by Bogart, Cagney, Edward G. Robinson and the like, he had evidently decided to act the astringent Yank. Because it would have sounded ludicrous in a New York or Chicago drawl, Rollo fell back on his native argot. He berated my father in purest Poplar, and the effect was extraordinarily chilling.

'Guv,' he snorted in a Humphrey Bogart growl. 'Why dja come tommin for the ole pussy darn in Rovverhive?'

I for one was startled by the linguistic transformation, not to speak of his patent hostility.

'Eh?' said Bill Geraghty. 'I don't think I –'

Rollo gesticulated indiscriminately as he explored his thwarted possibilities. He began to exaggerate the Poplar vowels for authentic *film noir* effect.

'Whyn't you stick in Oxfawd mongst yor oo-ah type? What'm I sayin? You upsets fings tommin wif slag wimmin darn ere. You put Lenny the orange-outing in a vilent fit, an you make his mad muvver twice as bleedin doolally. You even upset a crazy tart like Coco when er an er fizzical shams was wot it was all in ide of in the first place.'

My father blinked at this beardless child's bizarre histrionics. He turned to me, his embarrassed son, as if I might offer assistance or inspiration. I looked away from both of them and let him have his just deserts. I was hoping he would have to do grovelling obeisance to this trilbied slavering dwarf. Instead I was surprised by the complacent smirk that was hovering at his lips. It was as if he beheld youth itself as an infinitely absurd thing, and Rollo's Cagney-fied bluster as its stupidest manifestation to date.

'Mm?' he said politely, carefully putting his tie in order. 'Tomming?' he echoed with the supine innocence of a Trollope country parson. 'Pussy, you said, Inspector Rollo?'

The constable woke from his dream and translated. 'He means tom-catting. He means humping, guv. I think you can guess what pussy means. You can by the looks of you.'

My father rose slowly from his seat. With leisurely expansiveness he ignored Inspector Rollo and addressed his contemporary, the old policeman.

'I'm rarely baffled by slang, constable, and very little colloquial obscenity eludes me. You see I've a certain gift for languages and speak over sixty in all. This in part explains why I know what 'pussy' means, as I certainly didn't bandy the term during the house matches at my prep school. Every one of these languages I speak, from Slav Macedonian to the Munda of the Dravidian hill tribes, has feline and other zoological epithets for the *pudendum muliebris*. As for your Inspector's reference to rutting tom cats, it's quite inaccurate slander in this case. Tom cats fight tooth and nail over their territory, rather like Lenny here does in his primitive and repulsive way. Even if, paradoxically, Risley turns his ludicrous violence upon himself, a thing no self-respecting alley cat would ever do. In my whole life I've never fought with anyone over anything, thank God. As for your superior's abrasive gutter lexicon, as an educated man in the presence of the sensitive sex' – smiling at squinting, swearing, dribbling old Elsie Risley – 'of whatever uneducated and unalluring kind, I don't care to step into the same gutter.'

Rollo fingered the end of his exceptionally thin nose. He was frowning though he didn't know why exactly. It had something to do with all those languages and all those bloody words that he never used and never needed to. The constable tapped his helmet uneasily, as if to make all-round if meaningless conciliation. Lenny gazed uncomprehending at the toff cardsharp, while Coco sat chain-smoking in a quiet fury. I took Bill Geraghty's arm and indicated I was going to remove him to a place of safety some fifty miles from here. Inspector Rollo made no effort to stop me.

Twelve

My father died a month after the end of the War, one week short of his fifty-fifth birthday. His last breath was drawn in the arms of a slim young woman in a four-poster bed in a handsome art-deco guest house in Brighton. It was just as he would have wished it. At the inquest, which of course Hetty Geraghty did not attend, I listened to Mabel Torrance, a thirty-year-old hairdresser from Queen's Park, explain how my father had taken a fit of apoplexy while resting after the act rather than during it. A medical report confirmed that he had a weakness of the lungs consistent with his childhood tuberculosis. Also, unbeknownst to anyone, including his own doctor, he showed incipient heart disease. He went through about twenty cigars a day and had a considerable phlegmy cough according to Mrs Torrance. Mabel stated that the apoplexy had begun as a coughing fit brought on by laughing very hard at one of his own jokes. The coroner asked with real interest what the fatal joke might have been. Mabel blushed and said she couldn't remember. It wasn't blue or disgusting, it was a kind of intellectual joke which she didn't understand.

Mrs Torrance was more forthcoming when it came to unburdening herself to me. She and Bill had been seeing each other for almost a year and it had been a most tender liaison. Mabel had fine green eyes and a generous smile and a determined, resistant sort of attitude to almost everything. Her husband Dick had been killed in action in '42. They had no children but her husband's brother Mervyn, a Dollis Hill grocer, had taken her under his wing in a convincingly protective manner. Soon, though, he was acting very possessively, asking for detailed accounts of her daily movements and attempting to run her life for her. Incredibly he demanded to see her shopping receipts and castigated her for overspending on toilet rolls! He described to her, without a trace of irony, how it was possible, by a certain anatomical flexing and a certain way of folding, to use less paper. Simultaneously he began making sweating, unambiguous demands of her. Mervyn perspired because he was fat, though he had a very pleasant baby face and could be impulsively generous to everyone under the sun, with his time if not his money. He accused her of trifling with his feelings. He was twenty years older and had a loyal stout wife and four obese grown-up children. Bill had entered Mabel's life just as she had begun to barricade the door against her persistent brother-in-law. Bill soon frightened off Mervyn by telling him he would flypost his grocer's shop and indeed the whole of Dollis bloody Hill with details of his tyrannical pestering, including Mervyn's incredible advice on how to tighten the arsecheeks and tightly fold the bog roll in order to use less paper.

'Did he really die of a laughing fit?' I asked her in a busy Brighton coffee shop in a very low voice.

'Yes he did. He didn't die in the act, George, truthfully. It would have been so awful if he had. I've had dreams of just that ever since. But . . .'

She hesitated, embarrassed and sceptical about something, perhaps the enduring value of absolute candour.

'Please go on. I won't repeat anything. I won't tell my mother any of this.'

The revelation such as it was was mystifying rather than tragic. After their lovemaking in the four-poster bed, Bill had fished out a cigar and an Akkadian primer bought at a considerable price in Blackwell's second-hand department the previous week. Akkadian was his sixty-ninth tongue and from now on he intended to concentrate on dead ones, he had told her. Dead languages had a convincingly closed canonical feel to them. No more new idioms, no more neologisms, all done and dusted, what? Mabel looked in amazement at his musty old book written in German and printed in Leipzig in 1892. Then with simple naive curiosity she asked him why he liked foreign languages so much, why his own wasn't enough for him as it was for everyone else. After which she had lain there reasonably enthralled, swathed in aromatic cigar smoke as my father gave her a tender little lecture on the history of languages. He told her all about Indo-European and the migration of tribes from the Caucasus, then discussed the Semitic and Hamitic and Finno-Ugrian and Amerindian language 'families'. He made it simple and vivid and exciting. He told her about inflected and non-inflected languages, about cases and the absence of cases. Mabel, who could think only of suitcases and head-cases, asked for examples. Bill started on Latin, then feeling that sounded too remote for her, he moved on to Jerry, to German. The War was just finished and Mabel, who didn't know a word of German, was riveted on that account: to hear Bill quoting sonorous passages of Goethe and Lessing and Heine. It sounded beautiful, nothing at all like Adolf ranting. He told her all about the forms of the German genitive, also known as the possessive. He told her that there were eight prepositions that invariably took the possessive.

'Yen something . . .' she said, as she stubbed out a Weights.

'*Jenseits?*' I said with disproportionate excitement.

'That's it.'

'*Jenseits des Flusses*! That side of the river. Where my dead father is today perhaps.'

She looked at me warily. 'That's it. He tried to make me learn the bloody things. I tried but I couldn't say them. I was too shy, it all felt beyond my station.'

'*Jenseits, diesseits, ausserhalb, innerhalb, statt, wegen, während, trotz. Trotz des Krieges.* In spite of the war. In spite of the war, he still loved their language. He still talked it in bed with . . . with a woman he . . . cared about like you. Mabel, he made me learn the same list when I was eight years old. I can't forget it. I shall never forget it. He drove it into my skull. When I am old and senile I'll forget my name, but I'll never ever forget the lists of German prepositions that my father made me learn by rote.'

She wiped away two tiny drops from her sharp little eyes. 'He made his mark on me, your father. He ordered you about and told you what was what. But his heart was always kind.'

'It was to some. It was to most I suppose. It wasn't so kind to my mother.' I looked up from my empty cup and watched her flinch. Bright red, I drummed my fingers and persisted, 'What happened after that? After he'd talked about German?'

She frowned at her coffee as if to steel herself for something painful. She sighed loudly then said, 'He read a bit more of his old book, smoked another cigar, then suddenly he puts down the book and exclaims, "Well, that's it then."'

I leant towards her anxiously. 'You mean he said, that's it then, and promptly died?'

'No, no. That was just the start of it. After that I got lost a good bit. It was a really long speech he made about languages and countries and people. I only understood the simple bits. He was saying you couldn't get anything much more complicated in language terms than the dead stuff he was studying. But that the people who spoke it didn't think it was complicated. They just opened their ancient gobs (those were his own words) and out it came. And they were an old, very sophisticated civilisation who seemed remote and old-fashioned and beyond our understanding. But they didn't seem that way to themselves. They didn't see themselves as old at all. They thought they were the most modern, go-ahead one of all time. Just like we do now. Just like almost everyone does everywhere and at every time in history. And yet the Jerries, he said, and that's when he started laughing, they were determined to bulldoze the world into taking them as the biggest ever and best ever. They were going to wipe out the poor Jews and the poor Gypsies and the poor Slavs and the poor Blacks just to show they were the most go-ahead for all time. History would look back in thousands of years time from now and see that they'd got rid of the bits they didn't like. Somehow they imagined they'd be applauded for that, instead of being hated for it. And your pa said that the Jerries adopted the swastika which he said was originally from India, from old India, ancient India. I never knew that but he swore it was true. Now the Indians are darkies really, aren't they, a type of darkie and the Jerries hated all the darkies and yet they went about flaunting the same symbol as these Very Old Darkies.'

I was glued to her simple transcription. They were obviously not my father's words but they conveyed in their flavour enough of his music-hall argot to make the seriousness of the message all the more poignant. According to Mabel it was after this speech about the swastika, about the Master Race espousing classical precedent, that my father suffered a great laughing fit. When it turned to apoplexy and he was choking and Mabel couldn't do anything and was in a madness of panic, the last word she heard him say was 'fuck'. Of course Mabel couldn't say the word, any more than Bill would ever have used it in front of a woman in ordinary circumstances. No doubt as death was hovering over him and his lungs refused to save him, he was unable to exercise a gentleman's restraint.

The day after the George Grosz broadcast, I woke up expecting to feel terrible. The hangover was there, but to my surprise I discovered that last night's disappointment had almost entirely faded. I realised with some puzzling disorientation that it didn't particularly bother me my Grosz book was out of print, that the art world had all but forgotten me, that you had to be well over fifty to remember my notorious cartoons. Unfortunately this absence of chagrin left me discomfited rather than cheered. Shouldn't I be good and bitter this morning, shouldn't the indignation have survived more than a few paltry hours? What did it say about my capacity for felt passion and strong emotion in old age? Was I so ancient and clapped out, I hadn't the stomach to feel hatred and spleen any more? No wonder, I thought, that my occasional attempts at cartooning these days produced such spiritless dross. Self-evidently I needed to rediscover my bile.

I remembered how at fifty I had given up cigarettes without effort, then found if I attempted to smoke the occasional one it gave me no pleasure at all. I had been a fag smoker for thirty years and overnight, without struggle, I had lost the addiction. Cockeyed as it sounds, it didn't feel right, it felt extremely unnerving not to be wanting a fag all the time. Annoyed as well as baffled, I promptly smoked six in a row, trying as it were to readdict myself. But to no avail. None of the six gave me the slightest pleasure. After which I was down to one cigar a day with my evening whisky, and even then I needed to remind myself to smoke it.

Jane's insolent appraisal of my stagnant sex life was much more to the point. I had woken thinking not of Grosz and wartime celebrity and favourable book reviews, but of Wilhelina Van der Waal, of Giselle the handsome actress, of flighty Frankie Charne, and even of Jane Geraghty as an attractive young wife. Throughout the night I had been remembering Bill and his delirious addiction to women and the way that that had moulded my fate. I spent most of today brooding over my own addiction to women, and how different it was from his. My father's addiction didn't entail any jealousy, anguish, remorse or biblical guilt. He felt no moral turmoil, because he was a stranger to the truth, his only truth being his cruelly thwarted talent.

I'd always thought of him as a figure of fun and been ashamed of his flagrance and mendacity, not to speak of his lustful tortoise and his polyglot cockatoos. Thinking of which, at his sparsely attended funeral in North Oxford, I had suddenly felt my shoulders shaking. As the coffin had been lowered, I'd been seized by the image of Bill Geraghty blithely angling for nocturnal trout while blanketed Mildred fumed in a pitch-dark caravan. He was all for women, but he was all for trout as well. I began to laugh till the tears were streaming down my face . . .

Blank with horror, Hetty begged me to restrain myself and behave like a sensible adult . . .

Like an adult? I'd been laughing myself sick, but as she reproved me I was crying the purest sorrow. My father was dead and gone, and he was only fifty-four. I would never see him again, and would never hear his latest lie. I realised with an ineffable chill that I was really going to miss the cracked old bugger, the unrepentant adventurer. I saw that for a very long time I was going to be seriously addicted to his memory.

'I'm crying.' I hiccupped hysterically. 'I know it looks like laughing but I'm crying.'

Still reeling from the circumstances of his death, Hetty's patience was in short supply. To die in bloody Brighton, of all places, in the arms of some London tart! He had choked to death having sex and a simultaneous laughing fit. She hissed that if I didn't stop all that embarrassing bloody racket, I would end up going the same bloody way.

I blinked back to the present and glanced at my kitchen clock. It was ten to one of a Tuesday, and the year was 1992. That loyal old clock assured me who I was, what I was, where I was, where I always was. The march of time was such an invaluable and unassailable ally. Even this business of getting old and approaching one's death was a sovereign blessing surely . . .

Dead celebrities are that and nothing else, eh? You can't feel renown or ignominy in heaven. You can't take it with you, Jazz, I mean George . . .

Lunchtime Concert on the Third in ten minutes. Oh those timeless, transcendent anachronisms. *The Third. The Wireless. The Home Service.* Esmond Jell had been dead a quarter of a century, and Pablo the cat who'd scratched his gorgeous radio had not been sipping crème-de-menthe since 1950. Forty years later it was ten minutes to one, which meant I would be enjoying my tenth cup of coffee very soon. I am addicted to coffee as well as women, I always have been. It means that I piss a massive amount, but it is worth it. Afterwards, I shall take the winding walk down to Dodgsonstown Ford and the whispering River Lyne.

I drink too much coffee but let's not talk about existential armour, shall we? Anyone not a fool can guess at the frightening transcendence of the One Real Thing That Lasts. When you're seventy-two, you have no bloody choice. I know of this one worth knowing because of the epiphanies of North Cumbrian sunsets and the sweet white dust of summer on the old grey D road to Easton. I am an artist after all and I have been trained to use my eyes. These are the Debatable Lands where I live and behold the swaying of that red-headed goldfinch pecking at those scraggy thistleheads. Dodgsonstown Ford, Josef Haydn rampant on the wireless, those red and gold finches, all point in the one direction, needless to add. They are all fords over the trickling beck that in its lasting plenitude assures us the one above is a visionary architect. Alive with compassion and understanding, he is not a squiggle-and-dash cartoonist. Nor any more, thank God, am I.

About the author

John Murray was born in West Cumbria in 1950. He has published seven critically acclaimed novels and a collection of stories, *Pleasure*, which won the Dylan Thomas Award in 1988. *Jazz Etc.* was longlisted for the 2003 Man Booker Prize and his 2004 novel, *Murphy's Favourite Channels*, was a Novel of the Week in the *Daily Telegraph*. In 1984 he founded the celebrated fiction magazine *Panurge* which he and David Almond edited until 1996. He lives in Brampton, North Cumbria, and is married with one daughter.